JOSEPH CONRAD

Heart of Darkness

Edited with Introduction and Notes by
OWEN KNOWLES

The Congo Diary

Edited with Notes by
ROBERT HAMPSON

General Editor
J. H. STAPE
PENGUIN BOOKS

PENGUIN CLASSICS

Published by the Penguin Group
Penguin Books Ltd, 80 Strand, London WC2R ORL, England
Penguin Group (USA) Inc., 375 Hudson Street, New York, New York 10014, USA
Penguin Group (Canada), 90 Eglinton Avenue East, Suite 700, Toronto, Ontario, Canada M4P 2Y3
(a division of Pearson Penguin Canada Inc.)
Penguin Ireland, 25 St Stephen's Green, Dublin 2, Ireland
(a division of Penguin Books Ltd)
Penguin Group (Australia), 250 Camberwell Road, Camberwell, Victoria 3124, Australia
(a division of Pearson Australia Group Pty Ltd)
Penguin Books India Pvt Ltd, 11 Community Centre, Panchsheel Park, New Delhi – 110 017, India
Penguin Group (NZ), 67 Apollo Drive, Rosedale, North Shore 0632, New Zealand
(a division of Pearson New Zealand Ltd)
Penguin Books (South Africa) (Pty) Ltd, 24 Sturdee Avenue, Rosebank, Johannesburg 2196, South Africa

Penguin Books Ltd, Registered Offices: 80 Strand, London WC2R ORL, England

www.penguin.com

First published 1899
Published in Penguin Classics 2007

14 15 16 17 18 19 20

Heart of Darkness Introduction and Notes, A Note on the Texts, Glossary
copyright © Owen Knowles, 2007
'The Congo Diary' Introduction copyright © Owen Knowles, 2007
Notes copyright © Robert Hampson, 2007
Author Biography, Chronology copyright © J. H. Stape, 2007
Further Reading copyright © J. H. Stape, Owen Knowles and Robert Hampson, 2007
Map copyright © The Joseph Conrad Society (UK), 2007
All rights reserved

The moral right of the editors has been asserted

Set in 10.25/12.25 pt PostScript Adobe Sabon
Typeset by Rowland Phototypesetting Ltd, Bury St Edmunds, Suffolk

Except in the United States of America, this book is sold subject
to the condition that it shall not, by way of trade or otherwise, be lent,
re-sold, hired out, or otherwise circulated without the publisher's
prior consent in any form of binding or cover other than that in
which it is published and without a similar condition including this
condition being imposed on the subsequent purchaser

ISBN: 978-0-141-44167-2

PENGUIN  CLASSICS

HEART OF DARKNESS AND THE CONGO DIARY

JOSEPH CONRAD (Józef Teodor Konrad Korzeniowski) was born in December 1857 in Berdichev (now in the Ukraine) of Polish parents. His father, a poet and translator, and his mother were exiled for nationalist activities and died when he was a child. He grew up and was educated informally in Lemberg (now L'viv) and Cracow, which he left for Marseilles and a career at sea in 1874. After voyages to the French Antilles, he joined the British Merchant Service in 1878, sailing first in British coastal waters and then to the Far East and Australia. In 1886, he became a British subject and received his captaincy certificate. In 1890, he was briefly in the Congo with a Belgian company. After his career at sea ended in 1894, he lived mainly in Kent. He married in 1896 and had two sons.

Conrad began writing, in his third language, in 1886. His first novels, *Almayer's Folly* (1895) and *An Outcast of the Islands* (1896), were immediately hailed as the work of a significant new talent. He produced his major fiction from about 1897 to 1911, a period that saw the publication of *The Nigger of the 'Narcissus'* (1897), *Heart of Darkness* (1899), *Lord Jim* (1900) and the political novels *Nostromo* (1904), *The Secret Agent* (1907) and *Under Western Eyes* (1911). Considered 'difficult', his writing received considerable critical acclaim, but not until 1914 after the appearance of *Chance* did it win a wide public. The dazzling narrative experiments and thematic complexities of Conrad's earlier fiction are largely absent from his later writings, pitched to a more popular audience.

Fame saw the offer of honorary degrees and a knighthood (both declined) capped by a triumphal publicity tour in America in 1923. In addition to novels, Conrad produced short stories, plays, several essays and two autobiographical volumes, *The Mirror of the Sea* (1906) and *A Personal Record* (1908-9). He died in August 1924 at the age of sixty-six.

OWEN KNOWLES, Research Fellow in the University of Hull, is the author of *A Conrad Chronology* (1989), *An Annotated Critical Bibliography of Joseph Conrad* (1992) and the *Oxford Reader's*

Companion to Conrad (2000) (with Gene M. Moore). Advisory Editor of *The Conradian*, he has edited Conrad's *Almayer's Folly* (1995), and has co-edited *A Portrait in Letters: Correspondence to and about Joseph Conrad* (1996) and, for Cambridge University Press, Volumes VI and IX (2002 and forthcoming) of *The Collected Letters of Joseph Conrad*.

ROBERT HAMPSON is Professor of Modern Literature in the Department of English at Royal Holloway, University of London. A former editor of *The Conradian*, his publications include *Joseph Conrad: Betrayal and Identity* (1992) and *Cross-Cultural Encounters in Conrad's Malay Fiction* (2001). The author of numerous articles, he has also edited *Victory* and *Nostromo*, Rudyard Kipling's *Something of Myself* and *Soldiers Three/In Black and White* and Rider Haggard's *King Solomon's Mines* for Penguin.

J. H. STAPE has taught in universities in Canada, France and the Far East. Author of *The Several Lives of Joseph Conrad* (2007), he has edited *The Cambridge Companion to Joseph Conrad* (1996) and Conrad's *Notes on Life and Letters* (2004) and co-edited *A Personal Record* (2007) and Volumes VII and IX (2005 and forthcoming) of *The Collected Letters of Joseph Conrad* for Cambridge University Press. He has also co-edited Conrad's *An Outcast of the Islands* and *The Rover* for Oxford World's Classics, and has written on Thomas Hardy, Virginia Woolf, William Golding and Angus Wilson. He is Contributing Editor of *The Conradian: The Journal of the Joseph Conrad Society (UK)*.

Contents

Acknowledgements

Owen Knowles wishes to record that the task of preparing his edition of *Heart of Darkness* has been greatly eased by the generous advice of the general editor, J. H. Stape, and the late Hans van Marle. He is also indebted to the work of two of the most influential Conrad critics of recent decades, the late Ian Watt and Professor Cedric Watts.

Robert Hampson wishes to acknowledge the assistance of the late Hans van Marle in preparing the annotations to his edition of 'The Congo Diary'.

Our thanks are due to Donald J. Shewan for the preparation of the map.

Warmest thanks are due to Louisa Sladen for her help in preparing the manuscript.

Chronology

1857 Józef Teodor Konrad Korzeniowski, coat-of-arms Nałęcz, is born on 3 December in Berdichev (Ukraine), the only child of the Polish poet and translator Apollo Korzeniowski and Ewelina (or Ewa), née Bobrowska.

1862 Apollo Korzeniowski, his wife and son are exiled from Warsaw to Vologda, northern Russia.

1865 Ewa Korzeniowska dies of consumption.

1868–9 Permitted to leave Russia, Apollo Korzeniowski relocates to Austro-Hungarian territory with his son, first in Lemberg (now L'viv, Ukraine) and vicinity and then in Cracow, where he dies (May).

1870 Becomes the ward of his maternal grandmother and maternal uncle, Tadeusz Bobrowski, and begins private studies with Adam Pulman, a medical student at Cracow's Jagiellonian University.

1873 Tours Vienna, Swiss Alps and northern Italy with Pulman. Private studies in Lemberg.

1874–7 Arrives in Marseilles to work for the shippers Delestang et Fils, sailing to the French Antilles in the *Mont-Blanc* and *Saint-Antoine*. A period of biographical mystery ensues, involving a possible brief side voyage to Venezuela, gunrunning in the Basque country for the doomed cause of the pretender to the Spanish throne and smuggling near Marseilles.

1878 After amassing debts and gambling losses, attempts suicide (February or March). Leaves Marseilles in the British steamer *Mavis* for Mediterranean waters (Malta and Constantinople) and then lands at Lowestoft, Suffolk. Employed as ordinary seaman in the *Skimmer of the Sea* (Lowestoft to Newcastle).

1878–80 In the *Duke of Sutherland* (to Australia) and then the *Europa* (to Genoa, Sicily and Greece). Passes the British Merchant Service second mate's examination.

1880–85 Third mate in the *Loch Etive* (to Australia); second mate in the ill-fated *Palestine* (bound for Bangkok, but sinks in the Straits of Malacca), ships out of Singapore in the *Riversdale* (to Madras) and after crossing India by rail joins the *Narcissus* in Bombay (to Dunkirk). Passes the examination for first mate (1884).

1886 Second mate in the *Tilkhurst* (Hull to Wales, Singapore, Calcutta, Dundee). Submits first story, 'The Black Mate', to a competition for *Tit-Bits*. Becomes a British subject and passes the captaincy examination, receiving his 'Certificate of Competency as Master'.

1886–8 Second mate in the *Falconhurst* (London to Penarth); first mate in the *Highland Forest* (Amsterdam to Semarang) and *Vidar* (Singapore to Celebes and Borneo ports); captain of the *Otago* (to Bangkok, Australia and Mauritius).

1889 Living in Pimlico (London), begins *Almayer's Folly*. Visits Bobrowski in the Ukraine.

1890 In the Congo Free State, working for the Belgian company Société Anonyme du Haut-Congo; second-in-command, then temporarily captain, of Congo River steamer *Roi des Belges*.

1891 Recuperating from African experience in the German Hospital, London, then in Geneva for hydrotherapy. On return, works for warehouse and shippers Barr, Moering, Company.

1891–4 First mate in the passenger clipper *Torrens* (to Australia), meeting John Galsworthy (1893), later novelist and playwright awarded a Nobel Prize. Second mate in the *Adowa* (Rouen to Quebec and Montreal, but making only a return voyage from London to Rouen as the company collapses). Sea career ends.

1894 Tadeusz Bobrowski dies. Meets Edward Garnett, his literary mentor and advisor, and Jessie George, his future wife. Though still looking for a berth, turns to professional authorship in earnest.

1895 *Almayer's Folly.* In Geneva in the spring for hydrotherapy, and in Paris in August on business for Fountaine
(G. F. W.) Hope, his first English friend.

1896 *An Outcast of the Islands.* After marrying Jessie George,
honeymoons in Brittany (April–September), later settling in
Stanford-le-Hope, Essex, near Hope and family. Christmas
holidays in Cardiff.

1897 Meets Henry James. Writes 'The Return' and 'Karain: A
Memory'. Befriends American novelist Stephen Crane and
R. B. Cunninghame Graham, socialist and writer. *The Nigger
of the 'Narcissus'.*

1898 Alfred Borys Conrad born in Stanford. *Tales of Unrest.*
Becomes friendly with Ford Madox Hueffer (later Ford) and
H. G. Wells. In Glasgow, looks for a command. The Conrads
move to Pent Farm, near Hythe, Kent, sub-let from Ford.
'Youth, A Narrative' in *Blackwood's Magazine.*

1899 Works on *Lord Jim. Heart of Darkness* serialized in
Blackwood's Magazine. Meets Hugh Clifford, writer and
civil servant in Malaya. The Boer War begins.

1900 Becomes a client of J. B. Pinker's literary agency. Crane
dies. Working-holiday in Belgium with Ford. *Lord Jim.*

1901 Queen Victoria dies. Works on 'Amy Foster', 'Falk' and
Romance (with Ford). *The Inheritors* (with Ford).

1902 The Boer War ends. Writes 'The End of the Tether'.
Youth: A Narrative and Two Other Stories.

1903 Works on *Nostromo. Typhoon and Other Stories* and
Romance (with Ford) appear.

1904 Two-month sojourn in London. Engages 'typewriter'
Lilian M. Hallowes, his secretary on and off for twenty years.
Nostromo.

1905 In Capri (January–May). *One Day More* staged in
London. Writes sea papers and critical articles.

1906 In Montpellier (mid-February–mid-April). John Alexander Conrad born in London. *The Mirror of the Sea.*

1907 In Montpellier (January–May). Writes 'The Duel', and
then in Geneva (May–August). *The Secret Agent.* The
Conrads move to Luton, Bedfordshire.

1908 Works on *Under Western Eyes* (then 'Razumov').

Involved with Ford's *English Review*, in which 'Some Reminiscences' appears (later *A Personal Record*).

1909 The Conrads move to Aldington, Kent. *The Nature of a Crime*, with Ford, with whom he quarrels and breaks off relationship. Writes 'The Secret Sharer' and more of *Under Western Eyes*.

1910 Suffers a mental and physical breakdown, recovery extending into the summer. The Conrads move to Capel House, Orlestone, Kent. Reviews for the *Daily Mail* (July) and writes 'A Smile of Fortune' and 'The Partner'.

1911 Writes 'Freya of the Seven Isles' and works on *Chance*. Meets novelist André Gide, who later translates 'Typhoon' and oversees Conrad's French translations. *Under Western Eyes*.

1912 *A Personal Record* in America, then as *Some Reminiscences* in England. Writes two articles on the *Titanic*. *'Twixt Land and Sea*. Writes short stories. Meets Richard Curle, journalist and short-story writer, in effect the unofficial private secretary to Conrad's later career.

1913 *Chance*. Becomes friendly with Cambridge philosopher Bertrand Russell through Lady Ottoline Morrell. Works on 'The Planter of Malata', 'Because of the Dollars' and *Victory*.

1914 Visiting Cracow in late July, the Conrads are caught by the outbreak of war. Taking refuge in Zakopane in the Tatras, return home via Vienna and Genoa (October–November).

1915 Writes 'Poland Revisited'. *Victory* and *Within the Tides* appear. Borys Conrad in basic training in the Army Service Corps, and fights in France for the next few years.

1916 Writes 'The Warrior's Soul' and 'The Tale'. For the Admiralty, visits naval bases, tours in a minesweeper, takes a flight, and sails in a Q-ship in the North Sea.

1917 Writes prefaces for new editions of *Youth*, *Lord Jim* and *Nostromo*. *The Shadow-Line* appears. Meets London-based French music critic and journalist Jean Aubry ('G. Jean-Aubry'), later his first biographer, who succeeds Gide in overseeing the French translations.

1918 Becomes friendly with novelist Hugh Walpole. Writes

articles about the Merchant Service and Polish events for the
newspapers. Borys Conrad is shell-shocked and gassed. The
war ends (11 November).

1919 Basil MacDonald Hastings's adaptation of *Victory* has
a successful London run, including a royal performance.
Moves to Spring Grove, near Wye, Kent. *The Arrow of Gold*.
Moves to Oswalds, Bishopsbourne, near Canterbury.

1920 Polish relative Aniela Zagórska visits the Conrads for
six months. *The Rescue*. Writes, with Pinker, *Gaspar the
Strongman*, a film version of 'Gaspar Ruiz'. In December,
collected editions begin publication in England by Heinemann (in the early new year in America by Doubleday, Page).

1921 Conrad and wife sojourn in Corsica (January–April),
celebrating silver wedding anniversary in March. *Notes on
Life and Letters* (collected essays) appears.

1922 J. B. Pinker dies in New York on a business trip, his son
Eric taking over management of Conrad. Meets composer
Maurice Ravel and poet Paul Valéry. Dramatic version of
The Secret Agent flops in London (November).

1923 Triumphant publicity tour in New York, with excursions
to Connecticut and Massachusetts (May–June). Briefly in
Normandy to arrange for French immersion experience for
son John (September). *The Rover*.

1924 Declines a knighthood. Succumbs to fatal heart attack on
3 August. After Roman Catholic rites, is buried in Canterbury
Cemetery. *The Nature of a Crime* (with Ford) and *The
Shorter Tales*. Ford rushes out *Joseph Conrad: A Personal
Remembrance*.

1925–8 Posthumous works published: *Tales of Hearsay* and the
unfinished *Suspense* (1925); *Last Essays*, edited by Richard
Curle (1926); *Joseph Conrad: Life and Letters* (1927), edited
by G. Jean-Aubry; the unfinished *The Sisters* (1928).

Introduction to *Heart of Darkness*

New readers are advised that this Introduction
makes details of the plot explicit.

Mention the name of Joseph Conrad and the answering
response will commonly invoke his celebrated African novella
of 1899, *Heart of Darkness*. If the work has acquired an iconic
status comparable to that of Edvard Munch's painting *The
Scream* (1893), its title has by contrast become something of a
tired cliché in being so repeatedly used by newspaper headline-
makers. Conrad, who modestly hoped that the work might
have a continuing 'vibration', would have been astonished by
these contemporary reverberations.

The story's emergence as a twentieth-century 'classic' forms
a first stage in the history of its remarkable after-life. A key
moment arrived with T. S. Eliot's use of a fragment from *Heart
of Darkness* as an epigraph to his poem, 'The Hollow Men'
(1925). Eliot's epigraph signals a temporary kinship and estab-
lishes a bridge between the two works, but it also probably
signifies a more intangible sense of indebtedness – to Conrad
as an important founder-member of a tradition of British Modernist writing.

The story's major rediscovery dates from the 1950s when its
apocalyptic symbolism and existentialist uncertainty seem to
have entered the collective consciousness of a generation who
lived through the Second World War or were coming to terms
with its legacy. As one critic of the time put it, the story had
become 'a *Pilgrim's Progress* for our pessimistic and psycholog-
izing age' (Guerard, p. 33). Its more recent impact has been
equally dramatic, if more controversial. Now standing at the
centre of a wider contemporary debate about race, imperialism
and feminism, its aesthetic dimensions and experimental

character have almost been left behind. It has acquired the status of an awkward problem novel, a standard text in the classroom and – for better or worse – a litmus test for a variety of theoretical preoccupations. As a modern quest parable translated into many languages, it has simultaneously had a powerful generative effect upon twentieth-century writers and film-makers, inspiring emulations, adaptations and counter-versions.

I

Conrad's direct and indirect engagement with things African has a long pre-history. It extends as far back as his childhood, when the young Pole pored over maps of the continent, devoured tales of the first European explorers in Africa and vicariously shared the perils of Dr Livingstone's travels. Like all dreams of heroic adventure, this one was destined to meet with a rude awakening. In 1890, towards the end of his career as a merchant seaman, the thirty-three-year-old Conrad signed a long-term contract to work for a Belgian company in the Congo Free State. The country he entered had since 1885 been the personal possession of King Leopold II of Belgium, who, under the guise of a philanthropic concern to bring 'light' to the 'dark' continent, was brutally engaged in what Conrad later described as 'the vilest scramble for loot that ever disfigured the history of human conscience and geographical exploration'.[1]

Conrad's growing desire to return to Europe was unexpectedly realized when he suffered a physical breakdown: plagued with the after-effects of dysentery and malaria, he ended his stay after seven months, returned to a period of hospitalization in London and suffered a legacy of ill health for the rest of his life. His first-hand encounter with the effects of Leopold's rule in the Congo almost certainly left him with deeper scars: according to a close friend, the episode formed 'the turning-point in his mental life', shaped 'his transformation from a sailor to a writer' and 'swept away the generous illusions of his youth'.[2]

One of the products of this period was 'The Congo Diary' (included in this edition), Conrad's record of his daily move-

ments during the first part of his stay. Severely factual and never intended for publication, the diary nevertheless offers his earliest written account of a peopled Africa and may have been kept to preserve material that would be of use to the later writer.

Conrad's first African work, 'An Outpost of Progress', was composed six years later. A fine short story in its own right, 'An Outpost' also represents an important stage in Conrad's attempt to fashion a serious and grown-up colonial fiction distinct from the boyish adventure stories of G. A. Henty and Rider Haggard. From his early Eastern novels the story inherits the large spectacle of the European abroad, removed from the constraints of the Western 'crowd', isolated in the wilderness and undergoing swift collapse. Here, however, the predicament is shaped by an acutely political awareness, with the focus partly upon its two carefully chosen types (a bureaucrat and a soldier) and partly upon the representative imperialist fictions arriving from Europe with them.

The degeneration of the two supposed 'light-bringers' is remorseless: they arrive in Africa voicing the conventional view that as racially superior Europeans they have the right and duty to civilize 'backward' peoples, but ironies emerge when it transpires that, as two of Europe's failed rejects, they are happy to cultivate failure, content with their fellowship in idleness and oblivious to the civilized litter they leave around an increasingly inefficient trading-post. Ultimately, however, the strengths of the story as a polemic – its aloof omniscient narration, singleness of focus and sparkling sarcasm – also serve to define its limits. In Conrad's later view, 'An Outpost' was mainly an important stepping-stone towards *Heart of Darkness*, in which an English narrator, Marlow, agitatedly reflects upon an earlier visit to Africa and his quest there towards the charismatic European trader, Kurtz. According to Conrad, his return to an African subject coincided with a widening sense of its possibilities and was accompanied by an intense 'nightmare feeling' (*Collected Letters*, vol. II, p. 162).

II

Enigmatic though *Heart of Darkness* may finally prove to be, its early episodes are remarkable for their trenchant topicality. At the outset of its composition, Conrad described the story as being of 'our time distinc[t]ly' in its concern with the 'criminality of inefficiency and pure selfishness when tackling the civilizing work in Africa' (*Collected Letters*, vol. II, pp. 140–41). For his subject, he again returned to what was bluntly described in a coinage of 1884 as the 'Scramble for Africa', one resulting in the systematic annexation and exploitation of Africa by European powers during the last decades of the nineteenth century.

At an early point, the story offers a summary of these developments. The map of Central Africa available to the youthful Marlow presents it as a white blankness, an unexplored and unnamed *terra incognita*. To the older Marlow, the area has become, presumably as a result of European expansion, a more impenetrable and menacing 'place of darkness' (9), while yet another map of the continent presents him with a multi-coloured chart, its pattern the visible evidence of European territorial possessions. Even more topically, the story's opening sequences confronted its first readers with echoes of their most recent newspaper headlines – in references to the building of a railway or to expanding trade-syndicates or to increasing militarization in Africa, as signalled by the presence of mercenary soldiers and a blockading French gunboat.

This sense of topical issue is, however, most marked in Marlow's acerbic quarrel with manifestations of the period's sophisticated propaganda machinery, of which the popular press formed a crucial cog. *Heart of Darkness* was written against a background of recent imperial celebration of a feverishly utopian kind. Queen Victoria's diamond jubilee in 1897 occasioned an exaltation of the British Empire and the importance of the imperial idea to the country's future as an international power. In her diary for that year, Beatrice Webb summarized the social mood: 'Imperialism in the air! – all classes drunk with sight seeing and hysterical loyalty'.[3] Articles

in the *New Review* evoke the wider note of intoxicated eulogy in lauding the Queen as 'the Great White Mother, the fame of whose virtue has won the loyalty of native races as the genius of Alexander or a Napoleon never could' and characterizing the British imperial idea as an onerous religious destiny: 'Since the wise men saw the star in the East, Christianity has found no nobler expression'.[4] A stream of propaganda also emanated from Brussels, where, as Conrad later observed, Leopold had commandeered press opinion – by, in effect, colonizing its language – in order to engineer an outrageous 'newspaper "stunt"'.[5]

The story's early progress from Europe to Africa offers a virtual initiation into the contagious power of the period's official imperial propaganda – in the anonymous narrator's eulogy to the River Thames, in the colourful hyperbole picked up by Marlow's aunt from her newspapers and through a variety of European voices in Africa. Sharing his creator's sense of the power of the printed word, Marlow is acutely aware of its journalistic misuse in rendering people essentially blinkered and insentient. Its invasive power is further suggested by the fact that for most of these speakers such rhetoric is a reflexive act: they are not, on the whole, individuals seeking to use hyperbole to disguise an unsavoury truth, but inert victims and instruments of linguistic coercion.

Marlow's counter-response takes a number of forms: sometimes he simply speaks plainly of newspaper 'rot', often he notes the spurious authority given to bureaucratic functionaries in Africa by their naming (as in the case of the euphemistically styled 'Workers' or 'agents'), while elsewhere he is shocked by the outrageous incongruities thrown up by the unthinking use of cliché. For example, his grim mirth at hearing from The Harlequin that the heads on stakes belong to 'rebels' prompts the comment: 'Rebels! What would be the next definition I was to hear? There had been enemies, criminals, workers—and these were rebels. Those rebellious heads looked very subdued to me on their sticks' (73).

If much of the best imaginative literature thrives on the exposure of what George Orwell termed Newspeak, it also

abhors a vacuum 'silences usually prevailed in the popular press
of the 1890s about the exact nature of European rule in Africa
and its effect upon her indigenous peoples and customs. By
1897, however, damning facts about the Congo were beginning
to filter into British newspapers, as in *The Times* of 13 May,
which reported an ex-Congo missionary's testimony that 'gross
atrocities were perpetrated by the soldiers of the State on the
natives, amounting in some cases to shooting and in others to
mutilation, for refusal to labour in the gathering of india-
rubber. Whole villages were spoliated and destroyed'.[6] The first
part of Conrad's story belongs to this early move towards
silence-breaking: 'I have a voice . . . and for good or evil mine
is the speech that cannot be silenced' (44).

Marlow's initiation into Africa allots him a role not unlike
that of an on-the-spot foreign correspondent, with his own
independent sense of what is newsworthy: he watches, listens,
reports on his interviews and trusts in the power of hard,
definite particulars. The picture of Africa to emerge combines
the image of a messily organized scramble for 'loot' with that
of a chaotic war zone littered with upturned rusting trucks,
abandoned drainage pipes and gaping craters. He also allows
space for voices unheard in the newspapers of the time – those
of the European 'agents', traders and other hangers-on. These
voices range from the brickmaker and his version of justice
– 'Transgression—punishment—bang! Pitiless, pitiless. That's
the only way' (31) – to Marlow's companion and his reasons
for being in Africa – 'To make money, of course. What do you
think?' (24) – and include a description of the agents' collective
voice: 'The word "ivory" rang in the air, was whispered, was
sighed. You would think they were praying to it. A taint of
imbecile rapacity blew through it all, like a whiff from some
corpse' (27).

The sense given of a narrator wishing to recover an Africa
lost, ignored or silenced culminates in the description of the
'grove of death':

[The African workers] were dying slowly—it was very clear.
They were not enemies, they were not criminals, they were

nothing earthly now   nothing but black shadows of disease and
starvation, lying confusedly in the greenish gloom. Brought from
all the recesses of the coast in all the legality of time contracts,
lost in uncongenial surroundings, fed on unfamiliar food, they
sickened, became inefficient, and were then allowed to crawl
away and rest . . . Near the same tree two more, bundles of acute
angles, sat with their legs drawn up. One, with his chin propped
on his knees, stared at nothing, in an intolerable and appalling
manner: his brother phantom rested its forehead, as if overcome
with a great weariness; and all about others were scattered in
every pose of contorted collapse, as in some picture of a massacre
or a pestilence. (20)

Like a poem by Wilfred Owen from the First World War
battlefront, this heightened reportage quickly dispenses with
the rattle of official verbiage in order to recover unreported
facts – in this case, of wasted African lives. The sense of waste
is intensified by the wider context. Marlow has just passed
through a rubbish tip for discarded pipes and rusty machinery,
and the implication is that the worn-out Africans have been
similarly discarded: having served their function, they are
thrown away like disposable objects. Crass labels discarded,
Marlow assimilates the details of human waste into an extended
elegy, with an invitation to complete it by recalling a picture of
Bosch-like extremity.

In conjunction with other contemporary events, *Heart of
Darkness* played no small part in effecting a linguistic change
that, in turn, reflected a wider shift in attitudes. In 1897, the
words 'Imperial' and 'Imperialism' (both normally capitalized)
carried hardly any pejorative meanings and, with their Latin
equivalents (*Imperium et Libertas*), formed a natural part of
the period's rhetoric. But by 1903, in the aftermath of the Boer
War and when the scandal of the Congo caused E. D. Morel to
found the Congo Reform Association, the terms began to
acquire less reputable associations and could no longer be used
as a form of unthinking national self-congratulation.

III

During its composition, *Heart of Darkness* developed like 'genii from the bottle' in ways that seem to have surprised Conrad himself, prompting him later to feel that its last two instalments were 'wrapped up in secondary notions' (*Collected Letters*, vol. II, pp. 146, 157). One sign of its changing character is that Marlow, predominantly a detached figure in Part I, becomes with his journey upriver an involved participant, increasingly excited, feverish and panic-stricken. Simultaneously, he is obsessed by the charismatic voice of Kurtz, a spectral figure who actively dominates the later part of the story. With these developments, the pattern of the quest becomes more insistent. Marlow conceives of his journey as culminating in a meeting with Kurtz, who is himself engaged in a quest into unexplored regions: when the two make contact late in the story, they become, in effect, agents in each other's lives.

Successive generations of critics have been impelled to testify to the nature of the elusive developments following upon Marlow's upriver departure, and there is now virtually an interpretation of the story to suit every predilection – the psychoanalytic, philosophic, political, post-colonial and gender-based. Each generation has also thrown up a major dissenting critic. In the immediate post-1950 period, F. R. Leavis was highly influential with his claim that the story was marred by an 'adjectival insistence upon . . . inexpressible and incomprehensible mystery'.[7] Later generations have been overshadowed by the Nigerian novelist and critic Chinua Achebe, whose angry polemic of 1975 accused Conrad of virtually betraying his subject by eliminating 'the African as a human factor', lamented his 'preposterous and perverse arrogance in reducing Africa to the role of props for the break-up of one petty European mind' and condemned the author as a 'bloody racist'.[8]

Traditionally, the most immediate problem for readers has been that of adjusting to the tale's dramatically changing character. Although Part I anticipates some of the terms of Marlow's coming quest, it hardly foreshadows the ambitious symbolic method to be brought into play. In part, Marlow

himself becomes an active symbol-maker, constantly seeking a figurative equivalent for his feelings. But in addition, the obscure nightmare in which he is embroiled increasingly determines the character of the story and embraces Kurtz as a significant part of its structure: everywhere felt but only occasionally glimpsed, the latter emerges as a strangely protean presence, forming and re-forming like the genie from a bottle. Achebe regards the story as involving a single 'petty European', but the symbol of dark nightmare also has a strenuously generalizing effect in suggesting that *all* Europeans are involved in the breakdown of the imperial dream.

Symbolic method also brings with it a new, and in some ways, problematic range of 'secondary' interests. In moving away from the symptoms of colonial rowdyism in Part I, the tale is not thereby always less topical, but it now devises markedly wider tests in order to probe the credentials of the European mission in Africa. As a compendium of decadent excesses, the figure of Kurtz is obviously central to the tale's free-wheeling and – as some readers have felt – erratically widening scope. His is the most comprehensive test and the most spectacular fall; in one of his many guises, he offers access to what might be called Europe's political unconscious – into the underlying obsessions and needs that both fostered and found relief in the imperial project. And finally, when Marlow returns to Europe, he brings with him a Kurtzian legacy that helps to shape an even wider vision of Western civilization and its discontents.

Early in Part II, with the beginning of Marlow's journey to the interior, the tale signals that the narrator's own inherited British traditions will be the first to come under scrutiny. The terms of this ordeal would have been familiar to late-Victorian readers, since what is on trial is a principle at the very basis of their culture and underpinning its 'mission' in the colonies – the work ethic as an agency of order and progress. In Britain, the gospel of work was associated with the Victorian sage Thomas Carlyle, in whose writings the principle gathered numerous moral, religious and philosophic resonances. As a British merchant seaman, Marlow's tradition is a seamanly inflexion of the Carlylean gospel. Marlow spells out the tonalities of this humanistic ideal: 'I don't like work — no man does — but I like what is in the work — the chance to find yourself. Your own reality — for yourself, not for others' (35). For him, the notion brings with it a view of the seaman's life as involving the pursuit of an honourable vocation, the performance of a social obligation in the cause of human solidarity and the restraining of individuality by the collective ethic. Translated into the context of colonial 'work', the ethic also involves a tough, no-nonsense pragmatism – the ability, as Marlow puts it, to bury dead hippo without being too bothered by the smell.

But even an immunity to noxious smells cannot defend Marlow from being challenged on several fronts. He is quickly made aware, when he becomes 'one of the Workers, with a capital' (14), that a wider political machinery can itself be found to exploit the superficial rhetoric of the Carlylean work ethic to legitimize its ultimately criminal purpose. (In 1898, Leopold had required of his agents that they 'accustom the population to general laws, of which the most needful and the most salutary is assuredly that of work'.)[9] Once in Africa, he quickly learns that his work efforts are either rendered futile by a lawless inefficiency or part of a process ultimately devoted to base ends.

Even though Marlow tries to attend to practicalities involved with the job in hand – the problem of acquiring rivets, tracking river obstacles and efficient steering – he is increasingly forced to question how far the job-sense is a necessary avoidance of a painful knowledge of the self and world. At a crucial point in the narrative, two documents serve to bring home his crisis of choice: on the one hand, the clear seamanly purpose he finds in Towson's nautical manual, a symbolic reminder of his inherited traditions, or, on the other, the searing self-contradictions of Kurtz's pamphlet, a signpost to the possibility of different kinships and allegiances.

In more senses than one, Marlow loses navigational clarity and purpose. The pressures put upon him reflect more widely on a tradition of liberal humanism that, when faced by the flinty actualities of wider colonial politics, has commonly suffered painful defeat and been left with a legacy of nervous irritation, panic, hysteria and frustrated silence. At the point where Marlow's panic sets in, Kurtz becomes a more material presence; as the narrator begins to share empathically in Kurtz's ordeal, their crises intermesh.

From a point of hindsight, Conrad himself seems to have been aware of the dangerous risk involved in the treatment of the tale's presiding symbolic figure: 'What I distinctly admit is the fault of having made Kurtz too symbolic or rather symbolic at all' (*Collected Letters*, vol. II, p. 460). Even in the first part of the tale, the Kurtz who emerges through hearsay and gossip is a bewildering medley of possibilities – now universal genius, now noted ivory-hunter, now confirmed solitary with ambitious plans for Africa and now threatening spectre. The problem of Kurtz's shifting metamorphoses becomes more formidable as the tale progresses, since this figure will become part of the tumultuous content of Marlow's nightmare, shaping its form and providing its climax. With each of his metamorphoses, moreover, Kurtz also contributes to a shifting sense of the nature and location of the 'heart of darkness'. How various and plural are his main incarnations, and how are their meanings registered in Marlow's narrative?

One of Kurtz's symbolic identities memorably extends the 'dark' evidence of European rule in Part I. Several descriptions focus upon his extreme deformity and grotesque, puppet-like movements in order to bring home the sense in which, as Europe's offspring, he enacts the logic of its expansionist and acquisitive drives. In his restless energy as an explorer, conqueror and self-styled hero of Empire, he is a powerfully iconoclastic caricature. To the extent that he casts aside the need for any hypocritical pretence and unashamedly acts out the will to acquire vast amounts of ivory, he embodies a brute economic imperative as well as an unnatural idolatry of the material object.

Where some nations tended high-mindedly to regard overseas expansion as an organic extension of their destiny, *Heart of Darkness* can suggest a powerfully alternative vision: of imperialism as a historical deformation, whose working out involves an inevitable principle of degeneration. Central to this version

in the presentation of Kurtz as a malformed seven-foot-long puppet-creature, who enacts a grotesquely choreographed ceremony. Kurtz has become so enthralled to the commodity he seeks that he is himself commodified, as though 'an animated image of death carved out of old ivory had been shaking its hand' (74); or he is imaged as a grimacing open mouth, giving him 'a weirdly voracious aspect, as though he had wanted to swallow all the air, all the earth, all the men before him' (74). He also acts out with psychopathic intensity the urge towards an autocratically governed empire – ' "My Intended, my ivory, my station, my river, my—" Everything belonged to him' (60) – in which, as the veritable Antichrist of its making, he exacts complete submission from his subordinates and can envisage a policy of what nowadays would be called racial cleansing: 'Exterminate all the brutes!' (62). The iconoclastic power of this portrait depends upon our recognizing that the 'heart of darkness' has its roots firmly in Europe and that Kurtz, as its malformed outgrowth, strikes Marlow as a symbol of present and active degeneration.

But overlaying this incarnation is another one, the object of Marlow's most excited and unspecific fears – the spectacle of Kurtz as a 'lost soul'. This version presses us to attend to the fact that Kurtz has a pre-history. There had, it seems, been an 'original Kurtz' (no mere trader, but a person of considerable idealism and with talents as a painter, poet, musician, philosopher and orator), who in Africa has been exposed as a 'hollow sham' (85). This transplanted European, originally the product of a cultured society and identifying himself with the high-minded mission of bringing 'light' to Africa, has been betrayed by a naive belief in imperial watchwords and, with his inherited assumptions exposed as fictions, stands revealed as a morally bankrupt cipher. The image of Kurtz as a greedily devouring mouth is now replaced by one of inner vacancy: he was, says Marlow, strikingly, 'hollow at the core' (72).

But for Marlow, the spectacle does not end there: it carries with it the added implication that Kurtz has undergone a spectacular 'fall' in Africa – brought about by a hollowness so profound as to have resulted in his invasion by the dark atavistic forces of the land. Though the narrator has previously shown himself to have a healthy disrespect for potential obfuscation, he himself seems to acquire a taste for the *frisson* of metaphysical melodrama in describing how Kurtz's 'soul' has become a battleground for the competing forces of good and evil. Marlow's heated imaginings offer two possibilities: that Kurtz has been captured, as if in some illicit and vampirish love affair, by a 'wilderness' that had 'taken him, loved him, embraced him, got into his veins, consumed his flesh, and sealed his soul to its own by the inconceivable ceremonies of some devilish initiation' (59).

Alternatively, he pictures Kurtz's fall as involving a Faustian pact, in which the man has virtually sold his soul in order to enjoy 'a high seat amongst the devils of the land—I mean literally'. However, in the absence of substantiating evidence, the impact of the word 'literally' remains muted, and attention is instead re-focused on Marlow's horrified sense of the 'creepy': 'Everything belonged to him—but that was a trifle. The thing was to know what he belonged to, how many powers of darkness claimed him for their own. That was the reflection that made you creepy all over' (60).

There is some force in Achebe's objection that the Africa to emerge in parts of the story belongs to a conventional picture of the 'dark' continent, a place of 'creepy' horrors and the traditional site of the 'white man's grave'. Certainly many of Conrad's first reviewers, overlooking the disturbing implications of Kurtz's hollowness, could comfortably regard the story as a version of a familiar type of late-Victorian novel, in which Africa's strange 'devils' bring about the decivilization or 'going native' of a European colonist, who finally descends into madness.

To Marlow's excited imagination, Kurtz simultaneously metamorphoses into yet another symbolic incarnation, that of a charismatic, oracular 'voice' (58), whose utterances will eventually help to shape the spreading nightmare into significant form. Several problems accompany this fascination, not least the fact that Marlow is at such an early stage of his journey fugitively haunted by the sensation that its culmination will

~~are eventually entail a redeeming~~ 'talk with Kurtz' (58) and confirm the rightness of his unconscious loyalty to him. Further, it is not entirely clear why Kurtz's powerful voice – the grandiloquence of which is often the object of Marlow's suspicion – should be so quickly valued as an unambiguous gift. There is often some confusion in Marlow's mind about whether he has actively chosen a commitment to Kurtz's voice or whether he is its fated victim. If the latter is true, then Marlow is possibly nearer than he thinks to The Harlequin, whom he regards as being dangerously captive to the power of Kurtz's charismatic eloquence: '"We talked of everything," he said, quite transported at the recollection. "I forgot there was such a thing as sleep"' (69).

In addition, Marlow has a growing tendency to be so obsessed by Kurtz's 'gift' of eloquence as to relegate his actions to a secondary place: 'Hadn't I been told . . . that he had collected, bartered, swindled, or stolen more ivory than all the other agents together. That was not the point. The point was in his being a gifted creature, and that of all his gifts the one that stood out pre-eminently, that carried with it a sense of real presence, was his ability to talk, his words' (58). If there is some oddity here, it derives from the fact that the Marlow of the early narrative had learned that actions speak louder than words, which can rarely be taken at face value. Here he appears to be haunted by the growing idea that the promise of words from a special being can, in some sense, redeem or justify actions: the pathway to the 'heart of darkness', it seems, now leads to a powerful oracle.

As if in response to Marlow's deepest wishes, Kurtz does finally emerge – by means of a sudden deathbed redemption – as a significant 'voice' and hero of the spirit. Marlow's approach to the spectacle involves a somewhat awkward readjustment of his previous convictions. Perhaps drawing upon an established nineteenth-century view that genius and madness are closely allied, he tells us that Kurtz is no 'lunatic' because his 'intelligence' is perfectly clear, if intensely self-centred; but, he adds, 'his soul was mad' (83). In a darkened cabin, the terminally ill Kurtz is seemingly allowed the privilege of the dying man to survey his entire life in flashback, with Marlow, his disciple, in attendance to catch the whisper of his final words, 'The horror! The horror!', this severely bare exclamation being apparently an involuntary one, made in response to 'some image . . . some vision' (86). The emerging view of Kurtz combines elements of the Promethean quester, philosopher-outlaw and deranged genius, whose isolated self-absorption is the condition of both his eventual greatness and consuming madness. In addition, Kurtz's deathbed scene brings with it the vindicatory suggestion that the 'criminal hero' discovers in the ultimacy of evil redemptive possibilities not open to average pilgrims of the world ('It was an affirmation, a moral victory paid for by innumerable defeats, by abominable terrors' (88)) and is therefore able to see into the essence of things, like the hero described by Thomas Carlyle: 'A Hero, as I repeat, has this first distinction . . . That he looks through the shows of things into *things*. Use and wont, respectable hearsay, respectable formula: all these are good, or not good.'[10]

Given the scarcity of substantiating details about the wraith-like Kurtz, the problems posed by his metamorphoses are especially acute. How, for example, do we identify a logic that can explain the development of a figure 'hollow' at the core into a veritable hero of the spirit? Is it possible to find any secure foothold in a simulated nightmare where Kurtz seems at once 'without a substance' (57) and is, at the same time, everything and everywhere in its formation? Some of the best-known literary works are associated with what appear to be unfolding enigmas or riddles, like Samuel Taylor Coleridge's *The Rime of the Ancient Mariner* (1798), a poem echoed in the story, and the developing *Heart of Darkness* has some claim to belong to this tradition. In fact, Marlow himself uses the word 'riddle' to describe the form of 'ultimate wisdom' that makes of life a 'mysterious arrangement of merciless logic for a futile purpose' (87). He seems to imply that riddles can have a pattern or 'logic', but that the pattern does not really signify anything – it is fundamentally mysterious.

In many ways, the tale might be said to reproduce the riddle of a structured pattern that is growingly opaque. As Marlow's quest evolves, the relationship between its early beginnings and its developing 'secondary' intuitions becomes increasingly enigmatic. But the medley effect inherent in the later stages of Marlow's quest presents a further order of difficulty. As the spectral Kurtz forms and re-forms, some of his incarnations overlap and some have a parallel life, but others seem actively to quarrel with each other. This medley effect also, of course, makes for an uncommon mixture of styles and genres – ranging from the spare style of polemic, through the excited stream of consciousness of a confessional, to the breathless fear of a Victorian sensation novel.

The problem of how and what 'Kurtz' signifies raises other implications of a general nature. Leavis's complaint about a persistent 'magazineish' element[11] in *Heart of Darkness* acts as a reminder that the professional Conrad was writing the story for *Blackwood's Magazine*, a monthly that welcomed fiction of a colourful medley nature. According to a spoof by Edgar Allan Poe, it preferred a style 'elevated, diffusive, and interjectional', where the 'words must be all in a whirl, like a humming top . . . which answers remarkably well instead of meaning'.[12] Other readers have felt that the 'whirling' words of the story's later part are signally important in emphasizing that the final horror assailing Marlow is grounded in his discovery that it is impossible to disclose a central core or an essence, even a firm basis for what Kurtz has done and what he is.

In other words, Kurtz's protean incarnations reflect upon the insufficiency of language to express anything more than a frustrated desire for meaning. That such extreme linguistic scepticism should appear in an apparently topical work about Africa is foreshadowed in Conrad's comments upon a vitriolic attack on imperialism mounted by his friend R. B. Cunninghame Graham in 'Bloody Niggers' (1897): 'There are no converts to ideas of honour, justice, pity, freedom. There are only people who . . . drive themselves into a frenzy with words, repeat them, shout them out, imagine they believe in them . . . And words fly away; and nothing remains, do you understand? Absolutely nothing, oh man of faith!' (*Collected Letters*, vol. II, p. 70). If, finally, the figure of Kurtz may be taken as a summarizing rubric for a larger free-wheeling medley of styles and genres, then one other implication tends to emerge: the quest for a presumed unity in the story may turn out to be less rewarding than one focusing upon the elisions, tensions and even collisions in its negotiation with shiftingly plural 'hearts' of darkness.

IV

It is hardly surprising that *Heart of Darkness* is often used to pursue an inquiry into the more general nature and practice of reading, and particularly into the perils and pitfalls of reading a Modernist text. The early part of the story offers a fore-warning of challenges to come:

> The yarns of seamen have an effective simplicity, the whole meaning of which lies within the shell of a cracked nut. But, as has been said, Marlow was not typical (if his propensity to spin yarns be excepted), and to him the meaning of an episode was not inside like a kernel but outside, enveloping the tale which brought it out only as a glow brings out a haze, in the likeness of one of these misty halos that, sometimes, are made visible by the spectral illumination of moonshine. (6)

While offering a familiar point of reference in Marlow's incorrigible tendency to 'yarn', the description otherwise emphasizes an extreme version of the nebulous and penumbral – meaning inheres not in a glow, but as in a silhouette produced by a glow, which itself can be 'spectral'. So pictorial is the analogy here that some readers have been prompted to make a link with, for example, the chromatic vibrations and atmospheric mistiness in paintings by the early nineteenth-century painter J. M. W. Turner, in whose works an 'obscure' revelation is effected by means of intermingled light and shade, or *chiaroscuro* (from the Italian *chiaro* or 'clear' + *oscuro* or 'obscure').

The reference to a 'misty halo' serves as a reminder that a cognate image in the story is that of the veil, as in the opening description of the mist as being 'like a gauzy and radiant fabric

... draping the ~~how~~ ~~shows~~ in diaphanous folds' (4), with its
accompanying implication that moments of revelation only
arrive when the veil is lifted or torn. It also anticipates the ways
in which Marlow's characteristic acts of seeing are so literally
obstructed (the journey downriver in Part II finds him success-
ively peering through darkness, impenetrable fog and then
dark smoke from the steamer's funnel) that he is allowed only
glimpses of a 'veiled' kind. That the tale may also tease the
reader with something akin to optical illusion is perhaps also
hinted at in the word 'moonshine'.

An equivalent sense of expressive riddle inheres not only in
how we see things, but also in how we hear them. An episode
at the beginning of Part II presents Marlow drowsing on the
deck of his steamer and suddenly disturbed by broken frag-
ments of a conversation between The Manager and his nephew,
who are sometimes too far away for him to hear them properly.
Marlow's imperfect overhearing means that the conversation
emerges without a connective logic. It brings him revealing but
puzzling 'snatches' (39) that only serve to generate further
glimpses of Kurtz. A more important form of partial hearing
arrives through the constant ellipses that steadily invade Marlow's narration in the form of unfinished or interrupted sentences marked by agitated pauses and silences: 'And I heard—
him—it—this voice—other voices . . . Voices, voices—even the
girl herself—now——' (59). The problem of what and how we
hear operates at two levels here. Marlow's struggle to decipher
what he has 'heard' is directly relayed to readers as a problem
in how *we* decipher his chosen 'snatches'. Do his pauses signify
a persistent confusion, a willed determination to leave something unspoken, or a panic-stricken sense of the unspeakable?

The fashioning of such glimpses into a sequential narrative
has the constant effect of deferring any promise of full insight.
So, at one point, Marlow with typical indirection peers through
binoculars to catch sight of what appear to be carved balls
stuck on posts or discovers a book with a mysterious cipher
pencilled on its margins. Only later does it transpire, with an
accompanying shock and need for readjustment on the
observer's part, that the objects are shrunken heads and that

the cipher is a form of annotation in Russian made by The Harlequin. In the case of the discovered heads on sticks, a further trap awaits the reader, since one puzzle is solved only to generate another – when, that is, Marlow goes on to deem the heads to be 'symbolic' and adds that they were 'expressive and puzzling . . . food for thought' (71).

The most extreme forms of expressive puzzle arrive with Marlow's attempts to glimpse his own obscure motives. The causal logic of a narrative sequence usually depends upon the reader's more or less clear perception of human motive. But Marlow the aspiring narrative-maker is sometimes defeated by an inability to fathom even his own governing motives. No explanation is given for his desire to confront Kurtz in isolation ('to this day I don't know why I was so jealous of sharing with any one the peculiar blackness of that experience' (80)) or why he wishes to visit the Intended ('I had no clear perception of what it was I really wanted' (91)) or whether he has acquired the correct papers of Kurtz to hand to her ('I was not even sure whether he had given me the right bundle' (94)). Such deferrals of meaning could not, it might be supposed, prolong indefinitely. Yet the tale's ending tends to do just this when it returns to the point at which it began – with the narrator sitting among his friends aboard a boat on the River Thames – and implies that the end is but a beginning to another telling.

V

'Come and find out' (15). The African jungle's teasing invitation to Marlow is also projected to the story's readers with the implication that, even with a full command of the evidence it has to offer, they will need to read inferentially and conjecturally. The history of *Heart of Darkness* criticism vividly indicates how the invitation has been taken up by successive generations and how, in the process, the work has undergone constant renewal.

The responses of late-Victorian readers bear little similarity to those of modern ones. Nor, among modern readers, is there a comfortable consensus, since *Heart of Darkness* has the power to divide opinion sharply, particularly in its treatment of race and imperialism. Yet the story continues to find a wide audience by virtue of the subliminal power at work in its treatment of collapse and breakdown. As T. S. Eliot seems to have recognized in 1925, the work's path-finding significance lies in its use of a simulated nightmare-quest by which to dramatize the relationship between the self and the modern world, with its attendant feelings of moral and metaphysical panic: 'I asked myself what I was doing there, with a sensation of panic in my heart as though I had blundered into a place of cruel and absurd mysteries not fit for a human being to behold' (93). Written in 1898–9, a dark sentiment of this kind helps to explain why Conrad's 'line' in the twentieth century – from T. S. Eliot through Graham Greene, V. S. Naipaul, William Golding and beyond – has been such a powerful one.

Owen Knowles

NOTES

Works cited in the text of the Introduction can be found in Further Reading.

1. *Last Essays*, in *Dent's Collected Edition of the Works of Joseph Conrad*, 22 vols. (London: J. M. Dent & Sons, 1946–55), p. 17.
2. Edward Garnett, ed., *Letters from Conrad, 1895–1923* (London: Nonesuch, 1928), p. xii.
3. Beatrice Webb, *Our Partnership*, ed. Barbara Drake and Margaret Isobel Cole (London: Longmans Green, 1948), p. 140.
4. C. de Thierry, 'Imperialism', *New Review* 17 (1897), p. 318.
5. *Last Essays*, in *Works of Joseph Conrad*, p. 17.
6. *The Times*, 13 May 1897, p. 7.
7. F. R. Leavis, *The Great Tradition: George Eliot, Henry James, Joseph Conrad* (London: Chatto & Windus, 1948).
8. This lecture was first delivered by Chinua Achebe in 1975, but not published until two years later: 'An Image of Africa', *Massachusetts Review* 17.4 (1977), pp. 782–94.
9. Robert Kimbrough, ed., *Joseph Conrad: 'Heart of Darkness'*, 3rd edn (New York: Norton, 1988), p. 79.

10. Thomas Carlyle, *Sartor Resartus and On Heroes and Hero Workship*, ed. W. H. Hudson (London: Dent, 1967), p. 289.

11. Leavis, *The Great Tradition*, p. 180.

12. Edgar Allan Poe, 'How to Write a *Blackwood's Article*', *The Complete Tales and Poems of Edgar Allan Poe* (New York: Random House, 1938), p. 341.

Introduction to 'The Congo Diary'

'The Congo Diary' is the title given to one or both of two small, leather-bound notebooks in which Conrad kept notes about his travels in the Congo in 1890. The first notebook contains the diary reproduced in this edition. Covering the opening stage of a twelve-week journey inland to Stanley Falls in the Upper Congo, the entries begin on 13 June (the day after Conrad had arrived in Africa), record daily events during a 230-mile (320-kilometre) overland trek from Matadi to Nselemba, where they end on 1 August. At Kinchasa (modern-day Kinshasa), the River Congo becomes navigable, and from here on 3 August Conrad continued his remaining 1000-mile (1600-kilometre) journey aboard the *Roi des Belges* and began his second notebook. This more specialized document, 'The Up-river Book', is not reproduced here. Devoted exclusively to navigational notes, maps and sketches made during the first sixteen days of the river journey, it was written with the purely practical purpose of assisting Conrad when he might be called upon to navigate the steamer on some future upriver trip.

With only three of Conrad's letters from the Congo having survived, the diary reproduced here has an obvious biographical importance. Although revealing little about Conrad's responses, its jottings and sketches nevertheless show where he went, what he was doing, who he met and some of the things he saw and experienced during the first part of his six-month stay in Africa. Additionally, the diary furnishes an early example – albeit of limited range – of the Anglo-Polish author's command of English (his third language), which, with its occasional strange word like 'andulating', indicates a Polish influence and, with some eccentric spellings like 'ressemble' or 'mentionned', also echoes French orthography.

The question of the diary's further importance may be broached by asking why Conrad should have chosen to keep it at all since, though some of its details are of a practical kind, the overall purpose is not an obviously practical one. In Conrad's *Under Western Eyes* (1911), the narrator speaks of the variety of 'inscrutable motives' leading some individuals to keep diaries (Part First). In conditions of extreme loneliness and stress, the act of keeping a diary can be a form of consoling self-communication, as well as a way of establishing a familiar routine and of using written language to bring a modicum of structure to confusing and chaotic experiences. Some of these reasons may help to explain the existence of 'The Congo Diary'. But the more intriguing likelihood is that Conrad may have felt that the diary would be of future use to him as a writer. In other words, its contents might later be used to reactivate his memories and serve as a creative catalyst – the diary becoming, in effect, part of what Conrad later described as the literary 'spoil' he brought back from Africa ('Author's Note', 112).

Whether or not Conrad consulted the diary eight years later when he started to compose *Heart of Darkness* remains an open question, although the presence of a handful of half-echoes in the story suggests that he may well have re-acquainted himself with some of its striking definite images: '[T]he dead body of a Backongo. Shot? Horrid smell' (100); 'Saw another dead body lying by the path in an attitude of meditative repose' (102); 'On the road today passed a skeleton tied-up to a post. Also white man's grave – no name. Heap of stones in the form of a cross' (106); 'Chief came with a youth about 13 suffering from gun-shot wound in the head. Bullet entered about an inch above the right eyebrow and came out a little inside the roots of the hair' (108).

Ultimately, however, an approach to *Heart of Darkness* by way of 'The Congo Diary' can be misleading if it encourages the view that Conrad's story is merely a fuller autobiographical extension of the diary and its figures always dependent upon 'real-life' sources. Even Norman Sherry, the critic most associated with the study of the novella's biographical and historical origins, is forced to admit: 'For Conrad it [the overland journey to Kinshasa] must have been the most gruelling part of his Congo journey . . . yet the experience as passed on to Marlow is dealt with in one paragraph and is one of the least significant aspects of *his* experience.'[1] In this instance, the fiction is neither constrained nor even determined by events of the corresponding period described in the diary. Forms of displacement and reinvention are at work in the way that the creative writer's return in 1898 to earlier African experiences involves a significant act of self-withdrawal: Conrad the writer is not now overtly visible, his function being taken over by a dramatized actor-narrator, the English sea-captain, Charlie Marlow. In addition, the period covered by the diary is subject to a new proportioning, with the result that its events are severely compacted and remodelled: whereas Conrad's original journey, as recorded in the 'Diary', is full of references to specific times, places and named people, the later story dissolves strict clock-time, occupies an unspecific geography (with the Congo only implicitly identified as its setting) and names most individuals according to their professional or symbolic functions.

Such differences between factual source and fictional artefact should not occasion surprise, given Conrad's wider belief that all creative literature of any lasting worth is, whatever its origins in the writer's own life, essentially an imaginative re-entry into past experience in the quest for a more impersonal but human truth, whether of a moral, socio-political or philosophic kind. 'All the great creations of literature have been symbolic, and in that way have gained in complexity, in power, in depth and in beauty' (*Collected Letters*, vol. VI, p. 211). Indeed, the symbolic geography and quests of some of those 'great creations of literature' – the Bible, Virgil's *Aeneid*, Dante's *Inferno* and the Faust legends – are themselves repeatedly echoed in the tale's definite images and, collectively, have some claim to be regarded as one of the most important 'sources' of its complexity, power and depth.

Owen Knowles

NOTE

1. Norman Sherry, *Conrad's Western World* (Cambridge: Cambridge University Press, 1971), p. 37.

Further Reading

LETTERS

The Collected Letters of Joseph Conrad, ed. Frederick R. Karl
and Laurence Davies, with Owen Knowles (vol. VI),
J. H. Stape (vol. VII) and Gene M. Moore (vol. VIII), 8 vols.
(Cambridge: Cambridge University Press, 1983–).
*Conrad's Polish Background: Letters to and from Polish
Friends*, ed. Zdzisław Najder (London: Oxford University
Press, 1964).
A Portrait in Letters: Correspondence to and about Conrad,
ed. J. H. Stape and Owen Knowles (Amsterdam: Editions
Rodopi, 1996).

BIOGRAPHICAL STUDIES

Batchelor, John, *The Life of Joseph Conrad: A Critical Biography* (Oxford: Blackwell, 1994).
Knowles, Owen, *A Conrad Chronology* (Basingstoke: Macmillan, 1990).
Najder, Zdzisław, *Joseph Conrad: A Life*, trans. Halina Carroll-Najder (1983; revised edn London: Boydell, 2007).
Najder, Zdzisław, ed., *Conrad under Familial Eyes*, trans. Halina Carroll-Najder (Cambridge: Cambridge University Press, 1983).
Ray, Martin, ed., *Joseph Conrad: Interviews and Recollections* (Basingstoke: Macmillan, 1990).

Stape, J. H., *The Several Lives of Joseph Conrad* (London: Heinemann; New York: Knopf, 2007).

REFERENCE

Knowles, Owen, *An Annotated Critical Bibliography of Joseph Conrad* (Hemel Hempstead: Harvester/Wheatsheaf, 1992).
Knowles, Owen, and Gene M. Moore, *Oxford Reader's Companion to Conrad* (Oxford: Oxford University Press, 2000).
Sherry, Norman, ed., *Conrad: The Critical Heritage* (London: Routledge & Kegan Paul, 1973).

CRITICAL STUDIES

Berthoud, Jacques, *Conrad: The Major Phase* (Cambridge: Cambridge University Press, 1978).
Gordan, John D., *Joseph Conrad: The Making of a Novelist* (Cambridge, MA: Harvard University Press, 1941).
Guerard, Albert J., *Conrad the Novelist* (Cambridge, MA: Harvard University Press, 1958).
Lothe, Jakob, *Conrad's Narrative Method* (Oxford: Oxford University Press, 1989).
Moser, Thomas C., *Joseph Conrad: Achievement and Decline* (Cambridge, MA: Harvard University Press, 1957).
Najder, Zdzisław, *Conrad in Perspective: Essays on Art and Fidelity* (Cambridge: Cambridge University Press, 1997).
Simmons, Allan H., *Joseph Conrad* (London: Palgrave, 2006).
Stape, J. H., ed., *The Cambridge Companion to Joseph Conrad* (Cambridge: Cambridge University Press, 1996).
Watt, Ian, *Conrad in the Nineteenth Century* (London: Chatto & Windus, 1980).
Watts, Cedric, *Preface to Conrad* (London: Longman, 1990; 2nd edn 1993).

JOURNALS

The Conradian: The Journal of the Joseph Conrad Society (UK), published twice yearly by Rodopi of Amsterdam.

Conradiana: A Journal of Joseph Conrad Studies, published thrice yearly by Texas Tech University Press, Lubbock, Texas.

L'Époque Conradienne, published once yearly by the Société Conradienne Française at Les Presses Universitaires Limoges, Limoges, France.

ON *HEART OF DARKNESS*

Bloom, Harold, ed., *Joseph Conrad's 'Heart of Darkness'* (New York: Chelsea House, 1987).

Firchow, Peter Edgerly, *Envisioning Africa: Racism and Imperialism in Conrad's 'Heart of Darkness'* (Lexington: University Press of Kentucky, 2000).

Fothergill, Anthony, *'Heart of Darkness'*, Open Guides to Literature (Milton Keynes: Open University Press, 1989).

Moore, Gene M., ed., *Joseph Conrad, 'Heart of Darkness': A Casebook* (New York: Oxford University Press, 2004).

Murfin, Ross C., *'Heart of Darkness': A Case Study in Contemporary Criticism* (Boston, MA: Bedford Books, 1989; 2nd edn 1996).

Tredell, Nicolas, ed., *Joseph Conrad: 'Heart of Darkness'*, Icon Critical Guides (Cambridge: Icon Books, 1998).

Watts, Cedric, *Conrad's 'Heart of Darkness': A Critical and Contextual Discussion* (Milan: Mursia International, 1977).

A Note on the Texts

The copy-text for *Heart of Darkness* is that of the first English edition of 13 November 1902; that for 'The Congo Diary' is the manuscript held at the Houghton Library, Harvard University; and that for the 'Author's Note' is the text first published in the second English edition of the *Youth* volume in September 1917 (London: J. M. Dent & Sons).

Conrad composed *Heart of Darkness* during the period from mid-December 1898 to early February 1899 for the thousandth issue of *Blackwood's Magazine*. A nearly complete manuscript is held at the Beinecke Rare Book and Manuscript Library, Yale University, and a portion of revised typescript in the Berg Collection, New York Public Library.

Under the title 'The Heart of Darkness', the story was serialized in Britain during February–April 1899, and appeared in the United States in *The Living Age*, June–August 1900. Along with two other stories, 'Youth' and 'The End of the Tether', it was first collected in Britain in *Youth: A Narrative and Two Other Stories* (Edinburgh and London: William Blackwood & Sons, 1902) and in the United States by McClure, Phillips of New York (1903). In both editions the story was renamed 'Heart of Darkness'.

Although this is not a critical edition, emendations to the *Heart of Darkness* copy-text have been made to correct outright errors, repair typographical flaws and rationalize minor inconsistencies. The first English edition has been compared with earlier stages of the text, including the manuscript (MS) and typescript fragment (TS), in order to take into account the complex circumstances of its early drafting, typing and printing, and thus to rectify a number of transmissional errors, mainly originating in the typescript prepared by Conrad's wife, Jessie, and passing into all printed forms.

Some features of Blackwood's house-style have been silently modified. An occasional feature of Blackwood's house-style, a comma and em-dash in combination (,—), has been replaced by an em-dash only. In the case of some spellings, Conrad's habitual usage has been preferred to that in the first English edition: thus 'further', 'by the bye', 'by and bye' and 'entrusted' are preferred to 'farther', 'by-the-by', 'by-and-by' and 'intrusted'. Ambiguous hyphenation has been resolved on the basis of majority practice in the text, and, where no clear precedent exists, is determined by the spelling of the period.

Written during his visit to the Congo in 1890, Conrad's 'Diary' did not appear in print until after his death, when Richard Curle published an edited and annotated version in *Blue Peter* 5 (October 1925), pp. 319–25. This was later republished in his edition of Conrad's *Last Essays* (London: J. M. Dent & Sons, 1926).

The manuscript bears the typical signs of an informal private diary not intended for publication, notably in its irregular or missing punctuation, abbreviated words and occasional unusual spellings. The present text remains faithful to these features. Conrad's frequent use of dashes instead of full stops is preserved, and punctuation is supplied or emended sparingly and only at points of potential ambiguity or confusion (see the list below). Minor inconsistencies of spelling have not been standardized, and irregular spellings are signalled in the notes but not repaired. Likewise, the apparently random underlinings and superscript letters in the manuscript have been preserved in order to remain faithful to the form of the original document. In the case of abbreviations and shorthand symbols, letters missing from words are supplied in square brackets (as in 'off[ic]er' or 'comp[an]y').

In the 'Author's Note', Dent's house-style has been silently modified in only one respect: where the original text italicized the titles of short stories, this text places all such titles in inverted commas.

LIST OF EMENDATIONS

The rejected reading of the copy-text appears to the right of the square bracket.

Heart of Darkness

6:3	effective (MS)] direct
6:5	But, as has been said, (MS)] But,
6:9	that, sometimes, (TS)] that sometimes
6:21	of say (MS)] of
7:10	forests (MS)] forest
7:25	and for (MS)] for
8:1	on (MS)] in
9:38	etc., etc.] &c., &c.
12:31	these (TS)] those
13:15	callipers, (MS, TS)] calipers
14:3	*Adieu*] Adieu
14:4	*Adieu*] Adieu
14:9	many, many (MS)] many
14:17	two pence (MS)] two-penny
14:28	Charles (MS)] Charlie
14:30	are! (MS)] are.
15:18	along (MS)] away along
15:22	Settlements—settlements, (MS)] Settlements
15:33	Bassam,] Bassam
16:1	toils (MS)] toil
16:18	drooped (MS)] dropped
16:20	shiny (MS)] slimy
16:32	a day] a-day
17:1	thickening (MS)] thickened
17:20	a month] a-month
17:21	told (MS)] said to
17:28	"At] At
17:31	rapids (MS, TS)] the rapids
18:7	thick shade (MS)] shady spot
18:12	way of (MS, TS)] way or

18:28   the meagre (MS)] their meagre
20:30   more, (MS)] more
20:30   angles, (MS)] angles
21:8   clear silk (MS)] clear
21:21   head (MS)] hair
21:23   backbone! (MS)] backbone.
21:29   had, verily, (MS)] had verily
21:33   Caravans, strings (MS, TS)] Strings
21:35   brass wire] brass-wire
21:35   set off] set
21:38   tent (MS)] hut
22:9   'agent' (MS)] agent
22:10   was hurriedly (MS)] was
22:20   trading-post] trading post
22:35   these (MS)] those
22:36   death! (MS)] death.
23:17   an empty (MS)] the empty
23:30   sixty-pound (MS)] 60-lb.
25:10   Still . . .] Still. . . .
25:22   manner (MS)] manners
27:8   Kurtz!', broke] Kurtz!' broke
27:9   dumbfounded] dumfounded
27:10   take to——'] take to' . . .
27:18   borne (MS)] borne in
29:26   so sociable (MS)] sociable
29:34   became also (MS)] became
30:8   by, civilly] by civilly,
31:26   papier-mâché] papier-maché
34:37   Palmers] Palmer
35:31   shouted,] shouted
35:32   exclaiming,] exclaiming
35:38   empty hulk (MS)] hulk
38:26   jerked out (MS)] jerked
42:35   Unknown (MS)] unknown
43:1   'ivory'] ivory
43:22   this (MS)] it
45:24   shore] short
46:16   Towzer (MS)] Tower

46:22   Towzer (MS)] Towser
47:2   pilgrims,] pilgrims
49:31   said nodding (MS)] said
50:29   half-cooked cold (MS)] half-cooked
52:1   serious, very serious (MS)] very serious
54:17   just in (MS)] in
55:8   splashy (MS)] splashing
55:30   opened fire (MS)] opened
57:38   with . . .] with. . . .
58:34   tell . . .] tell. . . .
60:6   Everything] everything
61:32   etc., etc.] &c., &c.
66:5   Government] Goverment
68:22   impractical (MS)] unpractical
70:25   talk (MS)] take
71:16   lying here (MS)] lying
74:20   'short'] short
75:9   Shadow (MS)] shadow
75:36   leggins (MS)] leggings
76:33   in though (MS)] in
77:26   quarters (MS)] quarter
77:31   is (MS)] is
78:34   again . . .] again. . . .
79:16   etc., etc.] &c., &c.
82:2   Shadow (MS)] shadow
82:10   There] there
83:29   fiery (MS)] fierce
84:21   don't (MS)] don't!
84:21   someone (MS)] some one
85:14   Intended, my ivory, (MS)] Intended,
85:26   hand (MS)] you
88:17   all (MS)] all the
88:20   Invisible (MS)] invisible
89:21   not very (MS)] not
89:33   etc., etc.] &c., &c.
90:22   broad black (MS)] broad
90:25   the faith (MS)] faith

95:1   stood up;] stood up
95:21   never! (MS)] never.

The Congo Diary

99:14   hearty] Hearty
99:14   Kalla)] Kalla
100:10 well.] well
100:22 Danes] danes
101:29 that.] that
101:33 camped] Camped
102:8   villages.] villages
104:4   hills,] hills
105:10 Very] very
106:30 Heap] heap
107:10 hammock.] hammock

Author's Note

111:4   'Narcissus'] Narcissus

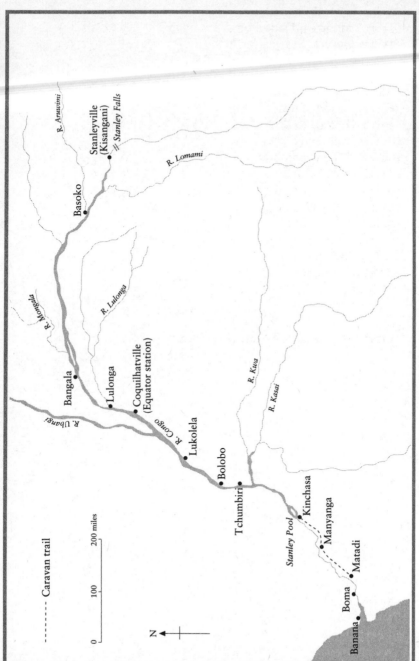

The River Congo

Heart of Darkness

I

The *Nellie*,[1] a cruising yawl, swung to her anchor without a flutter of the sails, and was at rest. The flood had made, the wind was nearly calm, and being bound down the river, the only thing for it was to come to and wait for the turn of the tide.

The sea-reach of the Thames stretched before us like the beginning of an interminable waterway. In the offing the sea and the sky were welded together without a joint, and in the luminous space the tanned sails of the barges drifting up with the tide seemed to stand still in red clusters of canvas sharply peaked, with gleams of varnished sprits. A haze rested on the low shores that ran out to sea in vanishing flatness. The air was dark above Gravesend,[2] and further back still seemed condensed into a mournful gloom, brooding motionless over the biggest, and the greatest, town on earth.

The Director of Companies was our captain and our host. We four[3] affectionately watched his back as he stood in the bows looking to seaward. On the whole river there was nothing that looked half so nautical. He resembled a pilot, which to a seaman is trustworthiness personified. It was difficult to realise his work was not out there in the luminous estuary, but behind him, within the brooding gloom.

Between us there was, as I have already said somewhere,[4] the bond of the sea. Besides holding our hearts together through long periods of separation, it had the effect of making us tolerant of each other's yarns—and even convictions. The Lawyer—the best of old fellows—had, because of his many years and many virtues, the only cushion on deck, and was lying on the only rug. The Accountant had brought out already a box of dominoes, and was toying architecturally with the bones.[5] Marlow sat cross-legged right aft, leaning against the mizzen-mast. He had sunken cheeks, a yellow complexion, a straight back, an ascetic aspect, and, with his arms dropped, the palms of hands outwards, resembled an idol.[6] The Director, satisfied the anchor had good hold, made his way aft and sat down amongst us. We exchanged a few words lazily. Afterwards there was silence on board the yacht. For some reason or other we did not begin that game of dominoes. We felt meditative, and fit for nothing but placid staring. The day was ending in a serenity of still and exquisite brilliance. The water shone pacifi-cally; the sky, without a speck, was a benign immensity of unstained light; the very mist on the Essex marshes was like a gauzy and radiant fabric, hung from the wooded rises inland, and draping the low shores in diaphanous folds. Only the gloom to the west, brooding over the upper reaches, became more sombre every minute, as if angered by the approach of the sun.

And at last, in its curved and imperceptible fall, the sun sank low, and from glowing white changed to a dull red without rays and without heat, as if about to go out suddenly, stricken to death by the touch of that gloom brooding over a crowd of men.[7]

Forthwith a change came over the waters, and the serenity became less brilliant but more profound. The old river in its broad reach rested unruffled at the decline of day, after ages of good service done to the race that peopled its banks, spread out in the tranquil dignity of a waterway leading to the uttermost ends of the earth. We looked at the venerable stream not in the vivid flush of a short day that comes and departs for ever, but in the august light of abiding memories. And indeed nothing is easier for a man who has, as the phrase goes, "followed the sea" with reverence and affection, than to evoke the great spirit of the past upon the lower reaches of the Thames. The tidal current runs to and fro in its unceasing service, crowded with memories of men and ships it had borne to the rest of home or to the battles of the sea. It had known and served all the men of whom the nation is proud, from Sir Francis Drake[8] to Sir John Franklin,[9] knights all, titled and untitled—the great knights-errant of the sea. It had borne all the ships whose names are like jewels flashing in the night of time, from the *Golden Hind* returning with her round flanks full of treasure, to be visited by the Queen's Highness and thus pass out of the gigantic tale, to the *Erebus* and *Terror*, bound on other conquests— and that never returned. It had known the ships and the men. They sailed from Deptford, from Greenwich, from Erith[10]—the adventurers and the settlers; kings' ships and the ships of men on 'Change;[11] captains, admirals, the dark "interlopers" of the Eastern trade, and the commissioned "generals" of East India fleets.[12] Hunters for gold or pursuers of fame, they all had gone out on that stream, bearing the sword, and often the torch, messengers of the might within the land, bearers of a spark from the sacred fire. What greatness had not floated on the ebb of that river into the mystery of an unknown earth! ... The dreams of men, the seed of commonwealths, the germs of empires.

The sun set; the dusk fell on the stream, and lights began to appear along the shore. The Chapman lighthouse,[13] a three-legged thing erect on a mudflat, shone strongly. Lights of ships moved in the fairway—a great stir of lights going up and going down. And further west on the upper reaches the place of the monstrous town was still marked ominously on the sky, a brooding gloom in sunshine, a lurid glare under the stars.

"And this also," said Marlow suddenly, "has been one of the dark places of the earth."[14]

He was the only man of us who still "followed the sea." The worst that could be said of him was that he did not represent his class. He was a seaman, but he was a wanderer too, while most seamen lead, if one may so express it, a sedentary life. Their minds are of the stay-at-home order, and their home is always with them—the ship; and so is their country—the sea. One ship is very much like another, and the sea is always the same. In the immutability of their surroundings the foreign shores, the foreign faces, the changing immensity of life, glide past, veiled not by a sense of mystery but by a slightly disdainful ignorance; for there is nothing mysterious to a seaman unless it be the sea itself, which is the mistress of his existence and as inscrutable as Destiny. For the rest, after his hours of work, a

casual stroll or a casual spree on shore suffices to unfold for
him the secret of a whole continent, and generally he finds the
secret not worth knowing. The yarns of seamen have an effective simplicity, the whole meaning of which lies within the shell
of a cracked nut. But, as has been said, Marlow was not typical
(if his propensity to spin yarns be excepted), and to him the
meaning of an episode was not inside like a kernel but outside,
enveloping the tale which brought it out only as a glow brings
out a haze, in the likeness of one of these misty halos that,
sometimes, are made visible by the spectral illumination of
moonshine.

His remark did not seem at all surprising. It was just like
Marlow. It was accepted in silence. No one took the trouble to
grunt even; and presently he said, very slow—

"I was thinking of very old times, when the Romans first
came here,[15] nineteen hundred years ago—the other day. . . .
Light came out of this river since—you say Knights? Yes; but
it is like a running blaze on a plain, like a flash of lightning in
the clouds. We live in the flicker—may it last as long as the old
earth keeps rolling! But darkness was here yesterday. Imagine
the feelings of say a commander of a fine—what d'ye call
'em?—trireme in the Mediterranean, ordered suddenly to the
north; run overland across the Gauls[16] in a hurry; put in charge
of one of these craft the legionaries—a wonderful lot of handy
men they must have been too—used to build, apparently by the
hundred, in a month or two, if we may believe what we read.[17]
Imagine him here—the very end of the world, a sea the colour
of lead, a sky the colour of smoke, a kind of ship about as rigid
as a concertina—and going up this river[18] with stores, or orders,
or what you like. Sandbanks, marshes, forests, savages—
precious little to eat fit for a civilised man, nothing but Thames
water to drink. No Falernian wine[19] here, no going ashore. Here
and there a military camp lost in a wilderness like a needle in a
bundle of hay—cold, fog, tempests, disease, exile, and death—
death skulking in the air, in the water, in the bush. They must
have been dying like flies here. Oh yes—he did it. Did it very
well, too, no doubt, and without thinking much about it either,
except afterwards to brag of what he had gone through in his

time, perhaps. They were men enough to face the darkness. And perhaps he was cheered by keeping his eye on a chance of promotion to the fleet at Ravenna,[20] by and bye, if he had good friends in Rome and survived the awful climate. Or think of a decent young citizen in a toga—perhaps too much dice, you know—coming out here in the train of some prefect,[21] or tax-gatherer, or trader even, to mend his fortunes. Land in a swamp, march through the woods, and in some inland post feel the savagery, the utter savagery, had closed round him—all that mysterious life of the wilderness that stirs in the forests, in the jungles, in the hearts of wild men. There's no initiation either into such mysteries. He has to live in the midst of the incomprehensible, which is also detestable. And it has a fascination, too, that goes to work upon him. The fascination of the abomination—you know. Imagine the growing regrets, the longing to escape, the powerless disgust, the surrender, the hate."

He paused.

"Mind," he began again, lifting one arm from the elbow, the palm of the hand outwards, so that, with his legs folded before him, he had the pose of a Buddha preaching in European clothes and without a lotus-flower—"Mind, none of us would feel exactly like this. What saves us is efficiency—the devotion to efficiency. But these chaps were not much account, really. They were no colonists; their administration was merely a squeeze, and nothing more, I suspect. They were conquerors, and for that you want only brute force—nothing to boast of, when you have it, since your strength is just an accident arising from the weakness of others. They grabbed what they could get and for the sake of what was to be got. It was just robbery with violence, aggravated murder on a great scale, and men going at it blind—as is very proper for those who tackle a darkness. The conquest of the earth, which mostly means the taking it away from those who have a different complexion or slightly flatter noses than ourselves, is not a pretty thing when you look into it too much. What redeems it is the idea only. An idea at the back of it; not a sentimental pretence but an idea; and an unselfish belief in the idea—something you can set up, and bow down before, and offer a sacrifice to. . . . ."

He broke off. Flames glided in on the river, small green flames, red flames, white flames,²² pursuing, overtaking, joining, crossing each other—then separating slowly or hastily. The traffic of the great city went on in the deepening night upon the sleepless river. We looked on, waiting patiently—there was nothing else to do till the end of the flood; but it was only after a long silence, when he said, in a hesitating voice, "I suppose you fellows remember I did once turn fresh-water sailor for a bit," that we knew we were fated, before the ebb began to run, to hear about one of Marlow's inconclusive experiences.

"I don't want to bother you much with what happened to me personally," he began, showing in this remark the weakness of many tellers of tales who seem so often unaware of what their audience would best like to hear; "yet to understand the effect of it on me you ought to know how I got out there, what I saw, how I went up that river to the place where I first met the poor chap. It was the furthest point of navigation and the culminating point of my experience. It seemed somehow to throw a kind of light on everything about me—and into my thoughts. It was sombre enough too—and pitiful—not extraordinary in any way—not very clear either. No, not very clear. And yet it seemed to throw a kind of light.

"I had then, as you remember, just returned to London after a lot of Indian Ocean, Pacific, China Seas—a regular dose of the East—six years or so, and I was loafing about, hindering you fellows in your work and invading your homes, just as though I had got a heavenly mission to civilise you. It was very fine for a time, but after a bit I did get tired of resting. Then I began to look for a ship—I should think the hardest work on earth. But the ships wouldn't even look at me. And I got tired of that game too.

"Now when I was a little chap I had a passion for maps.²³ I would look for hours at South America, or Africa, or Australia and lose myself in all the glories of exploration. At that time there were many blank spaces on the earth, and when I saw one that looked particularly inviting on a map (but they all look that) I would put my finger on it and say, When I grow up I will go there. The North Pole was one of these places,

I remember. Well, I haven't been there yet, and shall not try now. The glamour's off. Other places were scattered about the Equator, and in every sort of latitude all over the two hemispheres. I have been in some of them, and . . . well, we won't talk about that. But there was one yet—the biggest, the most blank, so to speak—that I had a hankering after.

"True, by this time it was not a blank space any more. It had got filled since my boyhood with rivers and lakes and names. It had ceased to be a blank space of delightful mystery—a white patch for a boy to dream gloriously over. It had become a place of darkness. But there was in it one river especially, a mighty big river, that you could see on the map, resembling an immense snake uncoiled, with its head in the sea, its body at rest curving afar over a vast country, and its tail lost in the depths of the land. And as I looked at the map of it in a shop-window, it fascinated me like a snake would a bird—a silly little bird. Then I remembered there was a big concern, a Company[24] for trade on that river. Dash it all! I thought to myself, they can't trade without using some kind of craft on that lot of fresh water—steamboats! Why shouldn't I try to get charge of one. I went on along Fleet Street, but could not shake off the idea. The snake had charmed me.

"You understand it was a Continental concern, that Trading society; but I have a lot of relations living on the Continent, because it's cheap and not so nasty as it looks, they say.

"I am sorry to own I began to worry them. This was already a fresh departure for me. I was not used to get things that way, you know. I always went my own road and on my own legs where I had a mind to go. I wouldn't have believed it of myself; but, then—you see—I felt somehow I must get there by hook or by crook. So I worried them. The men said 'My dear fellow,' and did nothing. Then—would you believe it?—I tried the women. I, Charlie Marlow, set the women to work—to get a job. Heavens! Well, you see, the notion drove me. I had an aunt, a dear enthusiastic soul. She wrote: 'It will be delightful. I am ready to do anything, anything for you. It is a glorious idea. I know the wife of a very high personage in the Administration, and also a man who has lots of influence with,' etc.,

etc. She was determined to make no end of fuss to get me appointed skipper of a river steamboat, if such was my fancy.

"I got my appointment—of course; and I got it very quick. It appears the Company had received news that one of their captains had been killed in a scuffle with the natives. This was my chance, and it made me the more anxious to go. It was only months and months afterwards, when I made the attempt to recover what was left of the body, that I heard the original quarrel arose from a misunderstanding about some hens. Yes, two black hens. Fresleven[25]—that was the fellow's name, a Dane—thought himself wronged somehow in the bargain, so he went ashore and started to hammer the chief of the village with a stick. Oh, it didn't surprise me in the least to hear this, and at the same time to be told that Fresleven was the gentlest, quietest creature that ever walked on two legs. No doubt he was; but he had been a couple of years already out there engaged in the noble cause, you know, and he probably felt the need at last of asserting his self-respect in some way. Therefore he whacked the old nigger mercilessly, while a big crowd of his people watched him, thunderstruck, till some man—I was told the chief's son—in desperation at hearing the old chap yell, made a tentative jab with a spear at the white man—and of course it went quite easy between the shoulder-blades. Then the whole population cleared into the forest, expecting all kinds of calamities to happen, while, on the other hand, the steamer Fresleven commanded left also in a bad panic, in charge of the engineer, I believe. Afterwards nobody seemed to trouble much about Fresleven's remains, till I got out and stepped into his shoes. I couldn't let it rest though; but when an opportunity offered at last to meet my predecessor, the grass growing through his ribs was tall enough to hide his bones. They were all there. The supernatural being had not been touched after he fell. And the village was deserted, the huts gaped black, rotting, all askew within the fallen enclosures. A calamity had come to it, sure enough. The people had vanished. Mad terror had scattered them, men, women, and children, through the bush, and they had never returned. What became of the hens I don't know either. I should think the cause of progress got them, anyhow. However, through this glorious affair I got my appointment, before I had fairly begun to hope for it.

"I flew around like mad to get ready, and before forty-eight hours I was crossing the Channel to show myself to my employers,[26] and sign the contract. In a very few hours I arrived in a city that always makes me think of a whited sepulchre.[27] Prejudice no doubt. I had no difficulty in finding the Company's offices. It was the biggest thing in the town, and everybody I met was full of it. They were going to run an over-sea empire, and make no end of coin by trade.

"A narrow and deserted street in deep shadow, high houses, innumerable windows with venetian blinds, a dead silence, grass sprouting between the stones, imposing carriage archways right and left, immense double doors standing ponderously ajar. I slipped through one of these cracks, went up a swept and ungarnished staircase, as arid as a desert, and opened the first door I came to. Two women, one fat and the other slim, sat on straw-bottomed chairs, knitting black wool.[28] The slim one got up and walked straight at me—still knitting with downcast eyes—and only just as I began to think of getting out of her way, as you would for a somnambulist, stood still, and looked up. Her dress was as plain as an umbrella-cover, and she turned round without a word and preceded me into a waiting-room. I gave my name, and looked about. Deal table in the middle, plain chairs all round the walls, on one end a large shining map, marked with all the colours of a rainbow.[29] There was a vast amount of red—good to see at any time, because one knows that some real work is done in there, a deuce of a lot of blue, a little green, smears of orange, and, on the East Coast, a purple patch, to show where the jolly pioneers of progress drink the jolly lager-beer. However, I wasn't going into any of these. I was going into the yellow. Dead in the centre. And the river was there—fascinating—deadly—like a snake. Ough! A door opened, a white-haired secretarial head, but wearing a compassionate expression, appeared, and a skinny forefinger beckoned me into the sanctuary. Its light was dim, and a heavy writing-desk squatted in the middle. From behind that structure came out an impression of pale plumpness in a frock-coat. The great man himself.[30] He was five feet six, I should judge, and had his grip on the handle-end of ever so many millions. He shook hands, I fancy, murmured vaguely, was satisfied with my French. *Bon voyage.*

"In about forty-five seconds I found myself again in the waiting-room with the compassionate secretary, who, full of desolation and sympathy, made me sign some document. I believe I undertook amongst other things not to disclose any trade secrets. Well, I am not going to.

"I began to feel slightly uneasy. You know I am not used to such ceremonies, and there was something ominous in the atmosphere. It was just as though I had been let into some conspiracy—I don't know—something not quite right; and I was glad to get out. In the outer room the two women knitted black wool feverishly. People were arriving, and the younger one was walking back and forth introducing them. The old one sat on her chair. Her flat cloth slippers were propped up on a foot-warmer, and a cat reposed on her lap. She wore a starched white affair on her head, had a wart on one cheek, and silver-rimmed spectacles hung on the tip of her nose. She glanced at me above the glasses. The swift and indifferent placidity of that look troubled me. Two youths with foolish and cheery countenances were being piloted over, and she threw at them the same quick glance of unconcerned wisdom. She seemed to know all about them and about me too. An eerie feeling came over me. She seemed uncanny and fateful. Often far away there I thought of these two, guarding the door of Darkness, knitting black wool as for a warm pall, one introducing, introducing continuously to the unknown, the other scrutinising the cheery and foolish faces with unconcerned old eyes. *Ave!* Old knitter of black wool. *Morituri te salutant.*[31] Not many of these she looked at ever saw her again—not half, by a long way.

"There was yet a visit to the doctor. 'A simple formality,' assured me the secretary, with an air of taking an immense part in all my sorrows. Accordingly a young chap wearing his hat over the left eyebrow, some clerk I suppose—there must have been clerks in the business, though the house was as still as a house in a city of the dead—came from somewhere up-stairs and led me forth. He was shabby and careless, with ink-stains on the sleeves of his jacket, and his cravat was large and billowy, under a chin shaped like the toe of an old boot. It was a little too early for the doctor, so I proposed a drink, and thereupon he developed a vein of joviality. As we sat over our vermuths he glorified the Company's business and by and bye I expressed casually my surprise at him not going out there. He became very cool and collected all at once. 'I am not such a fool as I look, quoth Plato to his disciples,'[32] he said sententiously, emptied his glass with great resolution, and we rose.

"The old doctor felt my pulse, evidently thinking of something else the while. 'Good, good for there,' he mumbled, and then with a certain eagerness asked me whether I would let him measure my head. Rather surprised, I said Yes, when he produced a thing like callipers and got the dimensions back and front and every way, taking notes carefully. He was an unshaven little man in a threadbare coat like a gaberdine, with his feet in slippers, and I thought him a harmless fool. 'I always ask leave, in the interests of science, to measure the crania[33] of those going out there,' he said. 'And when they come back too?' I asked. 'Oh, I never see them,' he remarked; 'and, moreover, the changes take place inside, you know.' He smiled, as if at some quiet joke. 'So you are going out there. Famous.[34] Interesting too.' He gave me a searching glance, and made another note. 'Ever any madness in your family?' he asked, in a matter-of-fact tone. I felt very annoyed. 'Is that question in the interests of science too?' 'It would be,' he said, without taking notice of my irritation, 'interesting for science to watch the mental changes of individuals, on the spot, but . . .' 'Are you an alienist?'[35] I interrupted. 'Every doctor should be—a little,' answered that original, imperturbably. 'I have a little theory which you Messieurs who go out there must help me to prove. This is my share in the advantages my country shall reap from the possession of such a magnificent dependency. The mere wealth I leave to others. Pardon my questions, but you are the first Englishman coming under my observation . . .' I hastened to assure him I was not in the least typical. 'If I were,' said I, 'I wouldn't be talking like this with you.' 'What you say is rather profound, and probably erroneous,' he said, with a laugh. 'Avoid irritation more than exposure to the sun. *Adieu*. How do you English say, eh? Goodbye. Ah! Goodbye. *Adieu*. In the tropics one must before everything keep calm.' ... He lifted a warning forefinger.... '*Du calme, du calme. Adieu*.'

"One thing more remained to do—say good-bye to my excellent aunt. I found her triumphant. I had a cup of tea—the last decent cup of tea for many, many days—and in a room that most soothingly looked just as you would expect a lady's drawing-room to look, we had a long quiet chat by the fireside. In the course of these confidences it became quite plain to me I had been represented to the wife of the high dignitary, and goodness knows to how many more people besides, as an exceptional and gifted creature—a piece of good fortune for the Company—a man you don't get hold of every day. Good heavens! and I was going to take charge of a two pence-halfpenny river-steamboat with a penny whistle attached! It appeared, however, I was also one of the Workers, with a capital[36]—you know. Something like an emissary of light, something like a lower sort of apostle. There had been a lot of such rot[37] let loose in print and talk just about that time, and the excellent woman, living right in the rush of all that humbug, got carried off her feet. She talked about 'weaning those ignorant millions from their horrid ways,' till, upon my word, she made me quite uncomfortable. I ventured to hint that the Company was run for profit.

"'You forget, dear Charles, that the labourer is worthy of his hire,' she said, brightly. It's queer how out of touch with truth women are! They live in a world of their own, and there had never been anything like it, and never can be. It is too beautiful altogether, and if they were to set it up it would go to pieces before the first sunset. Some confounded fact we men have been living contentedly with ever since the day of creation would start up and knock the whole thing over.

"After this I got embraced, told to wear flannel, be sure to write often, and so on—and I left. In the street—I don't know why—a queer feeling came to me that I was an impostor. Odd thing that I, who used to clear out for any part of the world at twenty-four hours' notice, with less thought than most men give to the crossing of a street, had a moment—I won't say of hesitation, but of startled pause, before this commonplace affair. The best way I can explain it to you is by saying that, for a second or two, I felt as though, instead of going to the centre of a continent, I were about to set off for the centre of the earth.

"I left in a French steamer, and she called in every blamed port they have out there, for, as far as I could see, the sole purpose of landing soldiers and custom-house officers. I watched the coast. Watching a coast as it slips by the ship is like thinking about an enigma. There it is before you—smiling, frowning, inviting, grand, mean, insipid, or savage, and always mute with an air of whispering, Come and find out. This one was almost featureless, as if still in the making, with an aspect of monotonous grimness. The edge of a colossal jungle, so dark-green as to be almost black, fringed with white surf, ran straight, like a ruled line, far, far along a blue sea whose glitter was blurred by a creeping mist. The sun was fierce, the land seemed to glisten and drip with steam. Here and there greyish-whitish specks showed up, clustered inside the white surf, with a flag flying above them perhaps. Settlements—settlements, some centuries old, and still no bigger than pin-heads on the untouched expanse of their background. We pounded along, stopped, landed soldiers; went on, landed custom-house clerks to levy toll in what looked like a God-forsaken wilderness, with a tin shed and a flag-pole lost in it; landed more soldiers—to take care of the custom-house clerks, presumably. Some, I heard, got drowned in the surf; but whether they did or not, nobody seemed particularly to care. They were just flung out there, and on we went. Every day the coast looked the same, as though we had not moved; but we passed various places— trading places—with names like Gran' Bassam, Little Popo,[38] names that seemed to belong to some sordid farce acted in front of a sinister backcloth. The idleness of a passenger, my isolation amongst all these men with whom I had no point of contact, the oily and languid sea, the uniform sombreness of the coast, seemed to keep me away from the truth of things, within the toils of a mournful and senseless delusion. The voice of the surf heard now and then was a positive pleasure, like the speech of a brother. It was something natural, that had its reason, that had a meaning. Now and then a boat from the shore gave one a momentary contact with reality. It was paddled by black fellows. You could see from afar the white of their eyeballs glistening. They shouted, sang; their bodies streamed with perspiration; they had faces like grotesque masks—these chaps; but they had bone, muscle, a wild vitality, an intense energy of movement, that was as natural and true as the surf along their coast. They wanted no excuse for being there. They were a great comfort to look at. For a time I would feel I belonged still to a world of straightforward facts; but the feeling would not last long. Something would turn up to scare it away. Once, I remember, we came upon a man-of-war anchored off the coast. There wasn't even a shed there, and she was shelling the bush. It appears the French had one of their wars[39] going on thereabouts. Her ensign drooped limp like a rag; the muzzles of the long eight-inch guns stuck out all over the low hull; the greasy, shiny swell swung her up lazily and let her down, swaying her thin masts. In the empty immensity of earth, sky, and water, there she was, incomprehensible, firing into a continent. Pop, would go one of the eight-inch guns; a small flame would dart and vanish, a little white smoke would disappear, a tiny projectile would give a feeble screech—and nothing happened. Nothing could happen. There was a touch of insanity in the proceeding, a sense of lugubrious drollery in the sight; and it was not dissipated by somebody on board assuring me earnestly there was a camp of natives—he called them enemies!—hidden out of sight somewhere.

"We gave her her letters (I heard the men in that lonely ship were dying of fever at the rate of three a day) and went on. We called at some more places with farcical names, where the merry dance of death and trade goes on in a still and earthy atmosphere as of an overheated catacomb; all along the formless coast bordered by dangerous surf, as if Nature herself had tried to ward off intruders; in and out of rivers, streams of death in life, whose banks were rotting into mud, whose waters, thickening into slime, invaded the contorted mangroves, that seemed to writhe at us in the extremity of an impotent despair. Nowhere did we stop long enough to get a particularised impression, but the general sense of vague and oppressive wonder grew upon me. It was like a weary pilgrimage amongst hints for nightmares.

"It was upwards of thirty days before I saw the mouth of the big river. We anchored off the seat of the government.⁴⁰ But my work would not begin till some two hundred miles further on. So as soon as I could I made a start for a place thirty miles higher up.

"I had my passage on a little sea-going steamer. Her captain was a Swede, and knowing me for a seaman, invited me on the bridge. He was a young man, lean, fair, and morose, with lanky hair and a shuffling gait. As we left the miserable little wharf, he tossed his head contemptuously at the shore. 'Been living there?' he asked. I said, 'Yes.' 'Fine lot these government chaps—are they not?' he went on, speaking English with great precision and considerable bitterness. 'It is funny what some people will do for a few francs a month. I wonder what becomes of that kind when it goes up country?' I told him I expected to see that soon. 'So-o-o!' he exclaimed. He shuffled athwart, keeping one eye ahead vigilantly. 'Don't be too sure,' he continued. 'The other day I took up a man who hanged himself on the road. He was a Swede, too.' 'Hanged himself! Why, in God's name?' I cried. He kept on looking out watchfully. 'Who knows? The sun too much for him, or the country perhaps.'

"At last we opened a reach. A rocky cliff appeared, mounds of turned-up earth by the shore, houses on a hill, others, with iron roofs, amongst a waste of excavations, or hanging to the declivity. A continuous noise of the rapids above hovered over this scene of inhabited devastation. A lot of people, mostly black and naked, moved about like ants. A jetty projected into the river. A blinding sunlight drowned all this at times in a sudden recrudescence of glare. 'There's your Company's station,'⁴¹ said the Swede, pointing to three wooden barrack-like structures hanging on the rocky slope. 'I will send your things up. Four boxes did you say? So. Farewell.'

"I came upon a boiler wallowing in the grass, then found a path leading up the hill. It turned aside for the boulders, and also for an undersized railway-truck lying there on its back with its wheels in the air. One was off. The thing looked as dead as the carcass of some animal. I came upon more pieces of decaying machinery, a stack of rusty rails. To the left a clump of trees made a thick shade, where dark things seemed to stir feebly. I blinked, the path was steep. A horn tooted to the right, and I saw the black people run. A heavy and dull detonation shook the ground, a puff of smoke came out of the cliff, and that was all. No change appeared on the face of the rock. They were building a railway.[42] The cliff was not in the way of anything; but this objectless blasting was all the work going on.

"A slight clinking behind me made me turn my head. Six black men advanced in a file, toiling up the path. They walked erect and slow, balancing small baskets full of earth on their heads, and the clink kept time with their footsteps. Black rags were wound round their loins, and the short ends behind wagged to and fro like tails. I could see every rib, the joints of their limbs were like knots in a rope; each had an iron collar on his neck, and all were connected together with a chain whose bights swung between them, rhythmically clinking. Another report from the cliff made me think suddenly of that ship of war I had seen firing into a continent. It was the same kind of ominous voice; but these men could by no stretch of imagination be called enemies. They were called criminals, and the outraged law, like the bursting shells, had come to them, an insoluble mystery from over the sea. All the meagre breasts panted together, the violently dilated nostrils quivered, the eyes stared stonily up-hill. They passed me within six inches, without a glance, with that complete, deathlike indifference of unhappy savages. Behind this raw matter one of the reclaimed, the product of the new forces at work, strolled despondently, carrying a rifle by its middle. He had a uniform jacket with one button off, and seeing a white man on the path, hoisted his weapon on to his shoulder with alacrity. This was simple prudence, white men being so much alike at a distance that he could not tell who I might be. He was speedily reassured, and with a large,

white, rascally grin, and a glance at his charge, seemed to take
me into partnership in his exalted trust. After all, I also was a
part of the great cause of these high and just proceedings.

"Instead of going up, I turned and descended to the left. My
idea was to let that chain-gang get out of sight before I climbed
the hill. You know I am not particularly tender; I've had to
strike and to fend off. I've had to resist and to attack sometimes—that's only one way of resisting—without counting the
exact cost, according to the demands of such sort of life as I
had blundered into. I've seen the devil of violence, and the devil
of greed, and the devil of hot desire; but, by all the stars!
these were strong, lusty, red-eyed devils, that swayed and drove
men—men, I tell you. But as I stood on this hillside, I foresaw
that in the blinding sunshine of that land I would become
acquainted with a flabby, pretending, weak-eyed devil of a
rapacious and pitiless folly. How insidious he could be, too, I
was only to find out several months later and a thousand miles
further. For a moment I stood appalled, as though by a warning. Finally I descended the hill, obliquely, towards the trees
I had seen.

"I avoided a vast, artificial hole somebody had been digging
on the slope, the purpose of which I found it impossible to
divine. It wasn't a quarry or a sandpit, anyhow. It was just a
hole. It might have been connected with the philanthropic desire
of giving the criminals something to do. I don't know. Then I
nearly fell into a very narrow ravine, almost no more than a
scar in the hillside. I discovered that a lot of imported drainage-
pipes for the settlement had been tumbled in there. There wasn't
one that was not broken. It was a wanton smash-up. At last I
got under the trees. My purpose was to stroll into the shade for
a moment; but no sooner within than it seemed to me I had
stepped into the gloomy circle of some Inferno.[43] The rapids
were near, and an uninterrupted, uniform, headlong, rushing
noise filled the mournful stillness of the grove, where not a
breath stirred, not a leaf moved, with a mysterious sound—as
though the tearing pace of the launched earth had suddenly
become audible.

"Black shapes crouched, lay, sat between the trees, leaning

against the trunks, clinging to the earth, half coming out, half effaced within the dim light, in all the attitudes of pain, abandonment, and despair. Another mine on the cliff went off, followed by a slight shudder of the soil under my feet. The work was going on. The work! And this was the place where some of the helpers had withdrawn to die.

"They were dying slowly—it was very clear. They were not enemies, they were not criminals, they were nothing earthly now—nothing but black shadows of disease and starvation, lying confusedly in the greenish gloom. Brought from all the recesses of the coast in all the legality of time contracts,[44] lost in uncongenial surroundings, fed on unfamiliar food, they sickened, became inefficient, and were then allowed to crawl away and rest. These moribund shapes were free as air—and nearly as thin. I began to distinguish the gleam of eyes under the trees. Then, glancing down, I saw a face near my hand. The black bones reclined at full length with one shoulder against the tree, and slowly the eyelids rose and the sunken eyes looked up at me, enormous and vacant, a kind of blind, white flicker in the depths of the orbs, which died out slowly. The man seemed young—almost a boy—but you know with them it's hard to tell. I found nothing else to do but to offer him one of my good Swede's ship's biscuits I had in my pocket. The fingers closed slowly on it and held—there was no other movement and no other glance. He had tied a bit of white worsted round his neck—Why? Where did he get it? Was it a badge—an ornament—a charm—a propitiatory act? Was there any idea at all connected with it? It looked startling round his black neck, this bit of white thread from beyond the seas.

"Near the same tree two more, bundles of acute angles, sat with their legs drawn up. One, with his chin propped on his knees, stared at nothing, in an intolerable and appalling manner: his brother phantom rested its forehead, as if overcome with a great weariness; and all about others were scattered in every pose of contorted collapse, as in some picture of a massacre or a pestilence. While I stood horror-struck, one of these creatures rose to his hands and knees, and went off on all-fours towards the river to drink. He lapped out of his hand, then sat up in the sunlight, crossing his shins in front of him, and after a time let his woolly head fall on his breastbone.

"I didn't want any more loitering in the shade, and I made haste towards the station. When near the buildings I met a white man, in such an unexpected elegance of get-up that in the first moment I took him for a sort of vision. I saw a high starched collar, white cuffs, a light alpaca jacket, snowy trousers, a clear silk necktie,[45] and varnished boots. No hat. Hair parted, brushed, oiled, under a green-lined parasol held in a big white hand. He was amazing, and had a penholder behind his ear.

"I shook hands with this miracle, and I learned he was the Company's chief accountant, and that all the book-keeping was done at this station. He had come out for a moment, he said, 'to get a breath of fresh air.' The expression sounded wonderfully odd, with its suggestion of sedentary desk-life. I wouldn't have mentioned the fellow to you at all, only it was from his lips that I first heard the name of the man who is so indissolubly connected with the memories of that time. Moreover, I respected the fellow. Yes; I respected his collars, his vast cuffs, his brushed head. His appearance was certainly that of a hairdresser's dummy; but in the great demoralisation of the land he kept up his appearance. That's backbone! His starched collars and got-up shirt-fronts were achievements of character. He had been out nearly three years; and, later on, I could not help asking him how he managed to sport such linen. He had just the faintest blush, and said modestly, 'I've been teaching one of the native women about the station. It was difficult. She had a distaste for the work.' Thus this man had, verily, accomplished something. And he was devoted to his books, which were in apple-pie order.

"Everything else in the station was in a muddle—heads, things, buildings. Caravans,[46] strings of dusty niggers with splay feet arrived and departed; a stream of manufactured goods, rubbishy cottons, beads, and brass wire[47] set off into the depths of darkness, and in return came a precious trickle of ivory.

"I had to wait in this station for ten days—an eternity. I lived in a tent in the yard, but to be out of the chaos I would sometimes get into the accountant's office. It was built of horizontal planks, and so badly put together that, as he bent over his high desk, he was barred from neck to heels with narrow strips of sunlight. There was no need to open the big shutter to see. It was hot there too; big flies buzzed fiendishly, and did not sting, but stabbed. I sat generally on the floor, while, of faultless appearance (and even slightly scented), perching on a high stool, he wrote, he wrote. Sometimes he stood up for exercise. When a truckle-bed[48] with a sick man (some invalided 'agent' from up country) was hurriedly put in there, he exhibited a gentle annoyance. 'The groans of this sick person,' he said, 'distract my attention. And without that it is extremely difficult to guard against clerical errors in this climate.'

"One day he remarked, without lifting his head, 'In the interior you will no doubt meet Mr Kurtz.'[49] On my asking who Mr Kurtz was, he said he was a first-class agent; and seeing my disappointment at this information, he added slowly, laying down his pen, 'He is a very remarkable person.' Further questions elicited from him that Mr Kurtz was at present in charge of a trading-post, a very important one, in the true ivory-country,[50] at 'the very bottom of there. Sends in as much ivory as all the others put together . . .' He began to write again. The sick man was too ill to groan. The flies buzzed in a great peace.

"Suddenly there was a growing murmur of voices and a great tramping of feet. A caravan had come in. A violent babble of uncouth sounds burst out on the other side of the planks. All the carriers were speaking together, and in the midst of the uproar the lamentable[51] voice of the chief agent was heard 'giving it up' tearfully for the twentieth time that day. . . . He rose slowly. 'What a frightful row,' he said. He crossed the room gently to look at the sick man, and returning, said to me, 'He does not hear.' 'What! Dead?' I asked, startled. 'No, not yet,' he answered, with great composure. Then, alluding with a toss of the head to the tumult in the station-yard, 'When one has got to make correct entries, one comes to hate these savages—hate them to the death!' He remained thoughtful for a moment. 'When you see Mr Kurtz,' he went on, 'tell him from me that everything here'—he glanced at the desk—'is very satisfactory. I don't like to write to him—with those messengers of ours you never know who may get hold of your letter—at that Central Station.'[52] He stared at me for a moment with his mild, bulging eyes. 'Oh, he will go far, very far,' he began again. 'He will be a somebody in the Administration before long. They, above—the Council in Europe, you know—mean him to be.'

"He turned to his work. The noise outside had ceased, and presently in going out I stopped at the door. In the steady buzz of flies the homeward-bound agent was lying flushed and insensible; the other, bent over his books, was making correct entries of perfectly correct transactions; and fifty feet below the doorstep I could see the still tree-tops of the grove of death.

"Next day I left that station at last, with a caravan of sixty men, for a two-hundred-mile tramp.[53]

"No use telling you much about that. Paths, paths, everywhere; a stamped-in network of paths spreading over an empty land, through long grass, through burnt grass, through thickets, down and up chilly ravines, up and down stony hills ablaze with heat; and a solitude, a solitude, nobody, not a hut. The population had cleared out a long time ago. Well, if a lot of mysterious niggers armed with all kinds of fearful weapons suddenly took to travelling on the road between Deal[54] and Gravesend, catching the yokels right and left to carry heavy loads for them, I fancy every farm and cottage thereabouts would get empty very soon. Only here the dwellings were gone too. Still I passed through several abandoned villages. There's something pathetically childish in the ruins of grass walls. Day after day, with the stamp and shuffle of sixty pair of bare feet behind me, each pair under a sixty-pound load. Camp, cook, sleep, strike camp, march. Now and then a carrier dead in harness, at rest in the long grass near the path, with an empty water-gourd and his long staff lying by his side. A great silence around and above. Perhaps on some quiet night the tremor of far-off drums, sinking, swelling, a tremor vast, faint; a sound weird, appealing, suggestive, and wild—and perhaps with as profound a meaning as the sound of bells in a Christian country. Once a white man in an unbuttoned uniform, camping on the

path with an armed escort of lank Zanzibaris,[55] very hospitable
and festive—not to say drunk. Was looking after the upkeep of
the road, he declared. Can't say I saw any road or any upkeep,
unless the body of a middle-aged negro, with a bullet-hole in
the forehead, upon which I absolutely stumbled three miles
further on, may be considered as a permanent improvement. I
had a white companion too, not a bad chap, but rather too
fleshy and with the exasperating habit of fainting on the hot
hillsides, miles away from the least bit of shade and water.
Annoying, you know, to hold your own coat like a parasol over
a man's head while he is coming-to. I couldn't help asking him
once what he meant by coming there at all. 'To make money,
of course. What do you think?' he said, scornfully. Then he got
fever, and had to be carried in a hammock slung under a pole.
As he weighed sixteen stone I had no end of rows with the
carriers. They jibbed, ran away, sneaked off with their loads in
the night—quite a mutiny. So, one evening, I made a speech in
English with gestures, not one of which was lost to the sixty
pairs of eyes before me, and the next morning I started the
hammock off in front all right. An hour afterwards I came upon
the whole concern wrecked in a bush—man, hammock, groans,
blankets, horrors. The heavy pole had skinned his poor nose.
He was very anxious for me to kill somebody, but there wasn't
the shadow of a carrier near. I remembered the old doctor—'It
would be interesting for science to watch the mental changes
of individuals, on the spot.' I felt I was becoming scientifically
interesting. However, all that is to no purpose. On the fifteenth
day I came in sight of the big river again, and hobbled into the
Central Station. It was on a back water surrounded by scrub
and forest, with a pretty border of smelly mud on one side, and
on the three others enclosed by a crazy fence of rushes. A
neglected gap was all the gate it had, and the first glance at the
place was enough to let you see the flabby devil was running
that show. White men with long staves in their hands appeared
languidly from amongst the buildings, strolling up to take a
look at me, and then retired out of sight somewhere. One of
them, a stout, excitable chap with black moustaches, informed
me with great volubility and many digressions, as soon as I told

him who I was, that my steamer was at the bottom of the river.
I was thunderstruck. What, how, why? Oh, it was 'all right.'
The 'manager himself' was there. All quite correct. 'Everybody
had behaved splendidly! splendidly!'—'you must,' he said in
agitation, 'go and see the general manager at once. He is
waiting!'

"I did not see the real significance of that wreck at once. I
fancy I see it now,[56] but I am not sure—not at all. Certainly the
affair was too stupid—when I think of it—to be altogether
natural. Still . . . But at the moment it presented itself simply as
a confounded nuisance. The steamer was sunk. They had started
two days before in a sudden hurry up the river with the manager
on board, in charge of some volunteer skipper, and before they
had been out three hours they tore the bottom out of her on
stones, and she sank near the south bank. I asked myself what
I was to do there, now my boat was lost. As a matter of fact, I
had plenty to do in fishing my command out of the river. I had
to set about it the very next day. That, and the repairs when
I brought the pieces to the station, took some months.

"My first interview with the manager was curious. He did
not ask me to sit down after my twenty-mile walk that morning.
He was commonplace in complexion, in feature, in manner,
and in voice. He was of middle size and of ordinary build. His
eyes, of the usual blue, were perhaps remarkably cold, and he
certainly could make his glance fall on one as trenchant and
heavy as an axe. But even at these times the rest of his person
seemed to disclaim the intention. Otherwise there was only an
indefinable, faint expression of his lips, something stealthy—a
smile—not a smile—I remember it, but I can't explain. It was
unconscious, this smile was, though just after he had said something it got intensified for an instant. It came at the end of his
speeches like a seal applied on the words to make the meaning
of the commonest phrase appear absolutely inscrutable. He
was a common trader,[57] from his youth up employed in these
parts—nothing more. He was obeyed, yet he inspired neither
love nor fear, nor even respect. He inspired uneasiness. That
was it! Uneasiness. Not a definite mistrust—just uneasiness—
nothing more. You have no idea how effective such a . . . a . . .

faculty can be. He had no genius for organising, for initiative, or for order even. That was evident in such things as the deplorable state of the station. He had no learning, and no intelligence. His position had come to him—why? Perhaps because he was never ill . . . He had served three terms of three years out there . . . Because triumphant health in the general rout of constitutions is a kind of power in itself. When he went home on leave he rioted on a large scale—pompously. Jack ashore[58]—with a difference—in externals only. This one could gather from his casual talk. He originated nothing, he could keep the routine going—that's all. But he was great. He was great by this little thing that it was impossible to tell what could control such a man. He never gave that secret away. Perhaps there was nothing within him. Such a suspicion made one pause—for out there there were no external checks. Once when various tropical diseases had laid low almost every 'agent' in the station, he was heard to say, 'Men who come out here should have no entrails.' He sealed the utterance with that smile of his, as though it had been a door opening into a darkness he had in his keeping. You fancied you had seen things—but the seal was on. When annoyed at meal-times by the constant quarrels of the white men about precedence, he ordered an immense round table to be made, for which a special house had to be built. This was the station's mess-room. Where he sat was the first place—the rest were nowhere. One felt this to be his unalterable conviction. He was neither civil nor uncivil. He was quiet. He allowed his 'boy'—an overfed young negro from the coast—to treat the white men, under his very eyes, with provoking insolence.

"He began to speak as soon as he saw me. I had been very long on the road. He could not wait. Had to start without me. The up-river stations had to be relieved. There had been so many delays already that he did not know who was dead and who was alive, and how they got on—and so on, and so on. He paid no attention to my explanations, and, playing with a stick of sealing-wax, repeated several times that the situation was 'very grave, very grave.' There were rumours that a very important station was in jeopardy, and its chief, Mr Kurtz, was ill. Hoped it was not true. Mr Kurtz was . . . I felt weary and

irritable. Hang Kurtz, I thought. I interrupted him by saying I
had heard of Mr Kurtz on the coast. 'Ah! So they talk of him
down there,' he murmured to himself. Then he began again,
assuring me Mr Kurtz was the best agent he had, an exceptional
man, of the greatest importance to the Company; therefore
I could understand his anxiety. He was, he said, 'very, very
uneasy.' Certainly he fidgeted on his chair a good deal, exclaimed, 'Ah, Mr Kurtz!', broke the stick of sealing-wax and
seemed dumbfounded by the accident. Next thing he wanted to
know 'how long it would take to——' I interrupted him again.
Being hungry, you know, and kept on my feet too, I was getting
savage. 'How could I tell?' I said. 'I hadn't even seen the wreck
yet—some months, no doubt.' All this talk seemed to me so
futile. 'Some months,' he said. 'Well, let us say three months
before we can make a start. Yes. That ought to do the affair.' I
flung out of his hut (he lived all alone in a clay hut with a sort
of verandah) muttering to myself my opinion of him. He was a
chattering idiot. Afterwards I took it back when it was borne
upon me startlingly with what extreme nicety he had estimated
the time requisite for the 'affair.'

"I went to work the next day, turning, so to speak, my back
on that station. In that way only it seemed to me I could keep
my hold on the redeeming facts of life. Still, one must look
about sometimes; and then I saw this station, these men strolling
aimlessly about in the sunshine of the yard. I asked myself
sometimes what it all meant. They wandered here and there
with their absurd long staves in their hands, like a lot of faithless
pilgrims bewitched inside a rotten fence. The word 'ivory' rang
in the air, was whispered, was sighed. You would think they
were praying to it. A taint of imbecile rapacity blew through it
all, like a whiff from some corpse. By Jove! I've never seen
anything so unreal in my life. And outside, the silent wilderness
surrounding this cleared speck on the earth struck me as something great and invincible, like evil or truth, waiting patiently
for the passing away of this fantastic invasion.

"Oh, these months! Well, never mind. Various things happened. One evening a grass shed full of calico, cotton prints,
beads, and I don't know what else, burst into a blaze so suddenly

that you would have thought the earth had opened to let an avenging fire consume all that trash. I was smoking my pipe quietly by my dismantled steamer, and saw them all cutting capers in the light, with their arms lifted high, when the stout man with moustaches came tearing down to the river, a tin pail in his hand, assured me that everybody was 'behaving splendidly, splendidly,' dipped about a quart of water and tore back again. I noticed there was a hole in the bottom of his pail.

"I strolled up. There was no hurry. You see the thing had gone off like a box of matches. It had been hopeless from the very first. The flame had leaped high, driven everybody back, lighted up everything—and collapsed. The shed was already a heap of embers glowing fiercely. A nigger was being beaten near by. They said he had caused the fire in some way; be that as it may, he was screeching most horribly. I saw him, later on, for several days, sitting in a bit of shade looking very sick and trying to recover himself: afterwards he arose and went out—and the wilderness without a sound took him into its bosom again. As I approached the glow from the dark I found myself at the back of two men, talking. I heard the name of Kurtz pronounced, then the words, 'take advantage of this unfortunate accident.' One of the men was the manager. I wished him a good evening. 'Did you ever see anything like it—eh? it is incredible,' he said, and walked off. The other man remained. He was a first-class agent, young, gentlemanly, a bit reserved, with a forked little beard and a hooked nose. He was stand-offish with the other agents, and they on their side said he was the manager's spy upon them. As to me, I had hardly ever spoken to him before. We got into talk, and by and bye we strolled away from the hissing ruins. Then he asked me to his room, which was in the main building of the station. He struck a match, and I perceived that this young aristocrat had not only a silver-mounted dressing-case but also a whole candle all to himself. Just at that time the manager was the only man supposed to have any right to candles. Native mats covered the clay walls; a collection of spears, assegais,[59] shields, knives was hung up in trophies. The business entrusted to this fellow was the making of bricks—so I had been informed; but there wasn't a fragment of a brick anywhere in the station, and he had been there more than a year—waiting. It seems he could not make bricks without something, I don't know what—straw maybe.[60] Anyway, it could not be found there, and as it was not likely to be sent from Europe, it did not appear clear to me what he was waiting for. An act of special creation[61] perhaps. However, they were all waiting—all the sixteen or twenty pilgrims of them—for something; and upon my word it did not seem an uncongenial occupation, from the way they took it, though the only thing that ever came to them was disease—as far as I could see. They beguiled the time by backbiting[62] and intriguing against each other in a foolish kind of way. There was an air of plotting about that station, but nothing came of it, of course. It was as unreal as everything else—as the philanthropic pretence of the whole concern, as their talk, as their government, as their show of work. The only real feeling was a desire to get appointed to a trading-post where ivory was to be had, so that they could earn percentages. They intrigued and slandered and hated each other only on that account—but as to effectually lifting a little finger—oh, no. By heavens! there is something after all in the world allowing one man to steal a horse while another must not look at a halter.[63] Steal a horse straight out. Very well. He has done it. Perhaps he can ride. But there is a way of looking at a halter that would provoke the most charitable of saints into a kick.

"I had no idea why he wanted to be so sociable, but as we chatted in there it suddenly occurred to me the fellow was trying to get at something—in fact, pumping me. He alluded constantly to Europe, to the people I was supposed to know there—putting leading questions as to my acquaintances in the sepulchral city, and so on. His little eyes glittered like mica discs—with curiosity—though he tried to keep up a bit of superciliousness. At first I was astonished, but very soon I became also awfully curious to see what he would find out from me. I couldn't possibly imagine what I had in me to make it worth his while. It was very pretty to see how he baffled himself, for in truth my body was full of chills, and my head had nothing in it but that wretched steamboat business. It was evident he took me for a perfectly shameless prevaricator. At last he got angry, and, to conceal a movement of furious annoyance, he yawned. I rose. Then I noticed a small sketch in oils, on a panel, representing a woman, draped and blindfolded, carrying a lighted torch.[64] The background was sombre—almost black. The movement of the woman was stately, and the effect of the torchlight on the face was sinister.

"It arrested me, and he stood by, civilly holding an empty half-pint champagne bottle (medical comforts) with the candle stuck in it. To my question he said Mr Kurtz had painted this—in this very station more than a year ago—while waiting for means to go to his trading-post. 'Tell me, pray,' said I, 'who is this Mr Kurtz?'

"'The chief of the Inner Station,' he answered in a short tone, looking away. 'Much obliged,' I said, laughing. 'And you are the brickmaker of the Central Station. Every one knows that.' He was silent for a while. 'He is a prodigy,' he said at last. 'He is an emissary of pity, and science, and progress, and devil knows what else. We want,' he began to declaim suddenly, 'for the guidance of the cause entrusted to us by Europe, so to speak, higher intelligence, wide sympathies, a singleness of purpose.' 'Who says that?' I asked. 'Lots of them,' he replied. 'Some even write that; and so *he* comes here, a special being, as you ought to know.' 'Why ought I to know?' I interrupted, really surprised. He paid no attention. 'Yes. To-day he is chief of the best station, next year he will be assistant-manager, two years more and . . . but I daresay you know what he will be in two years' time. You are of the new gang—the gang of virtue. The same people who sent him specially also recommended you. Oh, don't say no. I've my own eyes to trust.' Light dawned upon me. My dear aunt's influential acquaintances were producing an unexpected effect upon that young man. I nearly burst into a laugh. 'Do you read the Company's confidential correspondence?' I asked. He hadn't a word to say. It was great fun. 'When Mr Kurtz,' I continued severely, 'is General Manager, you won't have the opportunity.'

"He blew the candle out suddenly, and we went outside. The moon had risen. Black figures strolled about listlessly, pouring water on the glow, whence proceeded a sound of hissing; steam ascended in the moonlight, the beaten nigger groaned somewhere. 'What a row the brute makes!' said the indefatigable man with the moustaches, appearing near us. 'Serve him right. Transgression—punishment—bang! Pitiless, pitiless. That's the only way. This will prevent all conflagrations for the future. I was just telling the manager . . .' He noticed my companion, and became crestfallen all at once. 'Not in bed yet,' he said, with a kind of servile heartiness; 'it's so natural. Ha! Danger—agitation.' He vanished. I went on to the river-side, and the other followed me. I heard a scathing murmur at my ear, 'Heap of muffs⁶⁵—go to.' The pilgrims could be seen in knots gesticulating, discussing. Several had still their staves in their hands. I verily believe they took these sticks to bed with them. Beyond the fence the forest stood up spectrally in the moonlight, and through the dim stir, through the faint sounds of that lamentable courtyard, the silence of the land went home to one's very heart—its mystery, its greatness, the amazing reality of its concealed life. The hurt nigger moaned feebly somewhere near by, and then fetched a deep sigh that made me mend my pace away from there. I felt a hand introducing itself under my arm. 'My dear sir,' said the fellow, 'I don't want to be misunderstood, and especially by you, who will see Mr Kurtz long before I can have that pleasure. I wouldn't like him to get a false idea of my disposition. . . .'

"I let him run on, this papier-mâché Mephistopheles,⁶⁶ and it seemed to me that if I tried I could poke my forefinger through him, and find nothing inside but a little loose dirt, maybe. He, don't you see, had been planning to be assistant-manager by and bye under the present man, and I could see that the coming of that Kurtz had upset them both not a little. He talked precipitately, and I did not try to stop him. I had my shoulders against the wreck of my steamer, hauled up on the slope like a carcass of some big river animal. The smell of mud, of primeval mud, by Jove! was in my nostrils, the high stillness of primeval forests was before my eyes; there were shiny patches on the black creek. The moon had spread over everything a thin layer of silver—over the rank grass, over the mud, upon the wall of matted vegetation standing higher than the wall of a temple, over the great river I could see through a sombre gap glittering, glittering, as it flowed broadly by without a murmur. All this was great, expectant, mute, while the man jabbered about himself. I wondered whether the stillness on the face of the immensity looking at us two were meant as an appeal or as a menace. What were we who had strayed in here? Could we handle that dumb thing, or would it handle us? I felt how big, how confoundedly big, was that thing that couldn't talk, and perhaps was deaf as well. What was in there? I could see a little ivory coming out from there, and I had heard Mr Kurtz was in there. I had heard enough about it too—God knows! Yet somehow it didn't bring any image with it—no more than if I had been told an angel or a fiend was in there. I believed it in the same way one of you might believe there are inhabitants in the planet Mars. I knew once a Scotch sailmaker who was certain, dead sure, there were people in Mars. If you asked him for some idea how they looked and behaved, he would get shy and mutter something about 'walking on all-fours.' If you as much as smiled, he would—though a man of sixty—offer to fight you. I would not have gone so far as to fight for Kurtz, but I went for him near enough to a lie. You know I hate, detest, and can't bear a lie, not because I am straighter than the rest of us, but simply because it appals me. There is a taint of death, a flavour of mortality in lies—which is exactly what I hate and detest in the world—what I want to forget. It makes me miserable and sick, like biting something rotten would do. Temperament, I suppose. Well, I went near enough to it by letting the young fool there believe anything he liked to imagine as to my influence in Europe. I became in an instant as much of a pretence as the rest of the bewitched pilgrims. This simply because I had a notion it somehow would be of help to that Kurtz whom at the time I did not see—you understand. He was just a word for me. I did not see the man in the name any more than you do. Do you see him? Do you see the story? Do you see anything? It seems to me I am trying to tell you a dream—making a vain attempt, because no relation of a dream can convey the dream-sensation, that commingling of absurdity, surprise, and bewilderment in

a tremor of struggling revolt, that notion of being captured by the incredible which is of the very essence of dreams. . . ."
He was silent for a while.
". . . No, it is impossible; it is impossible to convey the life-sensation of any given epoch of one's existence—that which makes its truth, its meaning—its subtle and penetrating essence. It is impossible. We live, as we dream—alone. . . ."
He paused again as if reflecting, then added—
"Of course in this you fellows see more than I could then. You see me, whom you know. . . ."
It had become so pitch dark that we listeners could hardly see one another. For a long time already he, sitting apart, had been no more to us than a voice. There was not a word from anybody. The others might have been asleep, but I was awake. I listened, I listened on the watch for the sentence, for the word, that would give me the clue to the faint uneasiness inspired by this narrative that seemed to shape itself without human lips in the heavy night-air of the river.
". . . Yes—I let him run on," Marlow began again, "and think what he pleased about the powers that were behind me. I did! And there was nothing behind me! There was nothing but that wretched, old, mangled steamboat I was leaning against, while he talked fluently about 'the necessity for every man to get on.' 'And when one comes out here, you conceive, it is not to gaze at the moon.' Mr Kurtz was a 'universal genius,' but even a genius would find it easier to work with 'adequate tools—intelligent men.' He did not make bricks—why, there was a physical impossibility in the way—as I was well aware; and if he did secretarial work for the manager, it was because 'no sensible man rejects wantonly the confidence of his superiors.' Did I see it? I saw it. What more did I want? What I really wanted was rivets, by heaven! Rivets. To get on with the work—to stop the hole. Rivets I wanted. There were cases of them down at the coast—cases—piled up—burst—split! You kicked a loose rivet at every second step in that station yard on the hillside. Rivets had rolled into the grove of death. You could fill your pockets with rivets for the trouble of stoop-ing down—and there wasn't one rivet to be found where it was

wanted. We had plates that would do, but nothing to fasten them with. And every week the messenger, a lone negro, letter-bag on shoulder and staff in hand, left our station for the coast. And several times a week a coast caravan came in with trade goods—ghastly glazed calico that made you shudder only to look at it, glass beads value about a penny a quart, confounded spotted cotton handkerchiefs. And no rivets. Three carriers could have brought all that was wanted to set that steamboat afloat.

"He was becoming confidential now, but I fancy my unres-ponsive attitude must have exasperated him at last, for he judged it necessary to inform me he feared neither God nor devil, let alone any mere man. I said I could see that very well, but what I wanted was a certain quantity of rivets—and rivets were what really Mr Kurtz wanted, if he had only known it. Now letters went to the coast every week. . . . 'My dear sir,' he cried, 'I write from dictation.' I demanded rivets. There was a way—for an intelligent man. He changed his manner; became very cold, and suddenly began to talk about a hippopotamus; wondered whether sleeping on board the steamer (I stuck to my salvage night and day) I wasn't disturbed. There was an old hippo that had the bad habit of getting out on the bank and roaming at night over the station grounds. The pilgrims used to turn out in a body and empty every rifle they could lay hands on at him. Some even had sat up o' nights for him. All this energy was wasted, though. 'That animal has a charmed life,' he said; 'but you can say this only of brutes in this country. No man—you apprehend me?—no man here bears a charmed life.' He stood there for a moment in the moonlight with his delicate hooked nose set a little askew, and his mica eyes glittering without a wink, then, with a curt Good night, he strode off. I could see he was disturbed and considerably puzzled, which made me feel more hopeful than I had been for days. It was a great comfort to turn from that chap to my influential friend, the battered, twisted, ruined, tin-pot steamboat. I clambered on board. She rang under my feet like an empty Huntley & Palmers biscuit-tin[67] kicked along a gutter; she was nothing so solid in make, and rather less pretty in shape, but I had expended enough hard work on her to make me love her. No influential friend would have served me better. She had given me a chance to come out a bit—to find out what I could do. No, I don't like work. I had rather laze about and think of all the fine things that can be done. I don't like work—no man does—but I like what is in the work—the chance to find yourself. Your own reality—for yourself, not for others—what no other man can ever know. They can only see the mere show, and never can tell what it really means.

"I was not surprised to see somebody sitting aft, on the deck, with his legs dangling over the mud. You see I rather chummed with the few mechanics there were in that station, whom the other pilgrims naturally despised—on account of their imperfect manners, I suppose. This was the foreman—a boiler-maker by trade—a good worker. He was a lank, bony, yellow-faced man, with big intense eyes. His aspect was worried, and his head was as bald as the palm of my hand; but his hair in falling seemed to have stuck to his chin, and had prospered in the new locality, for his beard hung down to his waist. He was a widower with six young children (he had left them in charge of a sister of his to come out there), and the passion of his life was pigeon-flying. He was an enthusiast and a connoisseur. He would rave about pigeons. After work hours he used sometimes to come over from his hut for a talk about his children and his pigeons; at work, when he had to crawl in the mud under the bottom of the steamboat, he would tie up that beard of his in a kind of white serviette he brought for the purpose. It had loops to go over his ears. In the evening he could be seen squatted on the bank rinsing that wrapper in the creek with great care, then spreading it solemnly on a bush to dry.

"I slapped him on the back and shouted, 'We shall have rivets!' He scrambled to his feet exclaiming, 'No! Rivets!' as though he couldn't believe his ears. Then in a low voice, 'You . . . eh?' I don't know why we behaved like lunatics. I put my finger to the side of my nose and nodded mysteriously. 'Good for you!' he cried, snapped his fingers above his head, lifting one foot. I tried a jig. We capered on the iron deck. A frightful clatter came out of that empty hulk, and the virgin forest on the other bank of the creek sent it back in a thundering roll upon the sleeping station. It must have made some of the pilgrims sit up in their hovels. A dark figure obscured the lighted doorway of the manager's hut, vanished, then, a second or so after, the doorway itself vanished too. We stopped, and the silence driven away by the stamping of our feet flowed back again from the recesses of the land. The great wall of vegetation, an exuberant and entangled mass of trunks, branches, leaves, boughs, festoons, motionless in the moonlight, was like a rioting invasion of soundless life, a rolling wave of plants, piled up, crested, ready to topple over the creek, to sweep every little man of us out of his little existence. And it moved not. A deadened burst of mighty splashes and snorts reached us from afar, as though an ichthyosaurus[68] had been taking a bath of glitter in the great river. 'After all,' said the boiler-maker in a reasonable tone, 'why shouldn't we get the rivets?' Why not, indeed! I did not know of any reason why we shouldn't. 'They'll come in three weeks,' I said, confidently.

"But they didn't. Instead of rivets there came an invasion, an infliction, a visitation. It came in sections during the next three weeks, each section headed by a donkey carrying a white man in new clothes and tan shoes, bowing from that elevation right and left to the impressed pilgrims. A quarrelsome band of footsore sulky niggers trod on the heels of the donkey; a lot of tents, camp-stools, tin boxes, white cases, brown bales would be shot down in the courtyard, and the air of mystery would deepen a little over the muddle of the station. Five such instalments came, with their absurd air of disorderly flight with the loot of innumerable outfit shops and provision stores, that, one would think, they were lugging, after a raid, into the wilderness for equitable division. It was an inextricable mess of things decent in themselves but that human folly made look like the spoils of thieving.

"This devoted band called itself the Eldorado Exploring Expedition,[69] and I believe they were sworn to secrecy. Their talk, however, was the talk of sordid buccaneers: it was reckless without hardihood, greedy without audacity, and cruel without courage; there was not an atom of foresight or of serious intention in the whole batch of them, and they did not seem aware these things are wanted for the work of the world. To tear treasure out of the bowels of the land was their desire, with no more moral purpose at the back of it than there is in burglars breaking into a safe. Who paid the expenses of the noble enterprise I don't know; but the uncle of our manager was leader of that lot.

"In exterior he resembled a butcher in a poor neighbourhood, and his eyes had a look of sleepy cunning. He carried his fat paunch with ostentation on his short legs, and during the time his gang infested the station spoke to no one but his nephew. You could see these two roaming about all day long with their heads close together in an everlasting confab.[70]

"I had given up worrying myself about the rivets. One's capacity for that kind of folly is more limited than you would suppose. I said Hang!—and let things slide. I had plenty of time for meditation, and now and then I would give some thought to Kurtz. I wasn't very interested in him. No. Still, I was curious to see whether this man, who had come out equipped with moral ideas of some sort, would climb to the top after all, and how he would set about his work when there."

II

"One evening as I was lying flat on the deck of my steamboat, I heard voices approaching—and there were the nephew and the uncle strolling along the bank. I laid my head on my arm again, and had nearly lost myself in a doze, when somebody said in my ear, as it were: 'I am as harmless as a little child, but I don't like to be dictated to. Am I the manager—or am I not? I was ordered to send him there. It's incredible.' ... I became aware that the two were standing on the shore alongside the forepart of the steamboat, just below my head. I did not move; it did not occur to me to move: I was sleepy. 'It *is* unpleasant,' grunted the uncle. 'He has asked the Administration to be sent there,' said the other, 'with the idea of showing what he could do; and I was instructed accordingly. Look at the influence that man must have. Is it not frightful?' They both agreed it was frightful, then made several bizarre remarks: 'Make rain and fine weather[1]—one man—the Council—by the nose'—bits of absurd sentences that got the better of my drowsiness, so that I had pretty near the whole of my wits about me when the uncle said, 'The climate may do away with this difficulty for you. Is he alone there?' 'Yes,' answered the manager; 'he sent his assistant down the river with a note to me in these terms: "Clear this poor devil out of the country, and don't bother sending more of that sort. I had rather be alone than have the kind of men you can dispose of with me." It was more than a year ago. Can you imagine such impudence!' 'Anything since then?' asked the other, hoarsely. 'Ivory,' jerked out the nephew; 'lots of it— prime sort—lots—most annoying, from him.' 'And with that?' questioned the heavy rumble. 'Invoice,' was the reply fired out, so to speak. Then silence. They had been talking about Kurtz.

"I was broad awake by this time, but, lying perfectly at ease, remained still, having no inducement to change my position. 'How did that ivory come all this way?' growled the elder man, who seemed very vexed. The other explained that it had come with a fleet of canoes in charge of an English half-caste clerk Kurtz had with him; that Kurtz had apparently intended to return himself, the station being by that time bare of goods and stores, but after coming three hundred miles, had suddenly decided to go back, which he started to do alone in a small dug-out with four paddlers, leaving the half-caste to continue down the river with the ivory. The two fellows there seemed astounded at anybody attempting such a thing. They were at a loss for an adequate motive. As to me, I seemed to see Kurtz for the first time. It was a distinct glimpse: the dug-out, four paddling savages, and the lone white man turning his back suddenly on the headquarters, on relief, on thoughts of home— perhaps; setting his face towards the depths of the wilderness, towards his empty and desolate station. I did not know the motive. Perhaps he was just simply a fine fellow who stuck to his work for its own sake. His name, you understand, had not been pronounced once. He was 'that man.' The half-caste, who, as far as I could see, had conducted a difficult trip with great prudence and pluck, was invariably alluded to as 'that scoundrel.' The 'scoundrel' had reported that the 'man' had been very ill—had recovered imperfectly.... The two below me moved away then a few paces, and strolled back and forth at some little distance. I heard: 'Military post—doctor—two hundred miles—quite alone now—unavoidable delays—nine months—no news—strange rumours.' They approached again, just as the manager was saying, 'No one, as far as I know, unless a species of wandering trader—a pestilential fellow, snapping ivory from the natives.' Who was it they were talking about now? I gathered in snatches that this was some man supposed to be in Kurtz's district, and of whom the manager did not approve. 'We will not be free from unfair competition till one of these fellows is hanged for an example,' he said. 'Certainly,' grunted the other; 'get him hanged!² Why not?

Anything—anything can be done in this country. That's what I say; nobody here, you understand, *here*, can endanger your position. And why? You stand the climate—you outlast them all. The danger is in Europe; but there before I left I took care to——' They moved off and whispered, then their voices rose again. 'The extraordinary series of delays is not my fault. I did my possible.'³ The fat man sighed, 'Very sad.' 'And the pestiferous absurdity of his talk,' continued the other; 'he bothered me enough when he was here. "Each station should be like a beacon on the road towards better things, a centre for trade of course, but also for humanising, improving, instructing." Conceive you—that ass! And he wants to be manager! No, it's——' Here he got choked by excessive indignation, and I lifted my head the least bit. I was surprised to see how near they were—right under me. I could have spat upon their hats. They were looking on the ground, absorbed in thought. The manager was switching his leg with a slender twig: his sagacious relative lifted his head. 'You have been well since you came out this time?' he asked. The other gave a start. 'Who? I? Oh! Like a charm—like a charm. But the rest—oh, my goodness! All sick. They die so quick, too, that I haven't the time to send them out of the country—it's incredible!' 'H'm. Just so,' grunted the uncle. 'Ah! my boy, trust to this—I say, trust to this.' I saw him extend his short flipper of an arm for a gesture that took in the forest, the creek, the mud, the river—seemed to beckon with a dishonouring flourish before the sunlit face of the land a treacherous appeal to the lurking death, to the hidden evil, to the profound darkness of its heart. It was so startling that I leaped to my feet and looked back at the edge of the forest, as though I had expected an answer of some sort to that black display of confidence. You know the foolish notions that come to one sometimes. The high stillness confronted these two figures with its ominous patience, waiting for the passing away of a fantastic invasion.

"They swore aloud together—out of sheer fright, I believe—then pretending not to know anything of my existence, turned back to the station. The sun was low; and leaning forward side by side, they seemed to be tugging painfully uphill their two

ridiculous shadows of unequal length, that trailed behind them
slowly over the tall grass without bending a single blade.

"In a few days the Eldorado Expedition went into the patient
wilderness, that closed upon it as the sea closes over a diver.
Long afterwards the news came that all the donkeys were dead.
I know nothing as to the fate of the less valuable animals. They,
no doubt, like the rest of us, found what they deserved. I did
not inquire. I was then rather excited at the prospect of meeting
Kurtz very soon. When I say very soon I mean it comparatively.
It was just two months from the day we left the creek when we
came to the bank below Kurtz's station.

"Going up that river was like travelling back to the earliest
beginnings of the world, when vegetation rioted on the earth
and the big trees were kings. An empty stream, a great silence,
an impenetrable forest. The air was warm, thick, heavy, sluggish. There was no joy in the brilliance of sunshine. The long
stretches of the waterway ran on, deserted, into the gloom
of overshadowed distances. On silvery sandbanks hippos and
alligators sunned themselves side by side. The broadening
waters flowed through a mob of wooded islands; you lost your
way on that river as you would in a desert, and butted all day
long against shoals, trying to find the channel, till you thought
yourself bewitched and cut off for ever from everything you
had known once—somewhere—far away—in another existence perhaps. There were moments when one's past came back
to one, as it will sometimes when you have not a moment to
spare to yourself; but it came in the shape of an unrestful and
noisy dream, remembered with wonder amongst the overwhelming realities of this strange world of plants, and water,
and silence. And this stillness of life did not in the least resemble
a peace. It was the stillness of an implacable force brooding
over an inscrutable intention. It looked at you with a vengeful
aspect. I got used to it afterwards; I did not see it any more; I
had no time. I had to keep guessing at the channel; I had to
discern, mostly by inspiration, the signs of hidden banks; I
watched for sunken stones;[4] I was learning to clap my teeth
smartly before my heart flew out, when I shaved by a fluke
some infernal sly old snag that would have ripped the life out

of the tin-pot steamboat and drowned all the pilgrims; I had to keep a look-out for the signs of dead wood we could cut up in the night for next day's steaming. When you have to attend to things of that sort, to the mere incidents of the surface, the reality—the reality, I tell you—fades. The inner truth is hidden—luckily, luckily. But I felt it all the same; I felt often its mysterious stillness watching me at my monkey tricks, just as it watches you fellows performing on your respective tight-ropes for—what is it? half-a-crown a tumble——"

"Try to be civil, Marlow," growled a voice, and I knew there was at least one listener awake besides myself.

"I beg your pardon. I forgot the heartache which makes up the rest of the price. And indeed what does the price matter, if the trick be well done? You do your tricks very well. And I didn't do badly either, since I managed not to sink that steamboat on my first trip. It's a wonder to me yet. Imagine a blindfolded man set to drive a van over a bad road. I sweated and shivered over that business considerably, I can tell you. After all, for a seaman, to scrape the bottom of the thing that's supposed to float all the time under his care is the unpardonable sin. No one may know of it, but you never forget the thump—eh? A blow on the very heart. You remember it, you dream of it, you wake up at night and think of it—years after—and go hot and cold all over. I don't pretend to say that steamboat floated all the time. More than once she had to wade for a bit, with twenty cannibals[5] splashing around and pushing. We had enlisted some of these chaps on the way for a crew. Fine fellows—cannibals—in their place. They were men one could work with, and I am grateful to them. And, after all, they did not eat each other before my face: they had brought along a provision of hippo-meat which went rotten, and made the mystery of the wilderness stink in my nostrils. Phoo! I can sniff it now. I had the manager on board and three or four pilgrims[6] with their staves—all complete. Sometimes we came upon a station close by the bank, clinging to the skirts of the Unknown, and the white men rushing out of a tumble-down hovel, with great gestures of joy and surprise and welcome, seemed very strange—had the appearance of being held there captive by a spell. The word 'ivory' would ring in the air for a while—and on we went again into the silence, along empty reaches, round the still bends, between the high walls of our winding way, reverberating in hollow claps the ponderous beat of the stern-wheel. Trees, trees, millions of trees, massive, immense, running up high; and at their foot, hugging the bank against the stream, crept the little begrimed steamboat, like a sluggish beetle crawling on the floor of a lofty portico. It made you feel very small, very lost, and yet it was not altogether depressing that feeling. After all, if you were small, the grimy beetle crawled on—which was just what you wanted it to do. Where the pilgrims imagined it crawled to I don't know. To some place where they expected to get something, I bet! For me it crawled towards Kurtz—exclusively; but when the steam-pipes started leaking we crawled very slow. The reaches opened before us and closed behind, as if the forest had stepped leisurely across the water to bar the way for our return. We penetrated deeper and deeper into the heart of darkness. It was very quiet there. At night sometimes the roll of drums behind the curtain of trees would run up the river and remain sustained faintly, as if hovering in the air high over our heads, till the first break of day. Whether this meant war, peace, or prayer we could not tell. The dawns were heralded by the descent of a chill stillness; the wood-cutters slept, their fires burned low; the snapping of a twig would make you start. We were wanderers on a prehistoric earth, on an earth that wore the aspect of an unknown planet. We could have fancied ourselves the first of men taking possession of an accursed inheritance, to be subdued at the cost of profound anguish and of excessive toil. But suddenly, as we struggled round a bend, there would be a glimpse of rush walls, of peaked grass-roofs, a burst of yells, a whirl of black limbs, a mass of hands clapping, of feet stamping, of bodies swaying, of eyes rolling, under the droop of heavy and motionless foliage. The steamer toiled along slowly on the edge of a black and incomprehensible frenzy. The prehistoric man was cursing us, praying to us, welcoming us—who could tell? We were cut off from the comprehension of our surroundings; we glided past like phantoms, wondering and secretly appalled, as sane men would be before an enthusiastic outbreak in a madhouse. We could not understand, because we were too far and could not remember, because we were travelling in the night of first ages, of those ages that are gone, leaving hardly a sign—and no memories.

"The earth seemed unearthly. We are accustomed to look upon the shackled form of a conquered monster, but there— there you could look at a thing monstrous and free. It was unearthly, and the men were——No, they were not inhuman. Well, you know, that was the worst of it—this suspicion of their not being inhuman. It would come slowly to one. They howled, and leaped, and spun, and made horrid faces; but what thrilled you was just the thought of their humanity—like yours—the thought of your remote kinship with this wild and passionate uproar. Ugly. Yes, it was ugly enough; but if you were man enough you would admit to yourself that there was in you just the faintest trace of a response to the terrible frank-ness of that noise, a dim suspicion of there being a meaning in it which you—you so remote from the night of first ages—could comprehend. And why not? The mind of man is capable of anything[7]—because everything is in it, all the past as well as all the future. What was there after all? Joy, fear, sorrow, devotion, valour, rage—who can tell?—but truth—truth stripped of its cloak of time. Let the fool gape and shudder—the man knows, and can look on without a wink. But he must at least be as much of a man as these on the shore. He must meet that truth with his own true stuff—with his own inborn strength. Principles? Principles won't do. Acquisitions, clothes, pretty rags[8]—rags that would fly off at the first good shake. No; you want a deliberate belief. An appeal to me in this fiendish row—is there? Very well; I hear; I admit, but I have a voice too, and for good or evil mine is the speech that cannot be silenced. Of course, a fool, what with sheer fright and fine sentiments, is always safe. Who's that grunting? You wonder I didn't go ashore for a howl and a dance? Well, no—I didn't. Fine sentiments, you say? Fine sentiments, be hanged! I had no time. I had to mess about with white-lead[9] and strips of woollen blanket helping to put bandages on those leaky steam-pipes—

I tell you. I had to watch the steering, and circumvent those snags, and get the tin-pot along by hook or by crook. There was surface-truth enough in these things to save a wiser man. And between whiles I had to look after the savage who was fireman. He was an improved specimen; he could fire up a vertical boiler. He was there below me, and, upon my word, to look at him was as edifying as seeing a dog in a parody of breeches and a feather hat, walking on his hind-legs. A few months of training had done for that really fine chap. He squinted at the steam-gauge and at the water-gauge with an evident effort of intrepidity—and he had filed teeth too, the poor devil, and the wool of his pate shaved into queer patterns, and three ornamental scars on each of his cheeks. He ought to have been clapping his hands and stamping his feet on the bank, instead of which he was hard at work, a thrall to strange witchcraft, full of improving knowledge. He was useful because he had been instructed; and what he knew was this—that should the water in that transparent thing disappear, the evil spirit inside the boiler would get angry through the greatness of his thirst, and take a terrible vengeance.[10] So he sweated and fired up and watched the glass fearfully (with an impromptu charm, made of rags, tied to his arm, and a piece of polished bone, as big as a watch, stuck flatways through his lower lip), while the wooded banks slipped past us slowly, the shore noise was left behind, the interminable miles of silence—and we crept on, towards Kurtz. But the snags were thick, the water was treacherous and shallow, the boiler seemed indeed to have a sulky devil in it, and thus neither that fireman nor I had any time to peer into our creepy thoughts.

"Some fifty miles below the Inner Station we came upon a hut of reeds, an inclined and melancholy pole, with the unrecognisable tatters of what had been a flag of some sort flying from it, and a neatly stacked wood-pile. This was unexpected. We came to the bank, and on the stack of firewood found a flat piece of board with some faded pencil-writing on it. When deciphered it said: 'Wood for you. Hurry up. Approach cautiously.' There was a signature, but it was illegible—not Kurtz—a much longer word. Hurry up. Where? Up the river?

'Approach cautiously.' We had not done so. But the warning could not have been meant for the place where it could be only found after approach. Something was wrong above. But what—and how much? That was the question. We commented adversely upon the imbecility of that telegraphic style. The bush around said nothing, and would not let us look very far, either. A torn curtain of red twill hung in the doorway of the hut, and flapped sadly in our faces. The dwelling was dismantled; but we could see a white man had lived there not very long ago. There remained a rude table—a plank on two posts; a heap of rubbish reposed in a dark corner, and by the door I picked up a book. It had lost its covers, and the pages had been thumbed into a state of extremely dirty softness; but the back had been lovingly stitched afresh with white cotton thread, which looked clean yet. It was an extraordinary find. Its title was, 'An Inquiry into some Points of Seamanship,' by a man Towzer, Towson[11]— some such name—Master in his Majesty's Navy. The matter looked dreary reading enough, with illustrative diagrams and repulsive tables of figures, and the copy was sixty years old. I handled this amazing antiquity with the greatest possible tenderness, lest it should dissolve in my hands. Within, Towson or Towzer was inquiring earnestly into the breaking strain of ships' chains and tackle, and other such matters. Not a very enthralling book; but at the first glance you could see there a singleness of intention, an honest concern for the right way of going to work, which made these humble pages, thought out so many years ago, luminous with another than a professional light. The simple old sailor, with his talk of chains and purchases, made me forget the jungle and the pilgrims in a delicious sensation of having come upon something unmistakably real. Such a book being there was wonderful enough; but still more astounding were the notes pencilled in the margin, and plainly referring to the text. I couldn't believe my eyes! They were in cipher! Yes, it looked like cipher. Fancy a man lugging with him a book of that description into this nowhere and studying it—and making notes—in cipher at that! It was an extravagant mystery.

"I had been dimly aware for some time of a worrying noise,

and when I lifted my eyes I saw the wood-pile was gone, and
the manager, aided by all the pilgrims, was shouting at me from
the river-side. I slipped the book into my pocket. I assure you
to leave off reading was like tearing myself away from the
shelter of an old and solid friendship.

"I started the lame engine ahead. 'It must be this miserable
trader—this intruder,' exclaimed the manager, looking back
malevolently at the place we had left. 'He must be English,' I
said. 'It will not save him from getting into trouble if he is not
careful,' muttered the manager darkly. I observed with assumed
innocence that no man was safe from trouble in this world.

"The current was more rapid now, the steamer seemed at her
last gasp, the stern-wheel flopped languidly, and I caught myself
listening on tiptoe for the next beat of the float, for in sober
truth I expected the wretched thing to give up every moment.
It was like watching the last flickers of a life. But still we
crawled. Sometimes I would pick out a tree a little way ahead
to measure our progress towards Kurtz by, but I lost it invariably before we got abreast. To keep the eyes so long on one
thing was too much for human patience. The manager displayed
a beautiful resignation. I fretted and fumed and took to arguing
with myself whether or no I would talk openly with Kurtz; but
before I could come to any conclusion it occurred to me that
my speech or my silence, indeed any action of mine, would be
a mere futility. What did it matter what any one knew or
ignored? What did it matter who was manager? One gets sometimes such a flash of insight. The essentials of this affair lay
deep under the surface, beyond my reach, and beyond my
power of meddling.

"Towards the evening of the second day we judged ourselves
about eight miles from Kurtz's station. I wanted to push on;
but the manager looked grave, and told me the navigation up
there was so dangerous that it would be advisable, the sun
being very low already, to wait where we were till next morning.
Moreover, he pointed out that if the warning to approach
cautiously were to be followed, we must approach in daylight—
not at dusk, or in the dark. This was sensible enough. Eight
miles meant nearly three hours' steaming for us, and I could

also see suspicious ripples at the upper end of the reach. Nevertheless, I was annoyed beyond expression at the delay, and most
unreasonably too, since one night more could not matter much
after so many months. As we had plenty of wood, and caution
was the word, I brought up in the middle of the stream. The
reach was narrow, straight, with high sides like a railway cutting. The dusk came gliding into it long before the sun had set.
The current ran smooth and swift, but a dumb immobility sat
on the banks. The living trees, lashed together by the creepers
and every living bush of the undergrowth, might have been
changed into stone, even to the slenderest twig, to the lightest
leaf. It was not sleep—it seemed unnatural, like a state of
trance. Not the faintest sound of any kind could be heard. You
looked on amazed, and began to suspect yourself of being
deaf—then the night came suddenly, and struck you blind as
well. About three in the morning some large fish leaped, and
the loud splash made me jump as though a gun had been fired.
When the sun rose there was a white fog, very warm and
clammy, and more blinding than the night. It did not shift or
drive; it was just there, standing all round you like something
solid. At eight or nine, perhaps, it lifted as a shutter lifts. We
had a glimpse of the towering multitude of trees, of the immense
matted jungle, with the blazing little ball of the sun hanging
over it—all perfectly still—and then the white shutter came
down again, smoothly, as if sliding in greased grooves. I ordered
the chain, which we had begun to heave in, to be paid out
again. Before it stopped running with a muffled rattle, a cry, a
very loud cry, as of infinite desolation, soared slowly in the
opaque air. It ceased. A complaining clamour, modulated in
savage discords, filled our ears. The sheer unexpectedness of it
made my hair stir under my cap. I don't know how it struck
the others: to me it seemed as though the mist itself had
screamed, so suddenly, and apparently from all sides at once,
did this tumultuous and mournful uproar arise. It culminated
in a hurried outbreak of almost intolerably excessive shrieking,
which stopped short, leaving us stiffened in a variety of silly
attitudes, and obstinately listening to the nearly as appalling
and excessive silence. 'Good God! What is the meaning——?'

stammered at my elbow one of the pilgrims—a little fat man, with sandy hair and red whiskers, who wore side-spring boots, and pink pyjamas tucked into his socks. Two others remained open-mouthed a whole minute, then dashed into the little cabin, to rush out incontinently and stand darting scared glances, with Winchesters[12] at 'ready' in their hands. What we could see was just the steamer we were on, her outlines blurred as though she had been on the point of dissolving, and a misty strip of water, perhaps two feet broad, around her—and that was all. The rest of the world was nowhere, as far as our eyes and ears were concerned. Just nowhere. Gone, disappeared; swept off without leaving a whisper or a shadow behind.

"I went forward, and ordered the chain to be hauled in short, so as to be ready to trip the anchor and move the steamboat at once if necessary. 'Will they attack?' whispered an awed voice. 'We will be all butchered in this fog,' murmured another. The faces twitched with the strain, the hands trembled slightly, the eyes forgot to wink. It was very curious to see the contrast of expressions of the white men and of the black fellows of our crew, who were as much strangers to that part of the river as we, though their homes were only eight hundred miles away. The whites, of course greatly discomposed, had besides a curious look of being painfully shocked by such an outrageous row. The others had an alert, naturally interested expression; but their faces were essentially quiet, even those of the one or two who grinned as they hauled at the chain. Several exchanged short, grunting phrases, which seemed to settle the matter to their satisfaction. Their headman, a young, broad-chested black, severely draped in dark-blue fringed cloths, with fierce nostrils and his hair all done up artfully in oily ringlets, stood near me. 'Aha!' I said nodding, just for good fellowship's sake. 'Catch 'im,' he snapped, with a bloodshot widening of his eyes and a flash of sharp teeth—'catch 'im. Give 'im to us.' 'To you, eh?' I asked; 'what would you do with them?' 'Eat 'im!' he said, curtly, and, leaning his elbow on the rail, looked out into the fog in a dignified and profoundly pensive attitude. I would no doubt have been properly horrified, had it not occurred to me that he and his chaps must be very hungry: that they must have been growing increasingly hungry for at least this month past. They had been engaged for six months (I don't think a single one of them had any clear idea of time, as we at the end of countless ages have. They still belonged to the beginnings of time—had no inherited experience to teach them as it were), and of course, as long as there was a piece of paper written over in accordance with some farcical law or other made down the river, it didn't enter anybody's head to trouble how they would live. Certainly they had brought with them some rotten hippo-meat, which couldn't have lasted very long, anyway, even if the pilgrims hadn't, in the midst of a shocking hullabaloo, thrown a considerable quantity of it overboard. It looked like a high-handed proceeding; but it was really a case of legitimate self-defence. You can't breathe dead hippo waking, sleeping, and eating, and at the same time keep your precarious grip on existence. Besides that, they had given them every week three pieces of brass wire, each about nine inches long; and the theory was they were to buy their provisions with that currency in river-side villages. You can see how *that* worked. There were either no villages, or the people were hostile, or the director, who like the rest of us fed out of tins, with an occasional old he-goat thrown in, didn't want to stop the steamer for some more or less recondite reason. So, unless they swallowed the wire itself, or made loops of it to snare the fish with, I don't see what good their extravagant salary could be to them. I must say it was paid with a regularity worthy of a large and honourable trading company. For the rest, the only thing to eat—though it didn't look eatable in the least—I saw in their possession was a few lumps of some stuff like half-cooked cold dough,[13] of a dirty lavender colour, they kept wrapped in leaves, and now and then swallowed a piece of, but so small that it seemed done more for the looks of the thing than for any serious purpose of sustenance. Why in the name of all the gnawing devils of hunger they didn't go for us—they were thirty to five—and have a good tuck in for once, amazes me now when I think of it. They were big powerful men, with not much capacity to weigh the consequences, with courage, with strength, even yet, though their skins were no longer glossy and their muscles no longer hard. And I saw that something restraining, one of those human secrets that baffle probability, had come into play there. I looked at them with a swift quickening of interest—not because it occurred to me I might be eaten by them before very long, though I own to you that just then I perceived—in a new light, as it were—how unwholesome the pilgrims looked, and I hoped, yes, I positively hoped, that my aspect was not so—what shall I say?—so—unappetising: a touch of fantastic vanity which fitted well with the dream-sensation that pervaded all my days at that time. Perhaps I had a little fever too. One can't live with one's finger everlastingly on one's pulse. I had often a 'little fever,' or a little touch of other things—the playful paw-strokes of the wilderness, the preliminary trifling before the more serious onslaught which came in due course. Yes; I looked at them as you would on any human being, with a curiosity of their impulses, motives, capacities, weaknesses, when brought to the test of an inexorable physical necessity. Restraint! What possible restraint? Was it superstition, disgust, patience, fear— or some kind of primitive honour? No fear can stand up to hunger, no patience can wear it out, disgust simply does not exist where hunger is; and as to superstition, beliefs, and what you may call principles, they are less than chaff in a breeze. Don't you know the devilry of lingering starvation, its exasper-ating torment, its black thoughts, its sombre and brooding ferocity? Well, I do. It takes a man all his inborn strength to fight hunger properly. It's really easier to face bereavement, dishonour, and the perdition of one's soul—than this kind of prolonged hunger. Sad, but true. And these chaps too had no earthly reason for any kind of scruple. Restraint! I would just as soon have expected restraint from a hyena prowling amongst the corpses of a battlefield. But there was the fact facing me—the fact dazzling, to be seen, like the foam on the depths of the sea, like a ripple on an unfathomable enigma, a mystery greater— when I thought of it—than the curious, inexplicable note of desperate grief in this savage clamour that had swept by us on the river-bank, behind the blind whiteness of a fog.

"Two pilgrims were quarrelling in hurried whispers as to which bank. 'Left.' 'No, no; how can you? Right, right, of course.' 'It is serious, very serious,' said the manager's voice behind me; 'I would be desolated if anything should happen to Mr Kurtz before we came up.' I looked at him, and had not the slightest doubt he was sincere. He was just the kind of man who would wish to preserve appearances. That was his restraint. But when he muttered something about going on at once, I did not even take the trouble to answer him. I knew, and he knew, that it was impossible. Were we to let go our hold of the bottom, we would be absolutely in the air—in space. We wouldn't be able to tell where we were going to—whether up or down stream, or across—till we fetched against one bank or the other—and then we wouldn't know at first which it was. Of course I made no move. I had no mind for a smash-up. You couldn't imagine a more deadly place for a shipwreck. Whether drowned at once or not, we were sure to perish speedily in one way or another. 'I authorise you to take all the risks,' he said, after a short silence. 'I refuse to take any,' I said shortly; which was just the answer he expected, though its tone might have surprised him. 'Well, I must defer to your judgment. You are captain,' he said, with marked civility. I turned my shoulder to him in sign of my appreciation, and looked into the fog. How long would it last? It was the most hopeless look-out. The approach to this Kurtz grubbing for ivory in the wretched bush was beset by as many dangers as though he had been an enchanted princess sleeping in a fabulous castle. 'Will they attack, do you think?' asked the manager, in a confidential tone.

"I did not think they would attack, for several obvious reasons. The thick fog was one. If they left the bank in their canoes they would get lost in it, as we would be if we attempted to move. Still, I had also judged the jungle of both banks quite impenetrable—and yet eyes were in it, eyes that had seen us. The river-side bushes were certainly very thick; but the under-growth behind was evidently penetrable. However, during the short lift I had seen no canoes anywhere in the reach—certainly not abreast of the steamer. But what made the idea of attack inconceivable to me was the nature of the noise—of the cries we had heard. They had not the fierce character boding of immediate hostile intention. Unexpected, wild, and violent as they had been, they had given me an irresistible impression of sorrow. The glimpse of the steamboat had for some reason filled those savages with unrestrained grief. The danger, if any, I expounded, was from our proximity to a great human passion let loose. Even extreme grief may ultimately vent itself in violence—but more generally takes the form of apathy. . . .

"You should have seen the pilgrims stare! They had no heart to grin, or even to revile me; but I believe they thought me gone mad—with fright, maybe. I delivered a regular lecture. My dear boys, it was no good bothering. Keep a look-out? Well, you may guess I watched the fog for the signs of lifting as a cat watches a mouse; but for anything else our eyes were of no more use to us than if we had been buried miles deep in a heap of cotton-wool. It felt like it too—choking, warm, stifling. Besides, all I said, though it sounded extravagant, was absolutely true to fact. What we afterwards alluded to as an attack was really an attempt at repulse. The action was very far from being aggressive—it was not even defensive, in the usual sense: it was undertaken under the stress of desperation, and in its essence was purely protective.

"It developed itself, I should say, two hours after the fog lifted, and its commencement was at a spot, roughly speaking, about a mile and a half below Kurtz's station. We had just floundered and flopped round a bend, when I saw an islet, a mere grassy hummock of bright green, in the middle of the stream. It was the only thing of the kind; but as we opened the reach more, I perceived it was the head of a long sandbank, or rather of a chain of shallow patches stretching down the middle of the river. They were discoloured, just awash, and the whole lot was seen just under the water, exactly as a man's backbone is seen running down the middle of his back under the skin. Now, as far as I did see, I could go to the right or to the left of this. I didn't know either channel, of course. The banks looked pretty well alike, the depth appeared the same; but as I had been informed the station was on the west side, I naturally headed for the western passage.

"No sooner had we fairly entered it than I became aware it was much narrower than I had supposed. To the left of us there was the long uninterrupted shoal, and to the right a high, steep bank heavily overgrown with bushes. Above the bush the trees stood in serried ranks. The twigs overhung the current thickly, and from distance to distance a large limb of some tree projected rigidly over the stream. It was then well on in the afternoon, the face of the forest was gloomy, and a broad strip of shadow had already fallen on the water. In this shadow we steamed up—very slowly, as you may imagine. I sheered her well in-shore—the water being deepest near the bank, as the sounding-pole informed me.

"One of my hungry and forbearing friends was sounding in the bows just below me. This steamboat was exactly like a decked scow. On the deck there were two little teak-wood houses, with doors and windows. The boiler was in the fore-end, and the machinery right astern. Over the whole there was a light roof, supported on stanchions. The funnel projected through that roof, and just in front of the funnel a small cabin built of light planks served for a pilot-house. It contained a couch, two camp-stools, a loaded Martini-Henry[14] leaning in one corner, a tiny table, and the steering-wheel. It had a wide door in front and a broad shutter at each side. All these were always thrown open, of course. I spent my days perched up there on the extreme fore-end of that roof, before the door. At night I slept, or tried to, on the couch. An athletic black belonging to some coast tribe, and educated by my poor predecessor, was the helmsman. He sported a pair of brass earrings, wore a blue cloth wrapper from the waist to the ankles, and thought all the world of himself. He was the most unstable kind of fool I had ever seen. He steered with no end of a swagger while you were by; but if he lost sight of you, he became instantly the prey of an abject funk, and would let that cripple of a steamboat get the upper hand of him in a minute.

"I was looking down at the sounding-pole, and feeling much annoyed to see at each try a little more of it stick out of that river, when I saw my poleman give up the business suddenly, and stretch himself flat on the deck, without even taking the trouble to haul his pole in. He kept hold on it though, and it trailed in the water. At the same time the fireman, whom I could

also see below me, sat down abruptly before his furnace and
ducked his head. I was amazed. Then I had to look at the river
mighty quick, because there was a snag in the fairway. Sticks,
little sticks, were flying about—thick: they were whizzing
before my nose, dropping below me, striking behind me against
my pilot-house. All this time the river, the shore, the woods,
were very quiet—perfectly quiet. I could only hear the heavy
splashy thump of the stern-wheel and the patter of these things.
We cleared the snag clumsily. Arrows, by Jove! We were being
shot at! I stepped in quickly to close the shutter on the land-side.
That fool-helmsman, his hands on the spokes, was lifting his
knees high, stamping his feet, champing his mouth, like a
reined-in horse. Confound him! And we were staggering within
ten feet of the bank. I had to lean right out to swing the heavy
shutter, and I saw a face amongst the leaves on the level with my
own, looking at me very fierce and steady; and then suddenly, as
though a veil had been removed from my eyes, I made out,
deep in the tangled gloom, naked breasts, arms, legs, glaring
eyes—the bush was swarming with human limbs in movement,
glistening, of bronze colour. The twigs shook, swayed, and
rustled, the arrows flew out of them, and then the shutter came
to. 'Steer her straight,' I said to the helmsman. He held his head
rigid, face forward; but his eyes rolled, he kept on lifting and
setting down his feet gently, his mouth foamed a little. 'Keep
quiet!' I said in a fury. I might just as well have ordered a tree
not to sway in the wind. I darted out. Below me there was a
great scuffle of feet on the iron deck; confused exclamations;
a voice screamed, 'Can you turn back?' I caught sight of a
V-shaped ripple on the water ahead. What? Another snag! A
fusillade burst out under my feet. The pilgrims had opened fire
with their Winchesters, and were simply squirting lead into that
bush. A deuce of a lot of smoke came up and drove slowly
forward. I swore at it. Now I couldn't see the ripple or the snag
either. I stood in the doorway, peering, and the arrows came in
swarms. They might have been poisoned, but they looked as
though they wouldn't kill a cat. The bush began to howl. Our
wood-cutters raised a warlike whoop; the report of a rifle just
at my back deafened me. I glanced over my shoulder, and the

pilot-house was yet full of noise and smoke when I made a dash at the wheel. The fool-nigger had dropped everything, to throw the shutter open and let off that Martini-Henry. He stood before the wide opening, glaring, and I yelled at him to come back, while I straightened the sudden twist out of that steamboat. There was no room to turn even if I had wanted to, the snag was somewhere very near ahead in that confounded smoke, there was no time to lose, so I just crowded her into the bank—right into the bank, where I knew the water was deep.

"We tore slowly along the overhanging bushes in a whirl of broken twigs and flying leaves. The fusillade below stopped short, as I had foreseen it would when the squirts[15] got empty. I threw my head back to a glinting whizz[16] that traversed the pilot-house, in at one shutter-hole and out at the other. Looking past that mad helmsman, who was shaking the empty rifle and yelling at the shore, I saw vague forms of men running bent double, leaping, gliding, distinct, incomplete, evanescent. Something big appeared in the air before the shutter, the rifle went overboard, and the man stepped back swiftly, looked at me over his shoulder in an extraordinary, profound, familiar manner, and fell upon my feet. The side of his head hit the wheel twice, and the end of what appeared a long cane clattered round and knocked over a little camp-stool. It looked as though after wrenching that thing from somebody ashore he had lost his balance in the effort. The thin smoke had blown away, we were clear of the snag, and looking ahead I could see that in another hundred yards or so I would be free to sheer off, away from the bank; but my feet felt so very warm and wet that I had to look down. The man had rolled on his back and stared straight up at me; both his hands clutched that cane. It was the shaft of a spear that, either thrown or lounged[17] through the opening, had caught him in the side just below the ribs; the blade had gone in out of sight, after making a frightful gash; my shoes were full; a pool of blood lay very still, gleaming dark-red under the wheel; his eyes shone with an amazing lustre. The fusillade burst out again. He looked at me anxiously, gripping the spear like something precious, with an air of being afraid I would try to take it away from him. I had to make an effort to free my eyes from his gaze and attend to the steering. With one hand I felt above my head for the line of the steam-whistle,[18] and jerked out screech after screech hurriedly. The tumult of angry and warlike yells was checked instantly, and then from the depths of the woods went out such a tremulous and prolonged wail of mournful fear and utter despair as may be imagined to follow the flight of the last hope from the earth. There was a great commotion in the bush; the shower of arrows stopped, a few dropping shots rang out sharply—then silence, in which the languid beat of the stern-wheel came plainly to my ears. I put the helm hard a-starboard at the moment when the pilgrim in pink pyjamas, very hot and agitated, appeared in the doorway. 'The manager sends me——' he began in an official tone, and stopped short. 'Good God!' he said, glaring at the wounded man.

"We two whites stood over him, and his lustrous and inquiring glance enveloped us both. I declare it looked as though he would presently put to us some question in an understandable language; but he died without uttering a sound, without moving a limb, without twitching a muscle. Only in the very last moment, as though in response to some sign we could not see, to some whisper we could not hear, he frowned heavily, and that frown gave to his black death-mask an inconceivably sombre, brooding, and menacing expression. The lustre of inquiring glance faded swiftly into vacant glassiness. 'Can you steer?' I asked the agent eagerly. He looked very dubious; but I made a grab at his arm, and he understood at once I meant him to steer whether or no. To tell you the truth, I was morbidly anxious to change my shoes and socks. 'He is dead,' murmured the fellow, immensely impressed. 'No doubt about it,' said I, tugging like mad at the shoe-laces. 'And, by the way, I suppose Mr Kurtz is dead as well by this time.'

"For the moment that was the dominant thought. There was a sense of extreme disappointment, as though I had found out I had been striving after something altogether without a substance. I couldn't have been more disgusted if I had travelled all this way for the sole purpose of talking with Mr Kurtz. Talking with . . . I flung one shoe overboard, and became aware that that was exactly what I had been looking forward to—a talk with Kurtz. I made the strange discovery that I had never imagined him as doing, you know, but as discoursing. I didn't say to myself, 'Now I will never see him,' or 'Now I will never shake him by the hand,' but, 'Now I will never hear him.' The man presented himself as a voice. Not of course that I did not connect him with some sort of action. Hadn't I been told in all the tones of jealousy and admiration that he had collected, bartered, swindled, or stolen more ivory than all the other agents together. That was not the point. The point was in his being a gifted creature, and that of all his gifts the one that stood out pre-eminently, that carried with it a sense of real presence, was his ability to talk, his words—the gift of expression, the bewildering, the illuminating, the most exalted and the most contemptible, the pulsating stream of light, or the deceitful flow from the heart of an impenetrable darkness.

"The other shoe went flying unto the devil-god of that river. I thought, By Jove! it's all over. We are too late; he has vanished—the gift has vanished, by means of some spear, arrow, or club. I will never hear that chap speak after all—and my sorrow had a startling extravagance of emotion, even such as I had noticed in the howling sorrow of these savages in the bush. I couldn't have felt more of lonely desolation somehow, had I been robbed of a belief or had missed my destiny in life. . . . Why do you sigh in this beastly way, somebody? Absurd? Well, absurd. Good Lord! mustn't a man ever——Here, give me some tobacco." . . .

There was a pause of profound stillness, then a match flared, and Marlow's lean face appeared—worn, hollow, with downward folds and dropped eyelids, with an aspect of concentrated attention; and as he took vigorous draws at his pipe, it seemed to retreat and advance out of the night in the regular flicker of the tiny flame. The match went out.

"Absurd!" he cried. "This is the worst of trying to tell . . . Here you all are, each moored with two good addresses, like a hulk with two anchors, a butcher round one corner, a policeman round another, excellent appetites, and temperature normal—you hear—normal from year's end to year's end.

And you say, Absurd! Absurd be—exploded! Absurd! My dear
boys, what can you expect from a man who out of sheer ner-
vousness had just flung overboard a pair of new shoes. Now I
think of it, it is amazing I did not shed tears. I am, upon the
whole, proud of my fortitude. I was cut to the quick at the idea
of having lost the inestimable privilege of listening to the gifted
Kurtz. Of course I was wrong. The privilege was waiting for
me. Oh yes, I heard more than enough. And I was right, too. A
voice. He was very little more than a voice. And I heard—him—
it—this voice—other voices—all of them were so little more
than voices—and the memory of that time itself lingers around
me, impalpable, like a dying vibration of one immense jabber,
silly, atrocious, sordid, savage, or simply mean, without any
kind of sense. Voices, voices—even the girl herself—now——"
    He was silent for a long time.
    "I laid the ghost of his gifts at last with a lie," he began
suddenly. "Girl! What? Did I mention a girl? Oh, she is out of
it—completely. They—the women I mean—are out of it—
should be out of it. We must help them to stay in that beautiful
world of their own, lest ours gets worse. Oh, she had to be out
of it. You should have heard the disinterred body of Mr Kurtz
saying, 'My Intended.' You would have perceived directly then
how completely she was out of it. And the lofty frontal bone of
Mr Kurtz! They say the hair goes on growing[19] sometimes,
but this—ah—specimen, was impressively bald. The wilderness
had patted him on the head, and, behold, it was like a ball—an
ivory ball; it had caressed him, and—lo!—he had withered; it
had taken him, loved him, embraced him, got into his veins,
consumed his flesh, and sealed his soul to its own by the inconceivable ceremonies of some devilish initiation. He was its
spoiled and pampered favourite. Ivory? I should think so. Heaps
of it, stacks of it. The old mud shanty was bursting with it. You
would think there was not a single tusk left either above or
below ground in the whole country. 'Mostly fossil,' the manager
had remarked disparagingly. It was no more fossil than I am;
but they call it fossil when it is dug up. It appears these niggers
do bury the tusks sometimes—but evidently they couldn't bury
this parcel deep enough to save the gifted Mr Kurtz from his

fate. We filled the steamboat with it, and had to pile a lot on the deck. Thus he could see and enjoy as long as he could see, because the appreciation of this favour had remained with him to the last. You should have heard him say, 'My ivory.' Oh yes, I heard him. 'My Intended, my ivory, my station, my river, my——' Everything belonged to him. It made me hold my breath in expectation of hearing the wilderness burst into a prodigious peal of laughter that would shake the fixed stars in their places. Everything belonged to him—but that was a trifle. The thing was to know what he belonged to, how many powers of darkness claimed him for their own. That was the reflection that made you creepy all over. It was impossible—it was not good for one either—trying to imagine. He had taken a high seat amongst the devils of the land—I mean literally. You can't understand. How could you?—with solid pavement under your feet, surrounded by kind neighbours ready to cheer you or to fall on you, stepping delicately between the butcher and the policeman, in the holy terror of scandal and gallows and lunatic asylums—how can you imagine what particular region of the first ages a man's untrammelled feet may take him into by the way of solitude—utter solitude without a policeman—by the way of silence—utter silence, where no warning voice of a kind neighbour can be heard whispering of public opinion? These little things make all the great difference. When they are gone you must fall back upon your own innate strength, upon your own capacity for faithfulness. Of course you may be too much of a fool to go wrong—too dull even to know you are being assaulted by the powers of darkness. I take it, no fool ever made a bargain for his soul with the devil: the fool is too much of a fool, or the devil too much of a devil—I don't know which. Or you may be such a thunderingly exalted creature as to be altogether deaf and blind to anything but heavenly sights and sounds. Then the earth for you is only a standing place— and whether to be like this is your loss or your gain I won't pretend to say. But most of us are neither one nor the other. The earth for us is a place to live in, where we must put up with sights, with sounds, with smells too, by Jove!—breathe dead hippo, so to speak, and not be contaminated. And there, don't you see? your strength comes in, the faith in your ability for the digging of unostentatious holes to bury the stuff in— your power of devotion, not to yourself, but to an obscure, back-breaking business. And that's difficult enough. Mind, I am not trying to excuse or even explain—I am trying to account to myself for—for—Mr Kurtz—for the shade of Mr Kurtz. This initiated wraith from the back of Nowhere honoured me with its amazing confidence before it vanished altogether. This was because it could speak English to me. The original Kurtz had been educated partly in England, and—as he was good enough to say himself—his sympathies were in the right place. His mother was half-English, his father was half-French.[20] All Europe contributed to the making of Kurtz; and by and bye I learned that, most appropriately, the International Society for the Suppression of Savage Customs[21] had entrusted him with the making of a report, for its future guidance. And he had written it too. I've seen it. I've read it. It was eloquent, vibrating with eloquence, but too high-strung, I think. Seventeen pages of close writing he had found time for! But this must have been before his—let us say—nerves, went wrong, and caused him to preside at certain midnight dances ending with unspeakable rites, which—as far as I reluctantly gathered from what I heard at various times—were offered up to him—do you under- stand?—to Mr Kurtz himself. But it was a beautiful piece of writing. The opening paragraph, however, in the light of later information, strikes me now as ominous. He began with the argument that we whites, from the point of development we had arrived at, 'must necessarily appear to them [savages] in the nature of supernatural beings—we approach them with the might as of a deity,' and so on, and so on. 'By the simple exercise of our will we can exert a power for good practically unbounded,' etc., etc. From that point he soared and took me with him. The peroration was magnificent, though difficult to remember, you know. It gave me the notion of an exotic Immensity ruled by an august Benevolence. It made me tingle with enthusiasm. This was the unbounded power of elo- quence—of words—of burning noble words. There were no practical hints to interrupt the magic current of phrases, unless a kind of note at the foot of the last page, scrawled evidently much later, in an unsteady hand, may be regarded as the exposition of a method. It was very simple, and at the end of that moving appeal to every altruistic sentiment it blazed at you, luminous and terrifying, like a flash of lightning in a serene sky: 'Exterminate all the brutes!'[22] The curious part was that he had apparently forgotten all about that valuable postscriptum, because, later on, when he in a sense came to himself, he repeatedly entreated me to take good care of 'my pamphlet' (he called it), as it was sure to have in the future a good influence upon his career. I had full information about all these things, and, besides, as it turned out, I was to have the care of his memory. I've done enough for it to give me the indisputable right to lay it, if I choose, for an everlasting rest in the dust-bin of progress, amongst all the sweepings and, figuratively speaking, all the dead cats of civilisation. But then, you see, I can't choose. He won't be forgotten. Whatever he was, he was not common. He had the power to charm or frighten rudimentary souls into an aggravated witch-dance in his honour; he could also fill the small souls of the pilgrims with bitter misgivings: he had one devoted friend at least, and he had conquered one soul in the world that was neither rudimentary nor tainted with self-seeking. No; I can't forget him, though I am not prepared to affirm the fellow was exactly worth the life we lost in getting to him. I missed my late helmsman awfully—I missed him even while his body was still lying in the pilot-house. Perhaps you will think it passing strange this regret for a savage who was no more account than a grain of sand in a black Sahara. Well, don't you see, he had done something, he had steered; for months I had him at my back—a help—an instrument. It was a kind of partnership. He steered for me—I had to look after him, I worried about his deficiencies, and thus a subtle bond had been created, of which I only became aware when it was suddenly broken. And the intimate profundity of that look he gave me when he received his hurt remains to this day in my memory—like a claim of distant kinship affirmed in a supreme moment.

"Poor fool! If he had only left that shutter alone. He had no restraint, no restraint—just like Kurtz—a tree swayed by the wind. As soon as I had put on a dry pair of slippers, I dragged him out, after first jerking the spear out of his side, which operation I confess I performed with my eyes shut tight. His heels leaped together over the little door-step; his shoulders were pressed to my breast; I hugged him from behind desperately. Oh! he was heavy, heavy; heavier than any man on earth, I should imagine. Then without more ado I tipped him overboard. The current snatched him as though he had been a wisp of grass, and I saw the body roll over twice before I lost sight of it for ever. All the pilgrims and the manager were then congregated on the awning-deck about the pilot-house, chattering at each other like a flock of excited magpies, and there was a scandalised murmur at my heartless promptitude. What they wanted to keep that body hanging about for I can't guess. Embalm it, maybe. But I had also heard another, and very ominous, murmur on the deck below. My friends the wood-cutters were likewise scandalised, and with a better show of reason—though I admit that the reason itself was quite inadmissible. Oh, quite! I had made up my mind that if my late helmsman was to be eaten, the fishes alone should have him. He had been a very second-rate helmsman while alive, but now he was dead he might have become a first-class temptation, and possibly cause some startling trouble. Besides, I was anxious to take the wheel, the man in pink pyjamas showing himself a hopeless duffer at the business.

"This I did directly the simple funeral was over. We were going half-speed, keeping right in the middle of the stream, and I listened to the talk about me. They had given up Kurtz, they had given up the station; Kurtz was dead, and the station had been burnt—and so on—and so on. The red-haired pilgrim was beside himself with the thought that at least this poor Kurtz had been properly revenged. 'Say! We must have made a glorious slaughter of them in the bush. Eh? What do you think? Say?' He positively danced, the bloodthirsty little gingery beggar. And he had nearly fainted when he saw the wounded man! I could not help saying, 'You made a glorious lot of smoke, anyhow.' I had seen, from the way the tops of the bushes rustled and flew, that almost all the shots had gone too high. You can't hit anything unless you take aim and fire from the shoulder; but these chaps fired from the hip with their eyes shut. The retreat, I maintained—and I was right—was caused by the screeching of the steam-whistle. Upon this they forgot Kurtz, and began to howl at me with indignant protests.

"The manager stood by the wheel murmuring confidentially about the necessity of getting well away down the river before dark at all events, when I saw in the distance a clearing on the river-side and the outlines of some sort of building. 'What's this?' I asked. He clapped his hands in wonder. 'The station!'[23] he cried. I edged in at once, still going half-speed.

"Through my glasses I saw the slope of a hill interspersed with rare trees and perfectly free from undergrowth. A long decaying building on the summit was half buried in the high grass; the large holes in the peaked roof gaped black from afar; the jungle and the woods made a background. There was no enclosure or fence of any kind; but there had been one apparently, for near the house half-a-dozen slim posts remained in a row, roughly trimmed, and with their upper ends ornamented with round carved balls. The rails, or whatever there had been between, had disappeared. Of course the forest surrounded all that. The river-bank was clear, and on the water-side I saw a white man under a hat like a cart-wheel beckoning persistently with his whole arm. Examining the edge of the forest above and below, I was almost certain I could see movements—human forms gliding here and there. I steamed past prudently, then stopped the engines and let her drift down. The man on the shore began to shout, urging us to land. 'We have been attacked,' screamed the manager. 'I know—I know. It's all right,' yelled back the other, as cheerful as you please. 'Come along. It's all right. I am glad.'

"His aspect reminded me of something I had seen— something funny I had seen somewhere. As I manoeuvred to get alongside, I was asking myself, 'What does this fellow look like?' Suddenly I got it. He looked like a harlequin.[24] His clothes had been made of some stuff that was brown holland[25] probably, but it was covered with patches all over, with bright patches, blue, red, and yellow—patches on the back, patches on front, patches on elbows, on knees; coloured binding round his jacket, scarlet edging at the bottom of his trousers; and the sunshine made him look extremely gay and wonderfully neat withal, because you could see how beautifully all this patching had been done. A beardless, boyish face, very fair, no features to speak of, nose peeling, little blue eyes, smiles and frowns chasing each other over that open countenance like sunshine and shadow on a wind-swept plain. 'Look out, captain!' he cried; 'there's a snag lodged in here last night.' What! Another snag? I confess I swore shamefully. I had nearly holed my cripple, to finish off that charming trip. The harlequin on the bank turned his little pug nose up to me. 'You English?' he asked, all smiles. 'Are you?' I shouted from the wheel. The smiles vanished, and he shook his head as if sorry for my disappointment. Then he brightened up. 'Never mind!' he cried encouragingly. 'Are we in time?' I asked. 'He is up there,' he replied, with a toss of the head up the hill, and becoming gloomy all of a sudden. His face was like the autumn sky, overcast one moment and bright the next.

"When the manager, escorted by the pilgrims, all of them armed to the teeth, had gone to the house, this chap came on board. 'I say, I don't like this. These natives are in the bush,' I said. He assured me earnestly it was all right. 'They are simple people,' he added; 'well, I am glad you came. It took me all my time to keep them off.' 'But you said it was all right,' I cried. 'Oh, they meant no harm,' he said; and as I stared he corrected himself, 'Not exactly.' Then vivaciously, 'My faith, your pilot-house wants a clean up!' In the next breath he advised me to keep enough steam on the boiler to blow the whistle in case of any trouble. 'One good screech will do more for you than all your rifles. They are simple people,' he repeated. He rattled away at such a rate he quite overwhelmed me. He seemed to be trying to make up for lots of silence, and actually hinted, laughing, that such was the case. 'Don't you talk with Mr Kurtz?' I said. 'You don't talk with that man—you listen to him,' he exclaimed with severe exaltation. 'But now——' He waved his arm, and in the twinkling of an eye was in the uttermost depths of despondency. In a moment he came up again with a jump, possessed himself of both my hands, shook them continuously, while he gabbled: 'Brother sailor . . . honour . . . pleasure . . . delight . . . introduce myself . . . Russian . . . son of an arch-priest . . . Government of Tambov²⁶ . . . What? Tobacco! English tobacco; the excellent English tobacco! Now, that's brotherly. Smoke? Where's a sailor that does not smoke?'

"The pipe soothed him, and gradually I made out he had run away from school, had gone to sea in a Russian ship; ran away again; served some time in English ships; was now reconciled with the arch-priest. He made a point of that. 'But when one is young one must see things, gather experience, ideas; enlarge the mind.' 'Here!' I interrupted. 'You can never tell! Here I have met Mr Kurtz,' he said, youthfully solemn and reproachful. I held my tongue after that. It appears he had persuaded a Dutch trading-house²⁷ on the coast to fit him out with stores and goods, and had started for the interior with a light heart, and no more idea of what would happen to him than a baby. He had been wandering about that river for nearly two years alone, cut off from everybody and everything. 'I am not so young as I look. I am twenty-five,' he said. 'At first old Van Shuyten²⁸ would tell me to go to the devil,' he narrated with keen enjoyment; 'but I stuck to him, and talked and talked, till at last he got afraid I would talk the hind-leg off his favourite dog, so he gave me some cheap things and a few guns, and told me he hoped he would never see my face again. Good old Dutchman, Van Shuyten. I've sent him one small lot of ivory a year ago, so that he can't call me a little thief when I get back. I hope he got it. And for the rest I don't care. I had some wood stacked for you. That was my old house. Did you see?'

"I gave him Towson's book. He made as though he would kiss me, but restrained himself. 'The only book I had left, and I thought I had lost it,' he said, looking at it ecstatically. 'So many accidents happen to a man going about alone, you know. Canoes get upset sometimes—and sometimes you've got to clear out so quick when the people get angry.' He thumbed the pages. 'You made notes in Russian?' I asked. He nodded. 'I thought they were written in cipher,' I said. He laughed, then became serious. 'I had lots of trouble to keep these people off,' he said. 'Did they want to kill you?' I asked. 'Oh no!' he cried, and checked himself. 'Why did they attack us?' I pursued. He hesitated, then said shamefacedly, 'They don't want him to go.' 'Don't they?' I said, curiously. He nodded a nod full of mystery and wisdom. 'I tell you,' he cried, 'this man has enlarged my mind.' He opened his arms wide, staring at me with his little blue eyes that were perfectly round."

III

"I looked at him, lost in astonishment. There he was before me, in motley, as though he had absconded from a troupe of mimes, enthusiastic, fabulous. His very existence was improbable, inexplicable, and altogether bewildering. He was an insoluble problem. It was inconceivable how he had existed, how he had succeeded in getting so far, how he had managed to remain—why he did not instantly disappear. 'I went a little further,' he said, 'then still a little further—till I had gone so far that I don't know how I'll ever get back. Never mind. Plenty time. I can manage. You take Kurtz away quick—quick—I tell you.' The glamour of youth enveloped his particoloured rags, his destitution, his loneliness, the essential desolation of his futile wanderings. For months—for years—his life hadn't been worth a day's purchase; and there he was gallantly, thoughtlessly alive, to all appearance indestructible solely by the virtue of his few years and of his unreflecting audacity. I was seduced into something like admiration—like envy. Glamour urged him on, glamour kept him unscathed. He surely wanted nothing from the wilderness but space to breathe in and to push on through. His need was to exist, and to move onwards at the greatest possible risk, and with a maximum of privation. If the absolutely pure, uncalculating, impractical spirit of adventure had ever ruled a human being, it ruled this be-patched youth. I almost envied him the possession of this modest and clear flame. It seemed to have consumed all thought of self so completely, that, even while he was talking to you, you forgot that it was he—the man before your eyes—who had gone through these things. I did not envy him his devotion to Kurtz, though. He had not meditated over it. It came to him, and he accepted it with a sort of eager fatalism. I must say that to me it appeared about the most dangerous thing in every way he had come upon so far. "They had come together unavoidably, like two ships becalmed near each other, and lay rubbing sides at last. I suppose Kurtz wanted an audience, because on a certain occasion, when encamped in the forest, they had talked all night, or more probably Kurtz had talked. 'We talked of everything,' he said, quite transported at the recollection. 'I forgot there was such a thing as sleep. The night did not seem to last an hour. Everything! Everything! . . . Of love too.' 'Ah, he talked to you of love!' I said, much amused. 'It isn't what you think,' he cried, almost passionately. 'It was in general. He made me see things— things.'

"He threw his arms up. We were on deck at the time, and the headman of my wood-cutters, lounging near by, turned upon him his heavy and glittering eyes. I looked around, and I don't know why, but I assure you that never, never before, did this land, this river, this jungle, the very arch of this blazing sky, appear to me so hopeless and so dark, so impenetrable to human thought, so pitiless to human weakness. 'And, ever since, you have been with him, of course?' I said.

"On the contrary. It appears their intercourse had been very much broken by various causes. He had, as he informed me proudly, managed to nurse Kurtz through two illnesses (he alluded to it as you would to some risky feat), but as a rule Kurtz wandered alone, far in the depths of the forest. 'Very often coming to this station, I had to wait days and days before he would turn up,' he said. 'Ah, it was worth waiting for!— sometimes.' 'What was he doing? exploring or what?' I asked. 'Oh yes, of course'; he had discovered lots of villages, a lake too—he did not know exactly in what direction; it was dangerous to inquire too much—but mostly his expeditions had been for ivory. 'But he had no goods to trade with by that time,' I objected. 'There's a good lot of cartridges left even yet,' he answered, looking away. 'To speak plainly, he raided the country,' I said. He nodded. 'Not alone, surely!' He muttered something about the villages round that lake. 'Kurtz got the

tribe to follow him, did he?' I suggested. He fidgeted a little.
'They adored him,' he said. The tone of these words was so
extraordinary that I looked at him searchingly. It was curious
to see his mingled eagerness and reluctance to speak of Kurtz.
The man filled his life, occupied his thoughts, swayed his emotions. 'What can you expect?' he burst out; 'he came to them
with thunder and lightning, you know—and they had never
seen anything like it—and very terrible. He could be very terrible. You can't judge Mr Kurtz as you would an ordinary man.
No, no, no! Now—just to give you an idea—I don't mind
telling you, he wanted to shoot me too one day—but I don't
judge him.' 'Shoot you!' I cried. 'What for?' 'Well, I had a small
lot of ivory the chief of that village near my house gave me.
You see I used to shoot game for them. Well, he wanted it, and
wouldn't hear reason. He declared he would shoot me unless I
gave him the ivory and then cleared out of the country, because
he could do so, and had a fancy for it, and there was nothing
on earth to prevent him killing whom he jolly well pleased. And
it was true too. I gave him the ivory. What did I care! But
I didn't clear out. No, no. I couldn't leave him. I had to be
careful, of course, till we got friendly again for a time. He had
his second illness then. Afterwards I had to keep out of the way;
but I didn't mind. He was living for the most part in those
villages on the lake. When he came down to the river, sometimes
he would talk to me, and sometimes it was better for me to be
careful. This man suffered too much. He hated all this, and
somehow he couldn't get away. When I had a chance I begged
him to try and leave while there was time; I offered to go back
with him. And he would say yes, and then he would remain; go
off on another ivory hunt; disappear for weeks; forget himself
amongst these people—forget himself—you know.' 'Why! he's
mad,' I said. He protested indignantly. Mr Kurtz couldn't be
mad. If I had heard him talk, only two days ago, I wouldn't
dare hint at such a thing. . . . I had taken up my binoculars
while we talked, and was looking at the shore, sweeping the
limit of the forest at each side and at the back of the house. The
consciousness of there being people in that bush, so silent, so
quiet—as silent and quiet as the ruined house on the hill—made

me uneasy. There was no sign on the face of nature of this amazing tale that was not so much told as suggested to me in desolate exclamations, completed by shrugs, in interrupted phrases, in hints ending in deep sighs. The woods were unmoved, like a mask—heavy, like the closed door of a prison—they looked with their air of hidden knowledge, of patient expectation, of unapproachable silence. The Russian was explaining to me that it was only lately that Mr Kurtz had come down to the river, bringing along with him all the fighting men of that lake tribe. He had been absent for several months—getting himself adored, I suppose—and had come down unexpectedly, with the intention to all appearance of making a raid either across the river or down stream. Evidently the appetite for more ivory had got the better of the—what shall I say?—less material aspirations. However he had got much worse suddenly. 'I heard he was lying here helpless, and so I came up—took my chance,' said the Russian. 'Oh, he is bad, very bad.' I directed my glass to the house. There were no signs of life, but there was the ruined roof, the long mud wall peeping above the grass, with three little square window-holes, no two of the same size; all this brought within reach of my hand, as it were. And then I made a brusque movement, and one of the remaining posts of that vanished fence leaped up in the field of my glass. You remember I told you I had been struck at the distance by certain attempts at ornamentation, rather remarkable in the ruinous aspect of the place. Now I had suddenly a nearer view, and its first result was to make me throw my head back as if before a blow. Then I went carefully from post to post with my glass, and I saw my mistake. These round knobs were not ornamental but symbolic; they were expressive and puzzling, striking and disturbing—food for thought and also for the vultures if there had been any looking down from the sky; but at all events for such ants as were industrious enough to ascend the pole. They would have been even more impressive, those heads on the stakes,[1] if their faces had not been turned to the house. Only one, the first I had made out, was facing my way. I was not so shocked as you may think. The start back I had given was really nothing but a movement of surprise. I had expected to see a knob of wood there, you know. I returned deliberately to the first I had seen—and there it was, black, dried, sunken, with closed eyelids—a head that seemed to sleep at the top of that pole, and, with the shrunken dry lips showing a narrow white line of the teeth, was smiling too, smiling continuously at some endless and jocose dream of that eternal slumber.

"I am not disclosing any trade secrets. In fact the manager said afterwards that Mr Kurtz's methods had ruined the district. I have no opinion on that point, but I want you clearly to understand that there was nothing exactly profitable in these heads being there. They only showed that Mr Kurtz lacked restraint in the gratification of his various lusts, that there was something wanting in him—some small matter which, when the pressing need arose, could not be found under his magnificent eloquence. Whether he knew of this deficiency himself I can't say. I think the knowledge came to him at last—only at the very last. But the wilderness had found him out early, and had taken on him a terrible vengeance for the fantastic invasion. I think it had whispered to him things about himself which he did not know, things of which he had no conception till he took counsel with this great solitude—and the whisper had proved irresistibly fascinating. It echoed loudly within him because he was hollow at the core. . . . I put down the glass, and the head that had appeared near enough to be spoken to seemed at once to have leaped away from me into inaccessible distance.

"The admirer of Mr Kurtz was a bit crestfallen. In a hurried, indistinct voice he began to assure me he had not dared to take these—say, symbols—down. He was not afraid of the natives; they would not stir till Mr Kurtz gave the word. His ascendancy was extraordinary. The camps of these people surrounded the place, and the chiefs came every day to see him. They would crawl. . . . 'I don't want to know anything of the ceremonies used when approaching Mr Kurtz,' I shouted. Curious, this feeling that came over me that such details would be more intolerable than those heads drying on the stakes under Mr Kurtz's windows. After all, that was only a savage sight, while I seemed at one bound to have been transported into some lightless region of subtle horrors, where pure, uncomplicated savagery was a positive relief, being something that had a right to exist—obviously—in the sunshine. The young man looked at me with surprise. I suppose it did not occur to him Mr Kurtz was no idol of mine. He forgot I hadn't heard any of these splendid monologues on, what was it? on love, justice, conduct of life—or what not. If it had come to crawling before Mr Kurtz, he crawled as much as the veriest savage of them all. I had no idea of the conditions, he said: these heads were the heads of rebels. I shocked him excessively by laughing. Rebels! What would be the next definition I was to hear? There had been enemies, criminals, workers—and these were rebels. Those rebellious heads looked very subdued to me on their sticks. 'You don't know how such a life tries a man like Kurtz,' cried Kurtz's last disciple. 'Well, and you?' I said. 'I! I! I am a simple man. I have no great thoughts. I want nothing from anybody. How can you compare me to . . . ?' His feelings were too much for speech, and suddenly he broke down. 'I don't understand,' he groaned. 'I've been doing my best to keep him alive, and that's enough. I had no hand in all this. I have no abilities. There hasn't been a drop of medicine or a mouthful of invalid food for months here. He was shamefully abandoned. A man like this, with such ideas. Shamefully! Shamefully! I—I—haven't slept for the last ten nights. . . .'

"His voice lost itself in the calm of the evening. The long shadows of the forest had slipped down hill while we talked, had gone far beyond the ruined hovel, beyond the symbolic row of stakes. All this was in the gloom, while we down there were yet in the sunshine, and the stretch of the river abreast of the clearing glittered in a still and dazzling splendour, with a murky and overshadowed bend above and below. Not a living soul was seen on the shore. The bushes did not rustle.

"Suddenly round the corner of the house a group of men appeared, as though they had come up from the ground. They waded waist-deep in the grass, in a compact body, bearing an improvised stretcher in their midst. Instantly, in the emptiness of the landscape, a cry arose whose shrillness pierced the still air like a sharp arrow flying straight to the very heart of the land; and, as if by enchantment, streams of human beings—of naked human beings—with spears in their hands, with bows, with shields, with wild glances and savage movements, were poured into the clearing by the dark-faced and pensive forest. The bushes shook, the grass swayed for a time, and then everything stood still in attentive immobility.

"'Now, if he does not say the right thing to them we are all done for,' said the Russian at my elbow. The knot of men with the stretcher had stopped too, half-way to the steamer, as if petrified. I saw the man on the stretcher sit up, lank and with an uplifted arm, above the shoulders of the bearers. 'Let us hope that the man who can talk so well of love in general will find some particular reason to spare us this time,' I said. I resented bitterly the absurd danger of our situation, as if to be at the mercy of that atrocious phantom had been a dishonouring necessity. I could not hear a sound, but through my glasses I saw the thin arm extended commandingly, the lower jaw moving, the eyes of that apparition shining darkly far in its bony head that nodded with grotesque jerks. Kurtz—Kurtz—that means 'short' in German—don't it? Well, the name was as true as everything else in his life—and death. He looked at least seven feet long. His covering had fallen off, and his body emerged from it pitiful and appalling as from a winding-sheet. I could see the cage of his ribs all astir, the bones of his arm waving. It was as though an animated image of death carved out of old ivory had been shaking its hand with menaces at a motionless crowd of men made of dark and glittering bronze. I saw him open his mouth wide—it gave him a weirdly voracious aspect, as though he had wanted to swallow all the air, all the earth, all the men before him. A deep voice reached me faintly. He must have been shouting. He fell back suddenly. The stretcher shook as the bearers staggered forward again, and almost at the same time I noticed that the crowd of savages was vanishing without any perceptible movement of retreat, as if the forest that had ejected these beings so suddenly had drawn them in again as the breath is drawn in a long aspiration.

"Some of the pilgrims behind the stretcher carried his arms—two shot-guns, a heavy rifle, and a light revolver-carbine—the thunderbolts of that pitiful Jupiter.² The manager bent over him murmuring as he walked beside his head. They laid him down in one of the little cabins—just a room for a bed-place and a camp-stool or two, you know. We had brought his belated correspondence, and a lot of torn envelopes and open letters littered his bed. His hand roamed feebly amongst these papers. I was struck by the fire of his eyes and the composed languor of his expression. It was not so much the exhaustion of disease. He did not seem in pain. This Shadow looked satiated and calm, as though for the moment it had had its fill of all the emotions.

"He rustled one of the letters, and looking straight in my face said, 'I am glad.' Somebody had been writing to him about me. These special recommendations were turning up again. The volume of tone he emitted without effort, almost without the trouble of moving his lips, amazed me. A voice! a voice! It was grave, profound, vibrating, while the man did not seem capable of a whisper. However, he had enough strength in him— factitious no doubt—to very nearly make an end of us, as you shall hear directly.

"The manager appeared silently in the doorway; I stepped out at once and he drew the curtain after me. The Russian, eyed curiously by the pilgrims, was staring at the shore. I followed the direction of his glance.

"Dark human shapes could be made out in the distance, flitting indistinctly against the gloomy border of the forest, and near the river two bronze figures, leaning on tall spears, stood in the sunlight, under fantastic head-dresses of spotted skins, warlike and still in statuesque repose. And from right to left along the lighted shore moved a wild and gorgeous apparition of a woman.

"She walked with measured steps, draped in striped and fringed cloths, treading the earth proudly, with a slight jingle and flash of barbarous ornaments. She carried her head high; her hair was done in the shape of a helmet; she had brass leggins³ to the knee, brass wire gauntlets to the elbow, a crimson spot on her tawny cheek, innumerable necklaces of glass beads on her neck; bizarre things, charms, gifts of witch-men, that hung about her, glittered and trembled at every step. She must have had the value of several elephant tusks upon her. She was savage and superb, wild-eyed and magnificent; there was something ominous and stately in her deliberate progress. And in the hush that had fallen suddenly upon the whole sorrowful land, the immense wilderness, the colossal body of the fecund and mysterious life seemed to look at her, pensive, as though it had been looking at the image of its own tenebrous and passionate soul.

"She came abreast of the steamer, stood still, and faced us. Her long shadow fell to the water's edge. Her face had a tragic and fierce aspect of wild sorrow and of dumb pain mingled with the fear of some struggling, half-shaped resolve. She stood looking at us without a stir, and like the wilderness itself, with an air of brooding over an inscrutable purpose. A whole minute passed, and then she made a step forward. There was a low jingle, a glint of yellow metal, a sway of fringed draperies, and she stopped as if her heart had failed her. The young fellow by my side growled. The pilgrims murmured at my back. She looked at us all as if her life had depended upon the unswerving steadiness of her glance. Suddenly she opened her bared arms and threw them up rigid above her head, as though in an uncontrollable desire to touch the sky, and at the same time the swift shadows darted out on the earth, swept around on the river, gathering the steamer into a shadowy embrace. A formidable silence hung over the scene.

"She turned away slowly, walked on, following the bank, and passed into the bushes to the left. Once only her eyes gleamed back at us in the dusk of the thickets before she disappeared.

"'If she had offered to come aboard I really think I would have tried to shoot her,' said the man of patches, nervously. 'I had been risking my life every day for the last fortnight to keep her out of the house. She got in though one day and kicked up a row about those miserable rags I picked up in the storeroom to mend my clothes with. I wasn't decent. At least it must have been that, for she talked like a fury to Kurtz for an hour, pointing at me now and then. I don't understand the dialect of this tribe. Luckily for me, I fancy Kurtz felt too ill that day to

care, or there would have been mischief. I don't understand. . . .
No—it's too much for me. Ah, well, it's all over now.'
"At this moment I heard Kurtz's deep voice behind the curtain, 'Save me!—save the ivory, you mean. Don't tell me. Save
me! Why, I've had to save you. You are interrupting my plans
now. Sick! Sick! Not so sick as you would like to believe. Never
mind. I'll carry my ideas out yet—I will return. I'll show you
what can be done. You with your little peddling notions—you
are interfering with me. I will return. I . . .'
"The manager came out. He did me the honour to take me
under the arm and lead me aside. 'He is very low, very low,' he
said. He considered it necessary to sigh, but neglected to be
consistently sorrowful. 'We have done all we could for him—
haven't we? But there is no disguising the fact, Mr Kurtz has
done more harm than good to the Company. He did not see
the time was not ripe for vigorous action. Cautiously, cautiously—that's my principle. We must be cautious yet. The
district is closed to us for a time. Deplorable! Upon the whole,
the trade will suffer. I don't deny there is a remarkable quantity
of ivory—mostly fossil. We must save it, at all events—but
look how precarious the position is—and why? Because the
method is unsound.' 'Do you,' said I, looking at the shore, 'call
it "unsound method"?' 'Without doubt,' he exclaimed, hotly.
'Don't you?' . . . 'No method at all,' I murmured after a while.
'Exactly,' he exulted. 'I anticipated this. Shows a complete want
of judgment. It is my duty to point it out in the proper quarters.'
'Oh,' said I, 'that fellow—what's his name? —the brickmaker,
will make a readable report for you.' He appeared confounded
for a moment. It seemed to me I had never breathed an atmosphere so vile, and I turned mentally to Kurtz for relief—
positively for relief. 'Nevertheless I think Mr Kurtz *is* a remarkable man,' I said with emphasis. He started, dropped on
me a cold heavy glance, said very quietly, 'He *was*,' and turned
his back on me. My hour of favour was over. I found myself
lumped along with Kurtz as a partisan of methods for which
the time was not ripe. I was unsound! Ah! but it was something
to have at least a choice of nightmares.
"I had turned to the wilderness really, not to Mr Kurtz, who,

I was ready to admit, was as good as buried. And for a moment it seemed to me as if I also were buried in a vast grave full of unspeakable secrets. I felt an intolerable weight oppressing my breast, the smell of the damp earth, the unseen presence of victorious corruption, the darkness of an impenetrable night. . . . The Russian tapped me on the shoulder. I heard him mumbling and stammering something about 'brother seaman—couldn't conceal—knowledge of matters that would affect Mr Kurtz's reputation.' I waited. For him evidently Mr Kurtz was not in his grave. I suspect that for him Mr Kurtz was one of the immortals. 'Well!' said I at last, 'speak out. As it happens, I am Mr Kurtz's friend—in a way.'

"He stated with a good deal of formality that had we not been 'of the same profession,' he would have kept the matter to himself without regard to consequences. 'He suspected there was an active ill-will towards him on the part of these white men that——' 'You are right,' I said, remembering a certain conversation I had overheard. 'The manager thinks you ought to be hanged.' He showed a concern at this intelligence which amused me at first. 'I had better get out of the way quietly,' he said, earnestly. 'I can do no more for Kurtz now, and they would soon find some excuse. What's to stop them? There's a military post three hundred miles from here.' 'Well, upon my word,' said I, 'perhaps you had better go if you have any friends amongst the savages near by.' 'Plenty,' he said. 'They are simple people—and I want nothing, you know.' He stood biting his lip, then: 'I don't want any harm to happen to these whites here, but of course I was thinking of Mr Kurtz's reputation—but you are a brother seaman and——' 'All right,' said I, after a time. 'Mr Kurtz's reputation is safe with me.' I did not know how truly I spoke.

"He informed me, lowering his voice, that it was Kurtz who had ordered the attack to be made on the steamer. 'He hated sometimes the idea of being taken away—and then again . . . But I don't understand these matters. I am a simple man. He thought it would scare you away—that you would give it up, thinking him dead. I could not stop him. Oh, I had an awful time of it this last month.' 'Very well,' I said. 'He is all right now.' 'Ye-e-es,' he muttered, not very convinced apparently. 'Thanks,' said I; 'I shall keep my eyes open.' 'But quiet – eh?' he urged, anxiously. 'It would be awful for his reputation if anybody here——' I promised a complete discretion with great gravity. 'I have a canoe and three black fellows waiting not very far. I am off. Could you give me a few Martini-Henry cartridges?' I could, and did, with proper secrecy. He helped himself, with a wink at me, to a handful of my tobacco. 'Between sailors—you know—good English tobacco.' At the door of the pilot-house he turned round—'I say, haven't you a pair of shoes you could spare?' He raised one leg. 'Look.' The soles were tied with knotted strings sandal-wise under his bare feet. I rooted out an old pair, at which he looked with admiration before tucking it under his left arm. One of his pockets (bright red) was bulging with cartridges, from the other (dark blue) peeped 'Towson's Inquiry,' etc., etc. He seemed to think himself excellently well equipped for a renewed encounter with the wilderness. 'Ah! I'll never, never meet such a man again. You ought to have heard him recite poetry—his own too it was, he told me. Poetry!' He rolled his eyes at the recollection of these delights. 'Oh, he enlarged my mind!' 'Goodbye,' said I. He shook hands and vanished in the night. Sometimes I ask myself whether I had ever really seen him—whether it was possible to meet such a phenomenon! . . .

"When I woke up shortly after midnight his warning came to my mind with its hint of danger that seemed, in the starred darkness, real enough to make me get up for the purpose of having a look round. On the hill a big fire burned, illuminating fitfully a crooked corner of the station-house. One of the agents with a picket of a few of our blacks, armed for the purpose, was keeping guard over the ivory; but deep within the forest, red gleams that wavered, that seemed to sink and rise from the ground amongst confused columnar shapes of intense blackness, showed the exact position of the camp where Mr Kurtz's adorers were keeping their uneasy vigil. The monotonous beating of a big drum filled the air with muffled shocks and a lingering vibration. A steady droning sound of many men chanting each to himself some weird incantation came out from the black, flat wall of the woods as the humming of bees comes out of a hive, and had a strange narcotic effect upon my half-awake senses. I believe I dozed off leaning over the rail, till an abrupt burst of yells, an overwhelming outbreak of a pent-up and mysterious frenzy, woke me up in a bewildered wonder. It was cut short all at once, and the low droning went on with an effect of audible and soothing silence. I glanced casually into the little cabin. A light was burning within, but Mr Kurtz was not there.

"I think I would have raised an outcry if I had believed my eyes. But I didn't believe them at first—the thing seemed so impossible. The fact is I was completely unnerved by a sheer blank fright, pure abstract terror, unconnected with any distinct shape of physical danger. What made this emotion so over-powering was—how shall I define it?—the moral shock I received, as if something altogether monstrous, intolerable to thought and odious to the soul, had been thrust upon me unexpectedly. This lasted of course the merest fraction of a second, and then the usual sense of commonplace, deadly danger, the possibility of a sudden onslaught and massacre, or something of the kind, which I saw impending, was positively welcome and composing. It pacified me, in fact, so much, that I did not raise an alarm.

"There was an agent buttoned up inside an ulster[4] and sleeping on a chair on deck within three feet of me. The yells had not awakened him; he snored very slightly; I left him to his slumbers and leaped ashore. I did not betray Mr Kurtz—it was ordered I should never betray him—it was written I should be loyal to the nightmare of my choice. I was anxious to deal with this Shadow by myself alone—and to this day I don't know why I was so jealous of sharing with any one the peculiar blackness of that experience.

"As soon as I got on the bank I saw a trail—a broad trail through the grass. I remember the exultation with which I said to myself, 'He can't walk—he is crawling on all-fours—I've got him.' The grass was wet with dew. I strode rapidly with clenched fists. I fancy I had some vague notion of falling upon him and giving him a drubbing. I don't know. I had some

imbecile thoughts. The knitting old woman with tr
truded herself upon my memory as a most improper
be sitting at the other end of such an affair. I saw a
pilgrims squirting lead in the air out of Winchesters held
hip. I thought I would never get back to the steamer,
imagined myself living alone and unarmed in the woods to
advanced age. Such silly things—you know. And I remembe
confounded the beat of the drum with the béating of my hear
and was pleased at its calm regularity.

"I kept to the track though—then stopped to listen. The
night was very clear: a dark blue space, sparkling with dew and
starlight, in which black things stood very still. I thought I
could see a kind of motion ahead of me. I was strangely cocksure
of everything that night. I actually left the track and ran in a
wide semicircle (I verily believe chuckling to myself) so as to
get in front of that stir, of that motion I had seen—if indeed I
had seen anything. I was circumventing Kurtz as though it had
been a boyish game.

"I came upon him, and, if he had not heard me coming, I
would have fallen over him too; but he got up in time. He rose,
unsteady, long, pale, indistinct, like a vapour exhaled by the
earth, and swayed slightly, misty and silent before me; while at
my back the fires loomed between the trees, and the murmur
of many voices issued from the forest. I had cut him off cleverly;
but when actually confronting him I seemed to come to my
senses, I saw the danger in its right proportion. It was by no
means over yet. Suppose he began to shout? Though he could
hardly stand, there was still plenty of vigour in his voice. 'Go
away—hide yourself,' he said, in that profound tone. It was
very awful. I glanced back. We were within thirty yards from
the nearest fire. A black figure stood up, strode on long black
legs, waving long black arms, across the glow. It had horns—
antelope horns, I think—on its head. Some sorcerer, some
witch-man, no doubt: it looked fiend-like enough. 'Do you know
what you are doing?' I whispered. 'Perfectly,' he answered, raising his voice for that single word: it sounded to me far off and yet
loud, like a hail through a speaking-trumpet. If he makes a row
we are lost, I thought to myself. This clearly was not a case for

even apart from the very natural aversion I had to Shadow—this wandering and tormented thing. 'You ...ost,' I said—'utterly lost.' One gets sometimes such a : inspiration, you know. I did say the right thing, though ...d he could not have been more irretrievably lost than he at this very moment, when the foundations of our intimacy ...e being laid—to endure—to endure—even to the end— ...en beyond.

"'I had immense plans,' he muttered irresolutely. 'Yes,' said I; 'but if you try to shout I'll smash your head with——' There was not a stick or a stone near. 'I will throttle you for good,' I corrected myself. 'I was on the threshold of great things,' he pleaded, in a voice of longing, with a wistfulness of tone that made my blood run cold. 'And now for this stupid scoundrel——' 'Your success in Europe is assured in any case,' I affirmed, steadily. I did not want to have the throttling of him, you understand—and indeed it would have been very little use for any practical purpose. I tried to break the spell—the heavy, mute spell of the wilderness—that seemed to draw him to its pitiless breast by the awakening of forgotten and brutal instincts, by the memory of gratified and monstrous passions. This alone, I was convinced, had driven him out to the edge of the forest, to the bush, towards the gleam of fires, the throb of drums, the drone of weird incantations; this alone had beguiled his unlawful soul beyond the bounds of permitted aspirations. And, don't you see, the terror of the position was not in being knocked on the head—though I had a very lively sense of that danger too—but in this, that I had to deal with a being to whom I could not appeal in the name of anything high or low. I had, even like the niggers, to invoke him—himself—his own exalted and incredible degradation. There was nothing either above or below him, and I knew it. He had kicked himself loose of the earth. Confound the man! he had kicked the very earth to pieces. He was alone, and I before him did not know whether I stood on the ground or floated in the air. I've been telling you what we said—repeating the phrases we pronounced—but what's the good? They were common everyday words—the familiar, vague sounds exchanged on every waking day of life.

But what of that? They had behind them, to my mind, the terrific suggestiveness of words heard in dreams, of phrases spoken in nightmares. Soul! If anybody had ever struggled with a soul, I am the man. And I wasn't arguing with a lunatic either. Believe me or not, his intelligence was perfectly clear—concentrated, it is true, upon himself with horrible intensity, yet clear; and therein was my only chance—barring, of course, the killing him there and then, which wasn't so good, on account of unavoidable noise. But his soul was mad. Being alone in the wilderness, it had looked within itself, and, by heavens! I tell you, it had gone mad. I had—for my sins, I suppose—to go through the ordeal of looking into it myself. No eloquence could have been so withering to one's belief in mankind as his final burst of sincerity. He struggled with himself, too. I saw it—I heard it. I saw the inconceivable mystery of a soul that knew no restraint, no faith, and no fear, yet struggling blindly with itself. I kept my head pretty well; but when I had him at last stretched on the couch, I wiped my forehead, while my legs shook under me as though I had carried half a ton on my back down that hill. And yet I had only supported him, his bony arm clasped round my neck—and he was not much heavier than a child.

"When next day we left at noon, the crowd, of whose presence behind the curtain of trees I had been acutely conscious all the time, flowed out of the woods again, filled the clearing, covered the slope with a mass of naked, breathing, quivering bronze bodies. I steamed up a bit, then swung down-stream, and two thousand eyes followed the evolutions of the splashing, thumping, fiery river-demon beating the water with its terrible tail and breathing black smoke into the air. In front of the first rank, along the river, three men, plastered with bright red earth from head to foot, strutted to and fro restlessly. When we came abreast again, they faced the river, stamped their feet, nodded their horned heads, swayed their scarlet bodies; they shook towards the fierce river-demon a bunch of black feathers, a mangy skin with a pendant tail—something that looked like a dried gourd; they shouted periodically together strings of amazing words that resembled no sounds of human language; and the deep murmurs of the crowd, interrupted suddenly, were like the responses of some satanic litany.

"We had carried Kurtz into the pilot-house: there was more air there. Lying on the couch, he stared through the open shutter. There was an eddy in the mass of human bodies, and the woman with helmeted head and tawny cheeks rushed out to the very brink of the stream. She put out her hands, shouted something, and all that wild mob took up the shout in a roaring chorus of articulated, rapid, breathless utterance.

"'Do you understand this?' I asked.

"He kept on looking out past me with fiery, longing eyes, with a mingled expression of wistfulness and hate. He made no answer, but I saw a smile, a smile of indefinable meaning, appear on his colourless lips that a moment after twitched convulsively. "Do I not?" he said slowly, gasping, as if the words had been torn out of him by a supernatural power.

"I pulled the string of the whistle, and I did this because I saw the pilgrims on deck getting out their rifles with an air of anticipating a jolly lark. At the sudden screech there was a movement of abject terror through that wedged mass of bodies. "Don't! don't you frighten them away," cried someone on deck disconsolately. I pulled the string time after time. They broke and ran, they leaped, they crouched, they swerved, they dodged the flying terror of the sound. The three red chaps had fallen flat, face down on the shore, as though they had been shot dead. Only the barbarous and superb woman did not so much as flinch, and stretched tragically her bare arms after us over the sombre and glittering river.

"And then that imbecile crowd down on the deck started their little fun, and I could see nothing more for smoke.

"The brown current ran swiftly out of the heart of darkness, bearing us down towards the sea with twice the speed of our upward progress; and Kurtz's life was running swiftly too, ebbing, ebbing out of his heart into the sea of inexorable time. The manager was very placid, he had no vital anxieties now, he took us both in with a comprehensive and satisfied glance:

the 'affair' had come off as well as could be wished. I saw the
time approaching when I would be left alone of the party of
'unsound method.' The pilgrims looked upon me with dis-
favour. I was, so to speak, numbered with the dead. It is strange
how I accepted this unforeseen partnership, this choice of nightmares forced upon me in the tenebrous land invaded by these
mean and greedy phantoms.

"Kurtz discoursed. A voice! a voice! It rang deep to the very
last. It survived his strength to hide in the magnificent folds of
eloquence the barren darkness of his heart. Oh, he struggled!
he struggled! The wastes of his weary brain were haunted by
shadowy images now—images of wealth and fame revolving
obsequiously round his unextinguishable gift of noble and lofty
expression. My Intended, my ivory, my station, my career, my
ideas—these were the subjects for the occasional utterances of
elevated sentiments. The shade of the original Kurtz frequented
the bedside of the hollow sham, whose fate it was to be buried
presently in the mould of primeval earth. But both the diabolic
love and the unearthly hate of the mysteries it had penetrated
fought for the possession of that soul satiated with primitive
emotions, avid of lying fame, of sham distinction, of all the
appearances of success and power.

"Sometimes he was contemptibly childish. He desired to have
kings meet him at railway-stations[5] on his return from some
ghastly Nowhere, where he intended to accomplish great things.
'You show them you have in hand something that is really
profitable, and then there will be no limits to the recognition of
your ability,' he would say. 'Of course you must take care of
the motives—right motives—always.' The long reaches that
were like one and the same reach, monotonous bends that were
exactly alike, slipped past the steamer with their multitude of
secular[6] trees looking patiently after this grimy fragment of
another world, the forerunner of change, of conquest, of trade,
of massacres, of blessings. I looked ahead—piloting. 'Close the
shutter,' said Kurtz suddenly one day; 'I can't bear to look at
this.' I did so. There was a silence. 'Oh, but I will wring your
heart yet!' he cried at the invisible wilderness.

"We broke down—as I had expected—and had to lie up for

repairs at the head of an island. This delay was the first thing that shook Kurtz's confidence. One morning he gave me a packet of papers and a photograph—the lot tied together with a shoe-string. 'Keep this for me,' he said. 'This noxious fool' (meaning the manager) 'is capable of prying into my boxes when I am not looking.' In the afternoon I saw him. He was lying on his back with closed eyes, and I withdrew quietly, but I heard him mutter, 'Live rightly, die, die . . .'[7] I listened. There was nothing more. Was he rehearsing some speech in his sleep, or was it a fragment of a phrase from some newspaper article? He had been writing for the papers and meant to do so again, 'for the furthering of my ideas. It's a duty.'

"His was an impenetrable darkness. I looked at him as you peer down at a man who is lying at the bottom of a precipice where the sun never shines. But I had not much time to give him, because I was helping the engine-driver to take to pieces the leaky cylinders, to straighten a bent connecting-rod, and in other such matters. I lived in an infernal mess of rust, filings, nuts, bolts, spanners, hammers, ratchet-drills—-things I abominate, because I don't get on with them. I tended the little forge we fortunately had aboard; I toiled wearily in a wretched scrap-heap—unless I had the shakes too bad to stand.

"One evening coming in with a candle I was startled to hear him say a little tremulously, 'I am lying here in the dark waiting for death.' The light was within a foot of his eyes. I forced myself to murmur, 'Oh, nonsense!' and stood over him as if transfixed.

"Anything approaching the change that came over his features I have never seen before, and hope never to see again. Oh, I wasn't touched. I was fascinated. It was as though a veil had been rent. I saw on that ivory face the expression of sombre pride, of ruthless power, of craven terror—of an intense and hopeless despair. Did he live his life again in every detail of desire, temptation, and surrender during that supreme moment of complete knowledge? He cried in a whisper at some image, at some vision—he cried out twice, a cry that was no more than a breath—

" 'The horror! The horror!'[8]

"I blew the candle out and left the cabin. The pilgrims were dining in the mess-room, and I took my place opposite the manager, who lifted his eyes to give me a questioning glance, which I successfully ignored. He leaned back, serene, with that peculiar smile of his sealing the unexpressed depths of his meanness. A continuous shower of small flies streamed upon the lamp, upon the cloth, upon our hands and faces. Suddenly the manager's boy put his insolent black head in the doorway, and said in a tone of scathing contempt—

"'Mistah Kurtz—he dead.'

"All the pilgrims rushed out to see. I remained, and went on with my dinner. I believe I was considered brutally callous. However, I did not eat much. There was a lamp in there—light, don't you know—and outside it was so beastly, beastly dark. I went no more near the remarkable man who had pronounced a judgment upon the adventures of his soul on this earth. The voice was gone. What else had been there? But I am of course aware that next day the pilgrims buried something in a muddy hole.

"And then they very nearly buried me.

"However, as you see, I did not go to join Kurtz there and then. I did not. I remained to dream the nightmare out to the end, and to show my loyalty to Kurtz once more. Destiny. My destiny! Droll thing life is—that mysterious arrangement of merciless logic for a futile purpose. The most you can hope from it is some knowledge of yourself—that comes too late—a crop of unextinguishable regrets. I have wrestled with death. It is the most unexciting contest you can imagine. It takes place in an impalpable greyness, with nothing underfoot, with nothing around, without spectators, without clamour, without glory, without the great desire of victory, without the great fear of defeat, in a sickly atmosphere of tepid scepticism, without much belief in your own right, and still less in that of your adversary. If such is the form of ultimate wisdom, then life is a greater riddle than some of us think it to be. I was within a hair's-breadth of the last opportunity for pronouncement, and I found with humiliation that probably I would have nothing to say. This is the reason why I affirm that Kurtz was a remarkable

powerfull confidence

man. He had something to say. He said it. Since I had peeped over the edge myself, I understand better the meaning of his stare, that could not see the flame of the candle, but was wide enough to embrace the whole universe, piercing enough to penetrate all the hearts that beat in the darkness. He had summed up—he had judged. 'The horror!' He was a remarkable man. After all, this was the expression of some sort of belief; it had candour, it had conviction, it had a vibrating note of revolt in its whisper, it had the appalling face of a glimpsed truth—the strange commingling of desire and hate. And it is not my own extremity I remember best—a vision of greyness without form filled with physical pain, and a careless contempt for the evanescence of all things—even of this pain itself. No! It is his extremity that I seem to have lived through. True, he had made that last stride, he had stepped over the edge, while I had been permitted to draw back my hesitating foot. And perhaps in this is the whole difference; perhaps all wisdom, and all truth, and all sincerity, are just compressed into that inappreciable moment of time in which we step over the threshold of the Invisible. Perhaps! I like to think that my summing-up would not have been a word of careless contempt. Better his cry—much better. It was an affirmation, a moral victory paid for by innumerable defeats, by abominable terrors, by abominable satisfactions. But it was a victory! That is why I have remained loyal to Kurtz to the last, and even beyond, when a long time after I heard once more, not his own voice, but the echo of his magnificent eloquence thrown to me from a soul as translucently pure as a cliff of crystal.

"No, they did not bury me,[9] though there is a period of time which I remember mistily, with a shuddering wonder, like a passage through some inconceivable world that had no hope in it and no desire. I found myself back in the sepulchral city resenting the sight of people hurrying through the streets to filch a little money from each other, to devour their infamous cookery, to gulp their unwholesome beer, to dream their insignificant and silly dreams. They trespassed upon my thoughts. They were intruders whose knowledge of life was to me an irritating pretence, because I felt so sure they could not possibly

know the things I knew. Their bearing, which was simply the
bearing of commonplace individuals going about their business
in the assurance of perfect safety, was offensive to me like the
outrageous flauntings of folly in the face of a danger it is unable
to comprehend. I had no particular desire to enlighten them,
but I had some difficulty in restraining myself from laughing in
their faces, so full of stupid importance. I daresay I was not
very well at that time. I tottered about the streets—there were
various affairs to settle—grinning bitterly at perfectly respectable persons. I admit my behaviour was inexcusable, but then
my temperature was seldom normal in these days. My dear
aunt's endeavours to 'nurse up my strength' seemed altogether
beside the mark. It was not my strength that wanted nursing, it
was my imagination that wanted soothing. I kept the bundle of
papers given me by Kurtz, not knowing exactly what to do with
it. His mother had died lately, watched over, as I was told, by
his Intended. A clean-shaved man, with an official manner and
wearing gold-rimmed spectacles, called on me one day and
made inquiries, at first circuitous, afterwards suavely pressing,
about what he was pleased to denominate certain 'documents.'
I was not surprised, because I had had two rows with the
manager on the subject out there. I had refused to give up the
smallest scrap out of that package, and I took the same attitude
with the spectacled man. He became darkly menacing at last,
and with much heat argued that the Company had the right to
every bit of information about its 'territories.' And, said he,
'Mr Kurtz's knowledge of unexplored regions must have been
necessarily extensive and peculiar—owing to his great abilities
and to the deplorable circumstances in which he had been
placed: therefore——' I assured him Mr Kurtz's knowledge,
however extensive, did not bear upon the problems of commerce or administration. He invoked then the name of science.
'It would be an incalculable loss if,' etc., etc. I offered him
the report on the 'Suppression of Savage Customs,' with the
postscriptum torn off. He took it up eagerly, but ended by
sniffing at it with an air of contempt. 'This is not what we had
a right to expect,' he remarked. 'Expect nothing else,' I said.
'There are only private letters.' He withdrew upon some threat

of legal proceedings, and I saw him no more; but another fellow, calling himself Kurtz's cousin, appeared two days later, and was anxious to hear all the details about his dear relative's last moments. Incidentally he gave me to understand that Kurtz had been essentially a great musician. 'There was the making of an immense success,' said the man, who was an organist, I believe, with lank grey hair flowing over a greasy coat-collar. I had no reason to doubt his statement; and to this day I am unable to say what was Kurtz's profession, whether he ever had any—which was the greatest of his talents. I had taken him for a painter who wrote for the papers, or else for a journalist who could paint—but even the cousin (who took snuff during the interview) could not tell me what he had been—exactly. He was a universal genius—on that point I agreed with the old chap, who thereupon blew his nose noisily into a large cotton handkerchief and withdrew in senile agitation, bearing off some family letters and memoranda without importance. Ultimately a journalist anxious to know something of the fate of his 'dear colleague' turned up. This visitor informed me Kurtz's proper sphere ought to have been politics 'on the popular side.' He had furry straight eyebrows, bristly hair cropped short, an eye-glass on a broad black ribbon, and, becoming expansive, confessed his opinion that Kurtz really couldn't write a bit— 'but heavens! how that man could talk! He electrified large meetings. He had the faith—don't you see?—he had the faith. He could get himself to believe anything—anything. He would have been a splendid leader of an extreme party.' 'What party?' I asked. 'Any party,' answered the other. 'He was an—an— extremist.' Did I not think so? I assented. Did I know, he asked, with a sudden flash of curiosity, 'what it was that had induced him to go out there?' 'Yes,' said I, and forthwith handed him the famous Report for publication, if he thought fit. He glanced through it hurriedly, mumbling all the time, judged 'it would do,' and took himself off with this plunder.

"Thus I was left at last with a slim packet of letters and the girl's portrait. She struck me as beautiful—I mean she had a beautiful expression. I know that the sunlight can be made to lie too, yet one felt that no manipulation of light and pose could have conveyed the delicate shade of truthfulness upon those features. She seemed ready to listen without mental reservation, without suspicion, without a thought for herself. I concluded I would go and give her back her portrait and those letters myself. Curiosity? Yes; and also some other feeling perhaps.[10] All that had been Kurtz's had passed out of my hands: his soul, his body, his station, his plans, his ivory, his career. There remained only his memory and his Intended—and I wanted to give that up too to the past, in a way—to surrender personally all that remained of him with me to that oblivion which is the last word of our common fate. I don't defend myself. I had no clear perception of what it was I really wanted. Perhaps it was an impulse of unconscious loyalty, or the fulfilment of one of these ironic necessities that lurk in the facts of human existence. I don't know. I can't tell. But I went.

"I thought his memory was like the other memories of the dead that accumulate in every man's life—a vague impress on the brain of shadows that had fallen on it in their swift and final passage; but before the high and ponderous door, between the tall houses of a street as still and decorous as a well-kept alley in a cemetery, I had a vision of him on the stretcher, opening his mouth voraciously, as if to devour all the earth with all its mankind. He lived then before me; he lived as much as he had ever lived—a shadow insatiable of splendid appearances, of frightful realities; a shadow darker than the shadow of the night, and draped nobly in the folds of a gorgeous eloquence. The vision seemed to enter the house with me—the stretcher, the phantom-bearers, the wild crowd of obedient worshippers, the gloom of the forests, the glitter of the reach between the murky bends, the beat of the drum, regular and muffled like the beating of a heart—the heart of a conquering darkness. It was a moment of triumph for the wilderness, an invading and vengeful rush which, it seemed to me, I would have to keep back alone for the salvation of another soul. And the memory of what I had heard him say afar there, with the horned shapes stirring at my back, in the glow of fires, within the patient woods, those broken phrases came back to me, were heard again in their ominous and terrifying simplicity.

I remembered his abject pleading, his abject threats, the colossal scale of his vile desires, the meanness, the torment, the tempestuous anguish of his soul. And later on I seemed to see his collected languid manner, when he said one day, 'This lot of ivory now is really mine. The Company did not pay for it. I collected it myself at a very great personal risk. I am afraid they will try to claim it as theirs though. H'm. It is a difficult case. What do you think I ought to do—resist? Eh? I want no more than justice.' ... He wanted no more than justice—no more than justice. I rang the bell before a mahogany door on the first floor, and while I waited he seemed to stare at me out of the glassy panel—stare with that wide and immense stare embracing, condemning, loathing all the universe. I seemed to hear the whispered cry, 'The horror! The horror!'

"The dusk was falling. I had to wait in a lofty drawing-room with three long windows from floor to ceiling that were like three luminous and bedraped columns. The bent gilt legs and backs of the furniture shone in indistinct curves. The tall marble fireplace had a cold and monumental whiteness. A grand piano stood massively in a corner, with dark gleams on the flat surfaces like a sombre and polished sarcophagus.[11] A high door opened—closed. I rose.

"She came forward, all in black, with a pale head, floating towards me in the dusk. She was in mourning. It was more than a year since his death, more than a year since the news came; she seemed as though she would remember and mourn for ever. She took both my hands in hers and murmured, 'I had heard you were coming.' I noticed she was not very young—I mean not girlish. She had a mature capacity for fidelity, for belief, for suffering. The room seemed to have grown darker, as if all the sad light of the cloudy evening had taken refuge on her forehead. This fair hair, this pale visage, this pure brow, seemed surrounded by an ashy halo from which the dark eyes looked out at me. Their glance was guileless, profound, confident, and trustful. She carried her sorrowful head as though she were proud of that sorrow, as though she would say, I—I alone know how to mourn for him as he deserves. But while we were still shaking hands, such a look of awful desolation came upon her face that I perceived she was one of those creatures that are not the playthings of Time. For her he had died only yesterday. And, by Jove! the impression was so powerful that for me too he seemed to have died only yesterday—nay, this very minute. I saw her and him in the same instant of time—his death and her sorrow—I saw her sorrow in the very moment of his death. Do you understand? I saw them together—I heard them together. She had said, with a deep catch of the breath, 'I have survived'; while my strained ears seemed to hear distinctly, mingled with her tone of despairing regret, the summing-up whisper of his eternal condemnation. I asked myself what I was doing there, with a sensation of panic in my heart as though I had blundered into a place of cruel and absurd mysteries not fit for a human being to behold. She motioned me to a chair. We sat down. I laid the packet gently on the little table, and she put her hand over it.... 'You knew him well,' she murmured, after a moment of mourning silence.

"'Intimacy grows quick out there,' I said. 'I knew him as well as it is possible for one man to know another.'

"'And you admired him,' she said. 'It was impossible to know him and not to admire him. Was it?'

"'He was a remarkable man,' I said, unsteadily. Then before the appealing fixity of her gaze, that seemed to watch for more words on my lips, I went on, 'It was impossible not to——'

"'Love him,' she finished eagerly, silencing me into an appalled dumbness. 'How true! how true! But when you think that no one knew him so well as I! I had all his noble confidence. I knew him best.'

"'You knew him best,' I repeated. And perhaps she did. But with every word spoken the room was growing darker, and only her forehead, smooth and white, remained illumined by the unextinguishable light of belief and love.

"'You were his friend,' she went on. 'His friend,' she repeated, a little louder. 'You must have been, if he had given you this, and sent you to me. I feel I can speak to you—and oh! I must speak. I want you—you who have heard his last words—to know I have been worthy of him.... It is not pride.... Yes! I am proud to know I understood him better than any one on earth—he told me so himself. And since his mother died I have had no one—no one—to—to——'

"I listened. The darkness deepened. I was not even sure whether he had given me the right bundle. I rather suspect he wanted me to take care of another batch of his papers which, after his death, I saw the manager examining under the lamp. And the girl talked, easing her pain in the certitude of my sympathy; she talked as thirsty men drink. I had heard that her engagement with Kurtz had been disapproved by her people. He wasn't rich enough or something. And indeed I don't know whether he had not been a pauper all his life. He had given me some reason to infer that it was his impatience of comparative poverty that drove him out there.

"'... Who was not his friend who had heard him speak once?' she was saying. 'He drew men towards him by what was best in them.' She looked at me with intensity. 'It is the gift of the great,' she went on, and the sound of her low voice seemed to have the accompaniment of all the other sounds, full of mystery, desolation, and sorrow, I had ever heard—the ripple of the river, the soughing of the trees swayed by the wind, the murmurs of wild crowds, the faint ring of incomprehensible words cried from afar, the whisper of a voice speaking from beyond the threshold of an eternal darkness. 'But you have heard him! You know!' she cried.

"'Yes, I know,' I said with something like despair in my heart, but bowing my head before the faith that was in her, before that great and saving illusion that shone with an unearthly glow in the darkness, in the triumphant darkness from which I could not have defended her—from which I could not even defend myself.

"'What a loss to me—to us!'—she corrected herself with beautiful generosity; then added in a murmur, 'To the world.' By the last gleams of twilight I could see the glitter of her eyes, full of tears—of tears that would not fall.

"'I have been very happy—very fortunate—very proud,' she went on. 'Too fortunate. Too happy for a little while. And now I am unhappy for—for life.'

"She stood up; her fair hair seemed to catch all the remaining light in a glimmer of gold. I rose too.

"'And of all this,' she went on, mournfully, 'of all his promise, and of all his greatness, of his generous mind, of his noble heart, nothing remains—nothing but a memory. You and I——'

"'We shall always remember him,' I said, hastily.

"'No!' she cried. 'It is impossible that all this should be lost—that such a life should be sacrificed to leave nothing—but sorrow. You know what vast plans he had. I knew of them too—I could not perhaps understand—but others knew of them. Something must remain. His words, at least, have not died.'

"'His words will remain,' I said.

"'And his example,' she whispered to herself. 'Men looked up to him—his goodness shone in every act. His example——'

"'True,' I said; 'his example too. Yes, his example. I forgot that.'

"'But I do not. I cannot—I cannot believe—not yet. I cannot believe that I shall never see him again, that nobody will see him again, never, never, never!'[12]

"She put out her arms as if after a retreating figure, stretching them black and with clasped pale hands across the fading and narrow sheen of the window. Never see him! I saw him clearly enough then. I shall see this eloquent phantom as long as I live, and I shall see her too, a tragic and familiar Shade,[13] resembling in this gesture another one, tragic also, and bedecked with powerless charms, stretching bare brown arms over the glitter of the infernal stream, the stream of darkness. She said suddenly very low, 'He died as he lived.'

"'His end,' said I, with dull anger stirring in me, 'was in every way worthy of his life.'

"'And I was not with him,' she murmured. My anger subsided before a feeling of infinite pity.

"'Everything that could be done——' I mumbled.

"'Ah, but I believed in him more than any one on earth—more than his own mother, more than—himself. He needed

She doesn't really know him

me! Me! I would have treasured every sigh, every word, every
sign, every glance.'

"I felt like a chill grip on my chest.[14] 'Don't,' I said, in a
muffled voice.

"'Forgive me. I—I—have mourned so long in silence—in
silence. . . . You were with him—to the last? I think of his
loneliness. Nobody near to understand him as I would have
understood. Perhaps no one to hear . . .'

"'To the very end,' I said, shakily. 'I heard his very last
words. . . .' I stopped in a fright.

"'Repeat them,' she said in a heart-broken tone. 'I want—I
want—something—something—to—to live with.'

"I was on the point of crying at her, 'Don't you hear them?'
The dusk was repeating them in a persistent whisper all around
us, in a whisper that seemed to swell menacingly like the first
whisper of a rising wind. 'The horror! the horror!'

"'His last word—to live with,' she murmured. 'Don't you
understand I loved him—I loved him—I loved him!'

"I pulled myself together and spoke slowly.   ?

"'The last word he pronounced was—your name.'   ·

"I heard a light sigh, and then my heart stood still, stopped
dead short by an exulting and terrible cry, by the cry of inconceivable triumph and of unspeakable pain. 'I knew it—I was
sure!' . . . She knew. She was sure. I heard her weeping; she had
hidden her face in her hands. It seemed to me that the house
would collapse before I could escape, that the heavens would
fall upon my head. But nothing happened. The heavens do not
fall for such a trifle.[15] Would they have fallen, I wonder, if I
had rendered Kurtz that justice which was his due? Hadn't he
said he wanted only justice? But I couldn't. I could not tell her.
It would have been too dark—too dark altogether. . . ."

Marlow ceased, and sat apart, indistinct and silent, in the
pose of a meditating Buddha. Nobody moved for a time. "We
have lost the first of the ebb," said the Director, suddenly. I
raised my head. The offing was barred by a black bank of
clouds, and the tranquil waterway leading to the uttermost ends
of the earth flowed sombre under an overcast sky—seemed to
lead into the heart of an immense darkness.

The Congo Diary

Arrived at Matadi[1] on the 13th of June 1890. –
Mr Gosse[2] chief of the station (O.K.) retaining us for some reason of his own.

Made the acquaintance of Mr Roger Casement,[3] which I should consider as a great pleasure under any circumstances and now it becomes a positive piece of luck.

Thinks, speaks well, most intelligent and very sympathetic. – Feel considerably in doubt about the future. Think just now that my life amongst the people (white) around here can not be very comfortable. Intend avoid acquaintances as much as possible.

Through Mr R. C. Have made the acquaint[tan]^{ce} of Mr Underwood the manager of the English factory (Hatton & Cookson,[4] in Kalla Kalla). Av[era]^{ge} com[merci]^{al} – hearty and kind. Lunched there on the 21st. –

24th Gosse and R. C. gone with a large lot of ivory down to Boma. On G['s] return intend to start up the river. Have been myself busy packing ivory in casks. Idiotic employment. Health good up to now.

Wrote to Simpson,[5] to Gov. B.[6] to Purd.[7] to Hope,[8] to Cap Froud,[9] and to Mar.[10] Prominent characteristic of the social life here: People speaking ill of each other.[11] –

Saturday 28th June left Matadi with Mr Harou[12] and a caravan of 31 men. Parted with Casement in a very friendly manner. Mr Gosse saw us off as far as the State station. –
First halt. M'poso. 2 Danes[13] in Comp[a]ny.

Sund. 29th. Ascent of Palaballa. Sufficiently fatiguing – Camped
at 11ʰ am at Nsoke-River. Mosquitos.[14]

Monday. 30ᵗʰ to Congo da Lemba after passing black rocks
long ascent. Harou giving up. Bother. Camp bad. Water far.
Dirty. At night Harou better.

1st July.
    Tuesday. 1st. Left early in a heavy mist marching towards
Lufu River. – Part route through forest on the sharp slope of
a high mountain. Very long descent. Then, market place,
from where short walk to the bridge (good) and camp. V[ery]
G[ood]. Bath. Clear river. Feel well. Harou all right. 1st chicken.
2p.[m.]
    No sunshine today –

Wednesday 2ᵈ July –
    Started at 5ʰ 30 after a sleepless night. Country more open –
Gently andulating[15] hills. Road good in perfect order. (District
of Lukungu). Great market at 9.30. bought eggs & chickens –
    Feel not well today. Heavy cold in the head. Arrived at 11ʰ
at Banza Manteka. Camped on the market place. Not well
enough to call on the missionary.[16] Water scarce and bad –
Camp[in]ᵍ place dirty. –
    2 Danes still in company.

Thursday 3ᵈ July.
    Left at 6am. after a good night's rest. Crossed a low range of
hills and entered a broad valley or rather plain with a break in
the middle – Met an off[ic]er of the State inspecting. A few
minutes afterwards saw at a camp[in]ᵍ place the dead body of
a Backongo.[17] Shot? Horrid smell. – Crossed a range of mountains running NW-SE. by a low pass. Another broad flat valley
with a deep ravine through the centre. – Clay and gravel.
Another range parallel to the first-mentioned with a chain of
low foothills running close to it. Between the two came to camp
on the banks of the Luinzono River. Camp[in]ᵍ place clean.

River clear. Gov[ernmen]ᵗ Zanzibari[18] with register. Canoe. 2
Danes camp[in]ᵍ on the other bank. – Health good.

General tone of landscape grey yellowish (Dry grass) with
reddish patches (Soil) and clumps of dark green vegetation
scattered sparsely about. Mostly in steep gorges between the
higher mountains or in ravines cutting the plain – Noticed
Palma Christi[19] – Oil palm. Very straight tall and thick trees in
some places. Name not known to me. Villages quite invisible.
Infer their existence from cal[a]bashes[20] suspended to palm trees
for the 'malafu'.[21] –
    Good many caravans and travellers. No women unless on
the market place. –
    Bird notes charming – One especially a flute-like note.
Another kind of 'boom' ressembling[22] the very distant baying
of a hound. – Saw only pigeons and a few green parroquets;
very small and not many. No birds of prey seen by me. Up to
9am – sky clouded and calm – Afterwards gentle breeze from
the N[or]ᵗʰ generally and sky clearing – Nights damp and cool.
– White mists on the hills up about halfway. Water effects, very
beautiful this morning. Mists generally raising before sky clears.

    [Sketch: 'Section of today's road.' Marked on the sketch:
'Banza Manteka, 3 hills and Luinzono River.' Beneath the
sketch: 'Distance 15 miles. General direction NNE-SSW.']

Friday – 4ᵗʰ July. –
    Left camp at 6ʰ am – after a very unpleasant night – Marching
across a chain of hills and then in a maze of hills – At 8.15
opened out into an andulating plain. Took bearings of a break
in the chain of mountains on the other side – Bearing <u>NNE</u> –
Road passes through that. Sharp ascents up very steep hills not
very high. The higher mountains recede sharply and show a
low hilly country –
    At 9.30 Market place.
    At 10ʰ passed R. Lukanga and at 10.30 camped on the
Mpwe R.

[Sketch: 'Today's march.' Beneath title: 'Direction NNE½N
Dist[a]nce 13 miles.' Marked on sketch: 'Luinzono, Camp.']

Saw another dead body lying by the path in an attitude of
meditative repose. – In the evening 3 women of whom one
albino passed our camp – Horrid chalky white with pink
blotches. Red eyes. Red hair. Features very negroid and ugly. –
Mosquitos. At night when the moon rose heard shouts and
drumming in distant villages. Passed a bad night.

Saturday 5th July. [18]90.
    Left at 6.15. Morning cool, even cold and very damp –
Sky densely overcast. Gentle breeze from NE. Road through a
narrow plain up to R. Kwilu. Swift flowing and deep 50 yds
wide – Passed in canoes – After[war]^{ds} up and down very steep
hills intersected by deep ravines – Main chain of heights running
mostly NW-SE or W and E at times. Stopped at Manyamba.
    – Camp[in]^g place bad – in a hollow – Water very indifferent.
Tent set at 10^h 15^m

[Sketch: 'Section of today's road.' Underneath title: NNE
Dist[an]^{ce} 12^m.' Marked on sketch: 'Kwilu River, Camp
Manyamba.']

Today fell into a muddy puddle. Beastly. The fault of the man
that carried me. After camp[in]^g went to a small stream bathed
and washed clothes. – Getting jolly well sick of this fun. –
    Tomorrow expect a long march to get to Nsona. 2 days from
Manyanga. –
    No sunshine to-day. –

Sunday 6th July –
    Started at 5.40. – the route at first hilly then after a sharp descent
traversing a broad plain. At the end of it a large market place
    At 10^h sun came out. –
    After leaving the market passed another plain then walking
on the crest of a chain of hills passed 2 villages and at 11^h
arrived at Nsona. – Village invisible –

[Sketch: 'Section of day's march.' Sketch marked: 'Market, Camp Nsona.' Beneath: 'Direction about NNE Distance – 18 miles.']

In this camp (Nsona –) there is a good camp[in]^g place. Shady. Water far and not very good. – This night no mosquitos owing to large fires lit all round our tent. –
Afternoon very close
Night clear and starry.

Monday-7th July. –
Left at 6^h after a good night's rest on the road to Inkandu which is some distance past Lukungu gov[ernmen]^t station. – Route very accidented.^{23} Succession of round steep hills. At times walking along the crest of a chain of hills. –
Just before Lukunga our carriers took a wide sweep to the southward till the station bore N[or]th. – Walking through long grass for 1½ hours. – Crossed a broad river about 100 feet wide and 4 deep. – After another ½ hours walk through manioc plantations^{24} in good order rejoined our route to the E[astwar]^d of the Lukunga Sta[ti]^{on}. Walking along an undulating plain towards the Inkandu market on a hill. – Hot, thirsty and tired. At 11^h arrived on the m[ar]ketplace – About 200 people. – Brisk business. No water. No camp[in]^g place – After remaining for one hour left in search of a resting place. –
Row with carriers. – No water. At last about 1½ p.m. camped on an exposed hill side near a muddy creek. No shade. Tent on a slope. Sun heavy. Wretched.

[Untitled sketch of day's journey. Marked on sketch: 'Nsona, Lukunga, River bearing N[or]th, Inkandu, Camp.' Underneath: 'Direction NE by N. Distance 22 miles.']

Night miserably cold.
No sleep. Mosquitos –

Tuesday 8th July
Left at 6^h am

About ten minutes from camp left main gov[ernmen]^t path for the Manyanga track. Sky overcast. Road up and down all the time – Passing a couple of villages
The country presents a confused wilderness of hills, land slips on their sides showing red. Fine effect of red hill covered in places by dark green vegetation
½ hour before beginning the descent got a glimpse of the Congo. – Sky clouded.

[Sketch: 'Today's march – 3^h.' Marked on sketch: 'Camp, River, Hill, Congo, Manyanga.' Underneath: NbyE← SbyW General direction NbyE Dist[an]^{ce} 9½ miles.']

Arrived at Manyanga at 9^h a.m.
Received most kindly by Messrs Heyn & Jaeger.[25] –
Most comfortable and pleasant halt. –
Stayed here till the 25.[26] Both have been sick. – Most kindly care taken of us. Leave with sincere regret.

(Mafiela)

Frid^y 25th –	Nkenghe –	left
Sat. 26	Nsona	Nkendo K
Sund. 27	Nkandu	Luasi
Mond 28	Nkonzo	Nzungi (Ngoma)
Tues. 29	Nkenghe	Inkissi
Wedn: 30	Nsona mercredi	Stream
Thurs: 31	Nkandu	Luila
Frid^y 1st Aug	Nkonzo	Nselemba
Sat^y 2^d	Nkenghe	
Sund. 3^d	Nsona	
Mond. 4th	Nkandu	
Tues^d: 5th	Nkonzo.	
Wedn^y 6th	Nkenghe.[27]	

Friday the 5th July 1890. –
Left Manyanga at 2½ p.m – with plenty of hammock carriers.

H[arou] lame and not in very good form. Myself ditto but not lame. Walked as far as Mafiela and camped – 2ʰ

Saturday – 26ᵗʰ
Left very early – Road ascending all the time. – Passed villages. Country seems thickly inhabited. At 11ʰ arrived at large Market place. Left at noon and camped at 1ʰ pm.

[Untitled sketch of day's journey marked: 'Mafiela, Crocodile pond, mount, gov[ernmen]t path, market, a white man died here, camp.' Underneath: 'General direction E½N ← W½S. / Sun visible at 8 am. Very hot / distance – 18 miles.']

Sunday. 27ᵗʰ
Left at 8ʰ am. Sent luggage carriers straight on to Luasi and went ourselves round by the Mission of Sutili.
Hospitable reception by Mrs Comber[28] – all the missio[naries] absent. –
The looks of the whole establishment eminently civilized and very refreshing to see after lots of tumble down hovels in which the state & company agents are content to live. –
Fine buildings. Position on a hill. Rather breezy. –
Left at 3ʰ pm. At the first heavy ascent met Mr Davis[29] Miss[ionary] returning from a preaching trip. Rev. Bentley[30] away in the south with his wife. –
This being off the road no section given – Distance traversed about 15 miles – Gen[eral] Direction ENE. –
At Luasi we get on again on to the gov[ernmen]ᵗ road. –
Camped at 4½ pm. with Mr Heche in company. –
Today no sunshine –
Wind remarkably cold –
Gloomy day. –

Monday. 28ᵗʰ
Left camp at 6.30 after breakfasting with Heche –
Road at first hilly. Then walking along the ridges of hill chains with valleys on both sides. – The country more open and

there is much more trees[31] growing in large clumps in the ravines. –

Passed Nzungi and camped 11ʰ on the right bank of Ngoma. A rapid little river with rocky bed. Village on a hill to the right. –

[Untitled sketch. Marked: 'Camp, Luasi, River, Ridge, Wooded valleys, Nzungi, Ngoma River, Camp.' Underneath: 'General direction ENE / Distance – 14 miles.']

No sunshine. Gloomy cold day. Squalls.

Tuesday – 29ᵗʰ
Left camp at 7ʰ after a good night's rest. Continuous ascent; rather easy at first. – Crossed wooded ravines and the river Lunzadi by a very decent bridge –

At 9ʰ met Mr Louette escorting a sick agent of the Comp[an]ʸ back to Matadi – Looking very well – Bad news from up the river – All the steamers disabled. One wrecked.[32] – Country wooded – At 10.30 camped at Inkissi.

[Untitled sketch. Marked: 'Ngoma, Lunzadi River, Met Mr Louette, Inkissi River, Camp.' Underneath: 'General direction ENE / Dist[an]ce 15 miles.']

Sun visible at 6.30. Very warm day. –

29th
Inkissi River very rapid, is about 100 yards broad – Passage in canoes. – Banks wooded very densely and valley of the river rather deep but very narrow. –

Today did not set the tent but put up in gov[ernmen]ᵗ shimbek.[33]

Zanzibari in charge – Very obliging. – Met ripe pineapple for the first time. –

On the road today passed a skeleton tied-up to a post. Also white man's grave – No name. Heap of stones in the form of a cross.

Health good now –

<u>Wednesday – 30th.</u>
Left at 6 am intending to camp at Kinfumu – Two hours sharp walk brought me to Nsona na Nsefe – Market – ½ hour after Harou arrived very ill with billious [*sic*] attack and fever. – Laid him down in gov[ernmen]ᵗ shimbek – Dose of Ipeca.³⁴ Vomiting bile in enormous quantities. At 11ʰ gave him 1 gramme of quinine and lots of hot tea. Hot fit ending in heavy perspiration. At 9ʰ p.m. put him in hammock and started for Kinfumu – Row with carriers³⁵ all the way. Harou suffering much through the jerks of the hammock. Camped at a small stream. –
At 4ʰ Harou better. Fever gone. –

[Untitled sketch. Marked: 'Sward, A remarkable conical mountain bearing NE visible from here, Wood Lulufu River, Open, Wood, Stream, Nsona a Nsefe, Grass, Camp, Wooded.' Underneath: 'General direction NEbyE½E – / Distance 13 miles –']

Up till noon, sky clouded and strong NW wind very chilling. From 1ʰ pm to 4ʰ pm sky clear and very hot day. Expect lots of battles with carriers to-morrow – Had them all called and made a speech which they did not understand.³⁶ They promise good behaviour

<u>Thursday – 31st</u>
Left at 6ʰ – Sent Harou ahead and followed in ½ an hour. – Road presents several sharp ascents and a few others easier but rather long. Notice in places sandy surface soil instead of hard clay as heretofore; think however that the layer of sand is not very thick and that the clay would be found under it. Great difficulty in carrying Harou. – Too heavy. Bother! Made two long halts to rest the carriers. Country wooded in valleys and on many of the ridges.

[Sketch: 'Section of to-day's road.' Sketch marked: 'Camp, Nkenghe, Kinfumu River, Congo, Kinzilu River, Luila River, and NE½E.']

At 2.30 pm reached Luila at last and camped on right bank.
– Breeze from SW
General direction of march about NE½E
Distance e[a]st[war]$\underline{^d}$ – 16 miles
Congo very narrow and rapid. Kinzilu rushing in. A short
distance up from the mouth fine waterfall. –
– Sun rose red – From 9^h a.m. infernally hot day. –
Harou very little better.
Self rather seedy. Bathed.
Luila about 60 feet wide. Shallow

Friday – 1st of August 1890
Left at 6.30 am after a very indifferently passed night – Cold,
Heavy mists – Road in long ascents and sharp dips all the way
to Mfumu Mbé –
After leaving there a long and painful climb up a very steep hill;
then a long descent to Mfumu Koko where a long halt was made.
Left at 12.30pm – towards Nselemba. Many ascents – The
aspect of the country entirely changed – Wooded hills with
openings. – Path almost all the afternoon thro[ugh] a forest of
light trees with dense undergrowth. –
After a halt on a wooded hillside reached Nselemba at 4^h
10^m pm.

[Untitled sketch of day's march. Marked: 'Camp, Mfumu
Mbe, Koko, Stream, Stream, Mostly Wooded, Stream,
Nselemba, and Camp.']

Put up at gov[ernmen]^t shanty. –
Row between the carriers and a man stating himself in
gov[ernmen]^t employ, about a mat. – Blows with sticks raining
hard – Stopped it. Chief came with a youth about 13 suffering
from gunshot wound in the head. Bullet entered about an inch
above the right eyebrow and came out a little inside the roots
of the hair, fairly in the middle of the brow in a line with the
bridge of the nose – Bone not damaged apparently. Gave him
a little glycerine to put on the wound made by the bullet on
coming out.

Harou not very well. Mosquitos – Frogs – Beastly. Glad to see the end of this stupid tramp. Feel rather seedy.

Sun rose red – Very hot day – Wind S[ou]^th.

General direction of march – NEbyN

Distance about 17 miles

Appendix:
Author's Note

The three stories in this volume[1] lay no claim to unity of artistic purpose.[2] The only bond between them is that of the time in which they were written. They belong to the period immediately following the publication of the *Nigger of the 'Narcissus,'* and preceding the first conception of *Nostromo,*[3] two books which, it seems to me, stand apart and by themselves in the body of my work. It is also the period during which I contributed to 'Maga;'[4] a period dominated by *Lord Jim* and associated in my grateful memory with the late Mr William Blackwood's[5] encouraging and helpful kindness.

'Youth' was not my first contribution[6] to 'Maga.' It was the second. But that story marks the first appearance in the world of the man Marlow, with whom my relations have grown very intimate in the course of years.[7] The origins of that gentleman (nobody so far as I know has ever hinted that he was anything but that) – his origins have been the subject of some literary speculation of, I am glad to say, a friendly nature.

One would think that I am the proper person to throw a light on the matter; but in truth I find that it isn't so easy. It is pleasant to remember that nobody has charged him with fraudulent purposes or looked down on him as a charlatan; but apart from that he was supposed to be all sorts of things: a clever screen, a mere device, 'a personator,' a familiar spirit, a whispering 'daemon.'[8] I myself have been suspected of a mediated plan for his capture.

That is not so. I made no plans. The man Marlow and I came together in a casual manner of those health-resort acquaintances which sometimes ripen into friendships. This one has ripened. For all his assertiveness in matters of opinion he is not an intrusive person. He haunts my hours of solitude, when, in silence, we lay our heads together in great comfort and harmony; but as we part at the end of a tale I am never sure that it may not be for the last time. Yet I don't think that either of us would care much to survive the other. In his case, at any rate, his occupation would be gone[9] and he would suffer from that extinction, because I suspect him of some vanity in the Solomonian sense.[10] Of all my people he's the one that has never been a vexation to my spirit. A most discreet, understanding man. . . .

Even before appearing in book-form 'Youth' was very well received.[11] It lies on me to confess at last, and this is as good a place for it as another, that I have been all my life – all my two lives[12] – the spoiled adopted child of Great Britain and even of the Empire; for it was Australia that gave me my first command.[13] I break out into this declaration not because of a lurking tendency towards megalomania, but, on the contrary, as a man who has no very notable illusions about himself. I follow the instincts of vain-glory and humility natural to all mankind. For it can hardly be denied that it is not their own deserts that men are most proud of, but rather of their prodigious luck, of their marvellous fortune: of that in their lives for which thanks and sacrifices must be offered on the altars of the inscrutable gods.

'Heart of Darkness' also received a certain amount of notice from the first; and of its origins this much may be said: it is well known that curious men go prying into all sorts of places (where they have no business) and come out of them with all kinds of spoil. This story, and one other,[14] not in this volume, are all the spoil I brought out from the centre of Africa, where, really, I had no sort of business. More ambitious in its scope and longer in the telling, 'Heart of Darkness' is quite as authentic in fundamentals as 'Youth.' It is, obviously, written in another mood. I won't characterize the mood precisely, but anybody can see that it is anything but the mood of wistful regret, of reminiscent tenderness.

One more remark may be added. 'Youth' is a feat of memory. It is a record of experience; but that experience, in its facts, in its inwardness and in its outward colouring, begins and ends in myself. 'Heart of Darkness' is experience, too; but it is experience pushed a little (and only a very little) beyond the actual facts of the case for the perfectly legitimate, I believe, purpose of bringing it home to the minds and bosoms of the readers. There it was no longer a matter of sincere colouring. It was like another art altogether. That sombre theme had to be given a sinister resonance, a tonality of its own, a continued vibration that, I hoped, would hang in the air and dwell on the ear after the last note had been struck.

After saying so much there remains the last tale of the book, still untouched. 'The End of the Tether' is a story of sea-life in a rather special way; and the most intimate thing I can say of it is this; that having lived that life fully, amongst its men, its thoughts and sensations, I have found it possible, without the slightest misgiving, in all sincerity of heart and peace of conscience, to conceive the existence of Captain Whalley's personality and to relate the manner of his end. This statement acquires some force from the circumstance that the pages of that story – a fair half of the book – are also the product of experience. That experience belongs (like 'Youth''s) to the time before I ever thought of putting pen to paper.[15] As to its 'reality,' that is for the readers to determine. One had to pick up one's facts here and there. More skill would have made them more real and the whole composition more interesting. But here we are approaching the veiled region of artistic values which it would be improper and indeed dangerous for me to enter. I have looked over the proofs, have corrected a misprint or two, have changed a word or two – and that's all. It is not very likely that I shall ever read 'The End of the Tether' again. No more need be said. It accords best with my feelings to part from Captain Whalley in affectionate silence.

1917
J.C.

NOTES

1.   *volume*: *Heart of Darkness* was collected, with 'Youth' and 'The End of the Tether', in *Youth: A Narrative and Two Other Stories* (Edinburgh and London: William Blackwood & Sons, 1902).

2.   *unity of artistic purpose*: Conrad later revised his view that the volume had 'no claim to unity', writing to his American publisher F. N. Doubleday in February 1924: 'Or take the volume of *Youth*, which in its component parts presents the three ages of man (for that is what it really is, and I knew very well what I was doing when I wrote "The End of the Tether" to be the last of that trio). I can't somehow imagine any of those stories taken out of it and bound cheek and jowl with a story from another volume. It is in fact unthinkable' (*Joseph Conrad: Life and Letters*, ed. G. Jean-Aubry (London: Heinemann, 1927), vol. II, pp. 338–9).

3.   *They belong to the period . . . Nostromo*: That is, roughly from December 1897 to December 1902.

4.   *'Maga'*: A familiar abbreviation for *Blackwood's Magazine*, a Tory monthly founded in 1817. It published much of Conrad's fiction during the period 1898–1902.

5. *Blackwood's*: William Blackwood (1836–1912), grandson of the original publisher, headed the firm from 1879 until his death.

6. *first contribution*: The first contribution was 'Karain: A Memory', published in the November 1897 issue of *Blackwood's Magazine* and collected in *Tales of Unrest* (1898).

7. *Marlow*: In addition to his appearances in 'Youth' and *Heart of Darkness*, Marlow figures in *Lord Jim* (1900) and *Chance* (1913).

8. *daemon*: An inner or attendant spirit, often associated with the genius of creativity.

9. *his occupation would be gone*: Cf. 'Farewell! Othello's occupation's gone!', Shakespeare, *Othello*, III.iii.358.

10. *Solomonian sense*: The wise Solomon delivered many aphorisms on the vanity of human wishes (see Proverbs 1–29), although none describing vanity as a 'vexation' of the spirit. For this description, Conrad seems rather to echo Ecclesiastes 1:14: 'I have seen all the works that are done under the sun; and, behold, all *is* vanity and vexation of spirit.'

11. *well received*: Some three years before the publication of 'Youth' in book form, the critic and man of letters A. T. Quiller-Couch and the novelist Arnold Bennett, who had read the story in *Blackwood's Magazine*, praised it in print.

12. *my two lives*: That is, as a merchant seaman until 1894 and subsequently as a writer.

13. *my first command*: Conrad's only permanent command was of the Australian-owned barque, the *Otago*. He joined the ship in Bangkok on 24 January 1888, and arrived in Sydney on 7 May. This protracted voyage to Australia provides the basis for *The Shadow-Line*, while a later voyage in the *Otago*, from Australia to Mauritius, lies behind 'The Smile of Fortune'. Conrad resigned his command at the end of March 1889.

14. *one other*: 'An Outpost of Progress', written in 1896 and collected in *Tales of Unrest* (1898).

15. *the pages of that story … pen to paper*: If Conrad did indeed submit a short story, 'The Black Mate', to a *Tit-Bits* competition in 1886 (see Chronology), then this statement is not strictly true. Some of his South-East Asian experience that finds its way into 'The End of the Tether' belongs to the period immediately following 1886.

Notes

Topics adequately covered in a standard desk dictionary are not glossed here. The accompanying map identifies geographical places; where contextual or historical information might be useful it is added here. The Glossary deals with nautical terms. The Riverside Shakespeare (2nd edition, 1997) is used for quotations from Shakespeare's plays and biblical quotations are from the King James Bible.

Conrad drew on, and borrowed from, a large number of sources; the notes indicate the most important of these and do not attempt to catalogue all the source materials that he might have used.

All references to Conrad's works are to *Dent's Collected Edition of the Works of Joseph Conrad*, 22 vols. (London: J. M. Dent & Sons, 1946–55).

The notes are numbered for each part; cross-references, unless otherwise indicated, are to the same part.

Abbreviations

Glave	E. J. Glave, *In Savage Africa, Or Six Years of Adventure in Congo-Land* (New York: Russell, 1892).
Hochschild	Adam Hochschild, *King Leopold's Ghost: A Study of Greed, Terror, and Heroism in Colonial Africa* (London: Macmillan, 1999).
Kimbrough	*Joseph Conrad: 'Heart of Darkness'*, ed. Robert Kimbrough, Norton Critical Edition, 3rd edn (New York: Norton, 1988).
Letters	*The Collected Letters of Joseph Conrad*, ed. Frederick R. Karl and Laurence Davies, with Owen Knowles (vol. VI), J. H. Stape (vol. VII) and Gene M. Moore (vol. VIII), 8 vols. (Cambridge: Cambridge University Press, 1983–).
Sherry	Norman Sherry, *Conrad's Western World* (Cambridge: Cambridge University Press, 1971).

Stanley   Henry Morton Stanley, *The Congo and the Founding of Its Free State: A Story of Work and Exploration*, 2 vols. (London: Sampson Low, 1885).

Watts 1977   Cedric Watts, *Conrad's 'Heart of Darkness': A Critical and Contextual Discussion* (Milan: Mursia International, 1977).

Watts 1995   *'The Heart of Darkness'*, ed. Cedric Watts, Everyman Edition (London: J. M. Dent & Sons, 1995).

Watts 2002   *'Heart of Darkness' and Other Tales*, ed. Cedric Watts, Oxford World's Classics, 2nd edn (Oxford: Oxford University Press, 2002).

HEART OF DARKNESS

PART I

1. *Nellie*: The name of a small yacht owned by Conrad's friend George Fountaine Weare Hope (né Hopps, 1854–1930), an ex-seaman and company director, with whom Conrad made several excursions along the Thames estuary. Hope owned the *Nellie* from 1889 to 1892 (*Lloyd's Register*, 1889–93), and, given Conrad's absences from England, these outings took place in 1891.

2. *Gravesend*: A town and port on the south bank of the Thames opposite Tilbury Docks, approximately 20 miles (32 kilometres) east of London.

3. *We four*: Here and at the opening of 'Youth' Conrad recalls convivial excursions on the Thames in 1891 with his friends Hope (see note 1), Edward Gardner Mears (1857–1936), a meat salesman, and William Brock Keen (1861–1941), an accountant. Aside from Keen, all were ex-seamen and at different times in the 1870s had sailed in the *Duke of Sutherland*.

4. *said somewhere*: In the second paragraph of 'Youth': 'We all began life in the merchant service. Between the five of us there was the strong bond of the sea, and also the fellowship of the craft, which no amount of enthusiasm for yachting, cruising and so on can give, since one is only the amusement of life and the other is life itself.'

5. *bones*: A familiar term for dominoes, at the time often made of white ivory with black spots.

6. *an idol*: Conrad devises for Marlow a partly ironic variation of

one of the traditional poses of the Buddha, the 'Enlightened One' and founder of Buddhism: depicted sitting on a lotus, in a cross-legged position of meditation. The most sacred symbol in Buddhism, the lotus flower, variously signifies emergence into light from darkness, paradisiacal beauty, purity and spiritual grace.

7. *And at last . . . over a crowd of men*: This description of the sun's cooling and demise echoes the late-Victorian fascination with the spectacle of solar death and the wider prospect of *fin du globe* apocalypse. In the mid-nineteenth century, Lord Kelvin 'defined the thermodynamic principle of the dissipation of "available" energy; and the popularisation of this principle had disseminated the idea that the sun, like a Victorian coal-fire in the sky, was steadily burning itself out' (Watts 1977, p. 14).

8. *Sir Francis Drake*: The famous admiral (1540?–96) is cited here as the first Englishman to circumnavigate the world in the *Pelican* (later renamed the *Golden Hind*) and as founder of the British naval tradition. Departing from Plymouth in 1577, he returned in 1580, and in the following year was knighted by Elizabeth I on the deck of his ship at Deptford.

9. *Sir John Franklin*: The British naval explorer John Franklin (1786–1847; knighted 1825) took part in expeditions to Australia, the Arctic and northern Canada. In 1845, he left Greenhithe on an ill-fated voyage to look for the North-west Passage, he and his men all perishing in the Arctic wastes. The expedition had virtually found the Passage, but its ships – the *Erebus* and *Terror* – trapped in ice, were only discovered in 1859. In 1854, allegations that the last survivors had resorted to cannibalism created a public controversy, prompted Sir Leopold McClintock's return to the scene of the disaster and inspired his *Voyage of the 'Fox' in the Arctic Seas* (1859), a volume Conrad read as a boy (see note 23).

10. *Deptford . . . Erith*: Historical ports on the River Thames in London's eastern suburbs. The docks at Deptford were established by King Henry VIII, while Greenwich was also the site of a royal palace.

11. *men on 'Change*: Merchants, bankers and investors who transacted their business at such institutions as the Royal Exchange and the Stock Exchange.

12. *the dark 'interlopers' . . . East India fleets*: 'Interlopers' were traders who, engaged in smuggling, habitually trespassed on

the monopoly rights and royal charters held by large trading companies such as the East India Company; the commissioned 'generals' of the East India Company were the commanders of its fleet.

13.   *The Chapman lighthouse*: Built in 1849 on a mudflat off Canvey Island in the River Thames, west of Southend.

14.   *dark places of the earth*: Cf. 'Have respect unto the covenant: for the dark places of the earth are full of the habitations of cruelty' (Psalm 74:20). This biblical allusion has a long history in nineteenth-century abolitionist discourse in England and the United States and in religio-colonialist writing in general, as, for example, in the Reverend A. W. Pitzer's plea to his fellow Americans: 'The supreme duty of this nation is to realize her sublime providential mission, and bear the blessed light of the Gospel to all the dark places of the earth, to the habitations of men now filled with cruelty' (*Missionary Review*, November 1890, pp. 825–6). On the connection between late-Victorian England and Africa as 'dark places', see William Booth's provocative question, 'As there is a darkest Africa is there not also a darkest England?' (*In Darkest England and the Way Out*, London: Salvation Army, 1890, p. 11).

15.   *when the Romans first came here*: Comparisons between the Roman *imperium* and the British Empire were commonplace in late-Victorian debates about imperial policy. Conrad's close friend R. B. Cunninghame Graham, who repeatedly used such comparisons for ironic effect, denounced British imperialism in 'Bloody Niggers', scathingly: 'Material and bourgeois Rome, wolf-suckled ... filling the office in the old world that now is occupied so worthily by God's own Englishmen' (*The Social-Democrat: A Monthly Socialist Review* 1 (1897), p. 107).

16.   *the Gauls*: Inhabitants of ancient Gaul, a region of Europe corresponding to modern France, Belgium, the southern Netherlands, south-west Germany and northern Italy. Julius Caesar's forces completed the conquest of this region during the period 58–51 BC.

17.   *what we read*: Julius Caesar's *De bello gallico* claims that 628 ships were built in one winter by Romans preparing to invade Britain (Watts 2002, p. 203).

18.   *Imagine ... river*: Conrad's vision does not quite tally with historical facts, since 'the first Roman invaders, from Julius Caesar in 55 BC to Aulus Plautius in AD 43, did not enter what is now England through the Thames estuary, but landed on the shore of Kent' (Zdzisław Najder, ed., *The Mirror of the Sea and*

       A *Personal Record* (Oxford: Oxford University Press, 1988), p. 145).

19. *Falernian wine*: A famous ancient wine from the Falernus Ager district, inland from present-day Naples, mentioned reverentially by nearly every poet from Catullus to Propertius.

20. *Ravenna*: A city in north-east Italy, in AD 401 established as the capital of the Western Roman Empire; its port, Classis, was the largest Roman naval base on the Adriatic.

21. *prefect*: A senior Roman magistrate or military commander.

22. *green . . . white flames*: The 'flames' are the reflections of the ship's three differently coloured lights: a green light on the starboard (or right-hand side), a red one on the port (left) side and a white one on or in front of the foremast.

23. *a passion for maps*: In the account of his boyhood reading in 'Geography and Some Explorers', Conrad records how his attraction for Sir Leopold McClintock's *Voyage of the 'Fox' in the Arctic Seas* (1859) produced in him 'the taste for poring over maps' and a fascination with the 'exciting spaces of white paper' on maps of Africa (*Last Essays*, p. 17). Elsewhere, he observes: 'It was in 1868, when nine years old or thereabouts, that while looking at a map of Africa of the time and putting my finger on the blank space then representing the unsolved mystery of that continent, I said to myself with absolute assurance and an amazing audacity which are no longer in my character now: "When I grow up I shall go *there*"' (*A Personal Record*, p. 13). Boyhood fascination with the map of Africa is a common motif in travellers' accounts of the period.

24. *a Company*: One of several interlinked companies founded by Albert Thys (see note 30), the Société Anonyme Belge pour le Commerce du Haut-Congo (the Belgian Limited Company for Trade in the Upper Congo) was established in late 1888 to exploit the Congo's natural resources.

25. *Fresleven*: Johannes Freiesleben (1861?–90), a Danish ship captain in command of the *Floride*, was killed by tribesmen on 29 January 1890 at Tchumbiri. His remains were discovered almost two months later by a punitive expedition led by a Captain Duhst who found 'grass growing through the bones of the skeleton which lay where it had fallen' (Otto Lütken, 'Joseph Conrad in the Congo', *London Mercury*, 22 May 1930, p. 43). When Conrad's African posting was confirmed in late April 1890, he understood that he would be taking the deceased Freiesleben's place (Sherry, pp. 15–22, 375).

26. *show . . . employers*: In November 1889 and February 1890,
    Conrad was interviewed at the Société Anonyme du Haut-
    Congo's headquarters in Brussels with a view to a captaincy in
    one of the company's ships on the River Congo. He received
    confirmation of his appointment in April 1890 and left for Africa
    in May.

27. *city . . . whited sepulchre*: This description of (unnamed) Brussels
    echoes: 'Woe unto you, scribes and Pharisees, hypocrites! for ye
    are like unto whited sepulchres, which indeed appear beautiful
    outward, but are within full of dead *men's* bones, and of all
    uncleanness', Matthew 23:27. A cancelled typescript passage
    elaborates on Brussels: 'Its quiet streets empty decorum of its
    boulevards, all those big houses so intensely respectable to look
    at and so extremely tight closed suggest the reserve of discreet
    turpitudes.'

28. *Two women . . . black wool*: Resembling the Fates of Greek
    legend, Clotho and Lachesis, who, respectively, spin and measure
    out the thread of each life before Atropos cuts it. In Virgil's
    Aeneid (Book VI), the wise Cumaean Sibyl guards the door to
    the Underworld into which Aeneas will venture.

29. *a large shining map . . . all the colours of a rainbow*: An allusion
    to the colour-coding of territories on nineteenth-century world
    maps: British (red), French (blue), Portuguese (orange), Italian
    (green), German (purple) and Belgian (yellow). Marlow's journey
    into the 'yellow' takes him to the Congo Free State, officially
    created in 1885. The Berlin Conference of 1884–5 brought to-
    gether the European powers along with the United States to
    consider rival claims to some 2,400,000 square miles of African
    territory, including a plan to internationalize the Congo region
    under the African Association of Leopold II, King of the Belgians.
    The Conference recognized the Congo Free State as Leopold's
    personal property and confirmed him as its sovereign in return
    for guarantees of neutrality, free trade and opposition to slavery.
    Under the pretence of bringing Christian philanthropy and pro-
    gress, Leopold's rule inaugurated 'the vilest scramble for loot that
    ever disfigured the history of human conscience and geographical
    exploration' (Conrad, *Last Essays*, p. 17). In 1908, the Belgian
    state annexed the Congo region with the express purpose of
    righting the wrongs perpetrated by a regime that had brought
    Leopold an estimated fortune of $20 million.

30. *The great man himself*: This figure was probably prompted by
    Conrad's memories of his interviews in Brussels with General

Staff Major Albert Thys (1849–1915), aide-de-camp to Leopold II and managing director of the Société Anonyme du Haut-Congo. The 'great man' also spent several months in the Congo between 1887 and 1893 overseeing the development of the railway from Matadi to Kinchasa.

31. *Ave!* . . . *Morituri te salutant*: 'Hail [Caesar]! . . . Those who are about to die salute you', a traditional salutation to the Roman emperor by gladiators entering the arena.

32. *quoth* . . . *disciples*: A facetious attempt at banter rather than an authentic quotation.

33. *measure the crania*: An extension of the nineteenth-century interest in phrenology, the popular, if also controversial, pseudo-science of craniology involved measuring the shape and size of the human skull as indicators of brain capacity, in order to classify individuals according to racial type, intelligence and capacity for moral behaviour. Through his uncle, in 1881 Conrad received a request from Dr Izydor Kopernicki, a leading Polish anthropologist, to assist his studies by collecting native peoples' skulls during his travels, 'writing on each one whose skull it is and the place of origin', and sending them to the Museum of Craniology in Cracow (*Conrad's Polish Background: Letters to and from Polish Friends*, ed. Zdzisław Najder (London: Oxford University Press, 1964), p. 74).

34. *Famous*: A Gallicism, from *fameux*, 'first-rate' or 'splendid'.

35. *alienist*: The late-nineteenth-century term for a psychiatrist or mental pathologist.

36. *I was also one of the Workers, with a capital*: Thomas Carlyle (1795–1881), historian and political philosopher, venerated the gospel of work and 'Workers, with a capital [letter]'. Cf. *Past and Present* (1843): 'But it is to you, ye Workers . . . that the whole world calls for a new work and nobleness. Subdue mutiny, discord, wide-spread despair, by manfulness, justice, mercy and wisdom. . . . It is work for a God. Sooty Hell of mutiny and savagery and despair can, by man's energy, be made a kind of Heaven' (Book 4, chapter 8). This passage was also used by H. M. Stanley in 1898 in his defence of Leopold II as God's instrument in redeeming the Congo from its condition as a 'vast slave park' (quoted in Kimbrough, p. 79).

37. *such rot*: The populist rhetoric later attributed to Marlow's aunt most closely resembles H. M. Stanley's, who, echoing Luke 10:7, had written that in advanced nations 'every honest labourer is worthy of his hire' and that 'our principal aim is to open the

interior [of the Congo] by weaning the tribes below and above
from that savage and suspicious state which they are now in'
(Stanley, vol. I, pp. xiv, 30). Leopold II's widely reported speech
on 'The Sacred Mission of Civilization' was an example of such
propaganda (rpt. in Kimbrough, pp. 127–30).

38. *Gran' Bassam, Little Popo*: Grand Bassam is in the Ivory Coast
and Grand Popo in Dahomey (present-day Benin). Little Popo
(present-day Anecho) is in Togo, formerly Togoland. When
Conrad made his voyage to Africa in May 1890 in the French
steamer *Ville de Maceio*, the vessel called at these ports.

39. *It appears the French . . . wars*: Conrad observed: 'If I say that
the ship which bombarded the coast was French, it is quite simply
because *it was* a French ship. I recall its name – the *Seignelay*. It
was during the war (!) with Dahomey' (16 December 1903,
Letters, vol. II, p. 94). The vessel mentioned by Conrad does not
figure in numerous reports of the blockade in *The Times*,
although the French navy then included a cruiser named *Seignelay*, built in 1874 and wrecked in 1892 (www.battleships-
cruisers.co.uk). On 4 April 1890, the French began a blockade
'with a view to prevent the importation of arms and munition of
war into the Kingdom of Dahomey' (*The Times*, 12 April 1890,
p. 12), which resulted in Dahomey's becoming a French protec-
torate.

40. *the seat of the government*: Corresponding to Boma, 50 miles
(80 kilometres) upriver from the Congo estuary and then the
Congo Free State's capital. Conrad stayed there for a night on
arriving in Africa. In revising the typescript, Conrad deleted
a manuscript passage describing Boma's hotel, tramway and
government offices.

41. *Company's station*: Corresponding to the station at Matadi,
about 30 miles (48 kilometres) upstream from Boma and the
Lower Congo's terminal point of navigation.

42. *They were building a railway*: H. M. Stanley had argued that the
economic success of the Congo Free State depended on building
a 270-mile (432-kilometre) railway between Matadi and Kinchasa in order to bypass river cataracts. In 1887, Albert Thys
(see note 30) surveyed the route for the railway, and in that year
a charter for construction was granted to Thys's newly formed
Compagnie du Congo pour le Commerce et l'Industrie. Further
negotiations resulted in the creation of the Compagnie du
Chemin de fer du Congo in July 1889, with the first rails and
sleepers being shipped in the *Ville de Maceio* (see note 38).

During this same year, a decree by Leopold II allowed the railway company to establish a militia to press-gang workers from the surrounding area. Due to be completed in 1894, the railway was delayed by engineering difficulties, labour shortages and the high mortality rate of its workers. It was not finished until 1898.

43. *the gloomy circle of some Inferno*: A likely allusion to the topography of hell in *The Divine Comedy* by the Italian poet Dante Alighieri (1265–1321), whose work depicts the several circles of eternal damnation, where souls suffer punishments appropriate to their sins.

44. *Brought from all the recesses of the coast . . . of time contracts*: In 'A Report upon the Congo-State and Country to the President of the Republic of the United States of America' (1890), George Washington Williams explains that the majority of African employees in the Congo were recruited from the coastal regions and placed under contract: 'The soldiers serve three years, the workmen one year' (quoted in Kimbrough, p. 95).

45. *clear silk necktie*: Conrad's usage is probably influenced by the Polish *jasny* or French *clair*, both translated into English as 'clear' but connoting 'brightness' or 'lightness' of colour as English does not. Here, the manuscript version is preferred to 'a clear necktie' (first English edition) and 'a clean necktie' (a 'correction' in some later editions).

46. *Caravans*: Groups of travelling traders with their pack-animals.

47. *a stream of manufactured goods . . . brass wire*: Forms of currency used to pay the African workers. J. Rose Troup explains:

> The mitako, or brass rod, is the currency amongst the natives at Leopoldville and most of the regions of the Upper Congo. It is in general imported to the Congo by the State in large rolls or coils of 60 lbs. in weight. After its arrival at Leopoldville it is cut up into the regulation lengths (about 2 feet) . . . The value of each of these pieces . . . is reckoned at 1½d.
> (*With Stanley's Rear Column* (London: Chapman & Hall, 1890), pp. 103–4)

48. *a truckle-bed*: A low bed on wheels that can be stored under a larger bed.

49. *Mr Kurtz*: In the manuscript, Conrad's first four named allusions were to a 'Mr Klein', then cancelled and replaced by 'Mr Kurtz'. The original name was that of a French company agent, Georges-Antoine Klein (1863–90), who accompanied Conrad on his voy-

age downstream from Stanley Falls in the *Roi des Belges* in September 1890. He died on the journey and was buried at Tchumbiri. *Klein*, German for 'small', has an obvious link with the German *kurz* ('short').

50. *ivory-country*: The high value and low bulk of ivory made it especially attractive to European traders in the Congo. In 1886, H. M. Stanley reported: 'It may be presumed that there are about 200,000 elephants in about 15,000 herds in the Congo basin, each carrying, let us say, on an average 50 lbs. weight of ivory in his head, which would represent, when collected and sold in Europe, £5,000,000' (Stanley, vol. II, p. 354).

51. *lamentable*: A Gallicism nearer to the French meaning of the word, 'pitiful'.

52. *Central Station*: Corresponding to the station at Kinchasa, where, at the time of Conrad's stay, Camille Delcommune (see note 57) was the company's acting manager.

53. *two-hundred-mile tramp*: Marlow's trek to the Central Station corresponds geographically to Conrad's thirty-six-day overland journey with a caravan of thirty-one men from Matadi to Kinchasa between late June and early August 1890. Like Marlow, he was accompanied by a European companion (Prosper Harou), who fell ill and had to be carried by hammock.

54. *Deal*: An English port and a popular resort on the Kent coast.

55. *Zanzibaris*: In the late nineteenth century, European expeditions in Africa regularly used natives from this East African island as porters, mercenaries and policemen.

56. *I fancy I see it now*: This cryptic piece of information about the wrecked ship may form part of a probable 'covert plot' that has involved The Manager of the Central Station in arranging for the wreck to occur in order to delay the relief of the Inner Station until Kurtz, his main rival for promotion, has become mortally ill. After the steamer has been wrecked, The Manager obstructs the repairs for three months by intercepting Marlow's request for rivets. See Cedric Watts, *The Deceptive Text: An Introduction to Covert Plots* (Brighton: Harvester Press, 1984), pp. 119–20.

57. *common trader*: Marlow's animus here echoes Conrad's intense dislike of Camille Delcommune: 'The manager is a common ivory dealer with base instincts who considers himself a merchant although he is only a kind of African shop-keeper' (to Marguerite Poradowska, 26 September 1890, *Letters*, vol. I, p. 62).

58. *Jack ashore*: 'Jack tar' is a colloquial term for a sailor. The reference is to boisterous behaviour like that of a sailor on shore leave.

59. *assegais*: Slender iron-tipped spears, usually made of wood from the assegai tree.

60. *straw maybe*: The common adage 'to make bricks without straw' (that is, to be set an impossible task) originates from the form of punishment decreed by Pharaoh for the Israelites: 'Ye shall no more give the people straw to make brick, as heretofore: let them go and gather straw for themselves', Exodus 5:7.

61. *An act of special creation*: A sarcastic allusion to those who, in the vigorous nineteenth-century debate about evolution, upheld the biblical account of God as the creator of all living things, with species of an obviously later date, according to geological evidence, requiring special divine intervention.

62. *backbiting*: Cf. 'The Congo Diary': 'Prominent characteristic of the social life here: People speaking ill of each other' (99).

63. *one man to steal a horse . . . look at a halter*: A wittily sarcastic variation of the old adage 'One man may steal a horse, while another may not look over a hedge' – that is, one person may get away with any crime, while others are liable to punishment for trivialities.

64. *Then I noticed a small sketch . . . carrying a lighted torch*: Astraea, Roman goddess of justice, is often depicted as blindfolded (signifying her impartiality) and Liberty as holding a lighted torch. The images in Kurtz's painting are, however, rendered ambiguous by their links with more menacing colonial torch-bearers in the story. (A cancelled manuscript passage had also envisioned Kurtz as a 'man possessed of moral ideals holding a torch in the heart of darkness'.)

65. *muffs*: Bunglers, incompetents (slang).

66. *Mephistopheles*: The demonic tempter of Christopher Marlowe's *The Tragical History of Doctor Faustus* (probably first performed in 1588) and of Johann Wolfgang von Goethe's *Faust* (1808 and 1832).

67. *Huntley & Palmers biscuit-tin*: This famous biscuit-making firm at Reading advertised itself as being at the vanguard of imperial expansion. Their biscuits accompanied Captain Scott to the Antarctic and H. M. Stanley to Africa. Pointing out that some of their tins proclaimed that they were sold 'By Appointment to the King of the Belgians', Valentine Cunningham notes that the Reading Municipal Museum 'holds a photograph taken by a Reverend R. D. Darby of a Conrad-style Belgian trading steamer on the Upper Congo river. A large Huntley & Palmers tin is clearly visible on the roof of the vessel. The photograph is captioned "Huntley

& Palmers Biscuits foremost again"'' (*In the Reading Gaol: Post-modernity, Texts, and History*, Oxford: Blackwell, 1994, p. 253).

68. *ichthyosaurus*: An extinct marine reptile, resembling a dolphin, with streamlined body, toothed jaw, four flippers and a tail fin.

69. *Eldorado Exploring Expedition*: The Katanga Expedition led by Alexandre Delcommune, older brother of Camille, arrived at Kinchasa in three instalments on 20 and 23 September and 5 October 1890. See Conrad's essay 'Geography and Some Explorers', for comments on 'pertinaceous searchers for El Dorado' – that is, for the imaginary country (Spanish *el dorado* = 'the gilded [place]') supposed to abound in gold sought by the Spaniards in South America (*Last Essays*, p. 5).

70. *confab*: A shortened, colloquial form of 'confabulation', a chat or conversation.

PART II

1. *Make rain and fine weather*: This cryptic allusion seems to link Kurtz's extraordinary influence to the legendary power of ancient kings who were held by their followers to be man-gods, with supernatural powers to make rain and control the sun. Later, the Jupiter-like Kurtz is described by The Harlequin as having approached neighbouring African tribes 'with thunder and light-ning . . . and they had never seen anything like it—and very terrible' (70). James Frazer's chapter on 'The Magical Control of the Weather' in *The Golden Bough* (1890–1915) gives numerous examples of such beliefs among African tribes.

2. *'get him hanged! . . .'*: The intended victim of The Manager's threat seems to be The Harlequin, since Marlow later tells him: 'The manager thinks you ought to be hanged' (78). The reason for The Manager's animus becomes clear when it is revealed that The Harlequin is connected with a rival Dutch trading company and has been competing for ivory. The issue of punitive hanging in the Congo was a repeated item in the British press of the late 1890s, when relations between the British government and the Congo Free State were strained by the summary hanging in 1895 of Charles Henry Stokes, an Irish missionary turned trader, on the charge that he had supplied ammunition to the Arabs. The Congo government admitted that the execution was illegal and paid compensation, but the Belgian officer responsible, Captain Hubert Lothaire, was not punished.

3. *'I did my possible'*: This Gallicism from *J'ai fait mon possible*

and the neighbouring 'Conceive you—that ass!' indicate that the conversation takes place in French.

4. *I watched for sunken stones*: At the corresponding point of his own journey from Kinchasa to Stanley Falls in the *Roi des Belges*, Conrad began to make navigational notes and rough sketch-maps in a notebook labelled his 'Up-river book' in preparation for a time when he might take command of a company boat.

5. *twenty cannibals*: Probably members of the Bangala tribe who worked in Upper Congo steamers (Sherry, pp. 59–60).

6. *I had the manager* . . . *pilgrims*: On his journey upriver from Kinchasa to Stanley Falls in the *Roi des Belges*, Conrad was accompanied by six Europeans: Camille Delcommune, Captain Ludwig Rasmus Koch, three agents – Alphonse Keyaerts, E. F. L. Rollin and Van der Heyden – and a mechanic named Gossens (Sherry, p. 56). Conrad recalls Keyaerts by name in 'An Outpost of Progress' as Kayerts.

7. *The mind . . . anything*: Cf. the conclusion of Guy de Maupassant's short story 'La Chevelure' (1884): '*L'esprit de l'homme est capable de tout*' ('The mind of man is capable of everything').

8. *Principles won't do . . . pretty rags*: A similar sentiment is expressed in Thomas Carlyle's *Sartor Resartus* (1834), with civilized opinions and beliefs being likened to disposable clothing. The narrator declares that 'the solemnities and paraphernalia of civilised Life, which we make so much of, [are] nothing but so many Cloth-rags' (Book 1, chapter 10).

9. *white-lead*: A type of putty made by mixing lead carbonate and boiled linseed oil.

10. *terrible vengeance*: The African fireman's response here has been aptly compared with Azuma-zi's awed devotion to the 'Dynamo Deity' in H. G. Wells's tale 'The Lord of the Dynamos' (1894) (Watts 1995, p. 110).

11. *Towson*: Possibly derived from Nicholas Tinmouth's *An Inquiry Relative to Various Important Points of Seamanship, Considered as a Branch of Practical Science* (1845), which has several similarities to the *Inquiry* mentioned by Marlow, including a first chapter concerned with the relative strengths of various 'chains and tackle'. Tinmouth was not, however, a 'Master in his Majesty's Navy' but Master-Attendant at Her Majesty's Dockyard at Woolwich.

12. *Winchesters*: Breech-loading repeater rifles named after their American manufacturer, Oliver F. Winchester (1810–80).

13. *like half-cooked cold dough*: That is, cassava steeped and boiled

to form a stiff dough, and known as *kwanga*. H. M. Stanley
explains that 'the cassava or manioc, sweet and bitter kinds,
furnishes the main farinaceous food of the people along the main
river' (Stanley, vol. II, p. 357).

14. *Martini-Henry*: The British Army service rifle between 1871 and
1891, the Martini-Henry was a breech-action rifle, the breech-
mechanism designed by Friedrich von Martini and the barrel by
Alexander Henry.

15. *squirts*: Repeating rifles (slang).

16. *I threw . . . whizz*: This awkwardly constructed sentence appears
to call for a verb such as 'to avoid' ('to avoid the glinting whizz'),
but there is no textual authority for such emendation.

17. *lounged*: According to the *Oxford English Dictionary*, the verb
'lounge' as a variant spelling of 'lunge' (to make a thrust with a
foil or rapier) was apparently current in Britain up to the 1890s.

18. *steam-whistle*: Glave describes the Europeans' practice of using
a ship's whistle to alarm African tribesmen: 'We had a harmony
whistle on board which alarmed them a great deal . . . The poor
natives of Nkolé, superstitious, as all savages are, thought it was
some angry spirit who was kept by me to terrify people . . . The
natives on the beach beat a hasty retreat at this unusual sound,
and those in canoes lost all presence of mind' (p. 236).

19. *They say the hair . . . growing*: That is, on a corpse. Marlow has
just referred to the living Kurtz's 'disinterred body'.

20. *half-English . . . half-French*: Conrad later noted: 'I took great
care to give Kurtz a cosmopolitan origin' (16 December 1903,
Letters, vol. II, p. 94).

21. *International Society . . . Savage Customs*: During the period
1870 to 1900, Leopold II devised a number of similarly high-
sounding organizations to maintain the fiction that Belgium's
interest in the Congo was philanthropic or scientific. The 'International African Association' (1876) gave way to the 'Committee
for the Study of the Upper Congo' (1878) and then to the 'International Association of the Congo' (1883), the latter flatteringly
described by a Belgian correspondent in *The Times* as a sort of
'Society of the Red Cross . . . formed with the noble aim of
rendering lasting and disinterested services to the cause of progress' (28 March 1883, p. 3). In 1896, there followed the
'Commission for the Protection of the Natives'.

22. *'Exterminate all the brutes!'*: Cf. 'An Outpost of Progress', *Tales
of Unrest*, p. 108: 'Carlier . . . talked about the necessity of
exterminating all the niggers before the country could be made

habitable.' The terms used by Carlier and Kurtz echo the mid-nineteenth-century evolutionary debate about the possible extinction or 'extermination' of supposedly lesser equipped, non-European peoples summarized by Charles Darwin in *The Descent of Man* (1871), chapter 6: 'At some future period, not very distant as measured by centuries, the civilised races of man will almost certainly exterminate, and replace, the savage races throughout the world.' Earlier, W. Winwood Reade had speculated on the 'amiable task' of bringing European rule to Africa as one in which 'they [Africans] may possibly become exterminated': 'We must learn to look at this result with composure. It illustrates the beneficent law of Nature, that the weak must be devoured by the strong' (*Savage Africa*, London: Smith, Elder, 1863, p. 587).

23. *'The station!'*: Corresponding to the Inner Station at Stanley Falls.

24. *a harlequin*: Originally the leader of a nocturnal band of demon horsemen in French folk literature, this figure evolved into Arlecchino, the clown-like servant who played a leading role in the harlequinade of the Italian *commedia dell'arte*. In later English pantomimes he is a mute, acrobatic buffoon wearing a mask and multi-coloured costume, who is supposed to be invisible to the clown and other comic characters.

25. *brown holland*: An unbleached form of linen fabric.

26. *Tambov*: A city in south central Russia, capital of a province of the same name.

27. *Dutch trading-house*: According to H. M. Stanley (vol. I, pp. 72–3), the principal 'Dutch House' in the Congo of the 1880s was the Nieuwe Afrikaansche Handels Vennootschap (Dutch African Trading Company), based at Banana Point at the mouth of the River Congo and managed by A. de Bloeme.

28. *Van Shuyten*: 'Schuyten' is the more likely spelling for a Dutch name. A Belgian trading agent named Schouten worked in the Congo in the early 1890s (Sherry, p. 117).

PART III

1. *those heads on the stakes*: In 'Cruelty in the Congo Free State', E. J. Glave, who had worked in the Congo, described the aftermath of a punitive military expedition against some African rebels in Stanley Falls in 1895: 'Many women and children were taken, and twenty-one heads were brought to the falls, and have

been used by Captain Rom as a decoration round a flower-bed in front of his house' (*Century Illustrated Magazine* 54 (1897), p. 706). Edited details of Rom's 'decoration' were printed in Britain in the *Saturday Review* (17 December 1898), when Conrad was about to begin his African story. Léon Rom was a Belgian soldier and administrator in the Congo at the same time as Conrad. He went on to become district commissioner at Matadi and station manager at Stanley Falls.

2. *the thunderbolts of that pitiful Jupiter*: Chief Roman god and associated with thunderbolts and lightning as emblems of divine power, Jupiter also figured in the nickname *Jupiter tonans* given to the German philosopher Arthur Schopenhauer, (W. Wallace, *Life of Arthur Schopenhauer*, London and Newcastle: Walter Scott Publishing, 1890, p. 89). For a succinct account of Schopenhauer's direct and indirect influence on *Heart of Darkness*, see Owen Knowles and Gene M. Moore, *Oxford Reader's Companion to Conrad* (Oxford: Oxford University Press, 2000), pp. 326–7.

3. *leggins*: A still-current variant spelling of 'leggings' (a protective cover for the lower leg).

4. *buttoned up . . . ulster*: A man's heavy, double-breasted overcoat with a belt at the back (so called because it was first produced in Northern Ireland).

5. *He desired to have kings . . . railway-stations*: Echoing the climax of H. M. Stanley's regal procession from Africa to Europe in January 1878, when he was formally received and lionized by envoys of Leopold II at Marseilles railway station. On the occasion of an anti-slavery conference in Brussels in late 1889, Stanley was accommodated 'in the gilt and scarlet rooms at the Royal Palace normally reserved for visiting royalty' (Hochschild, p. 94).

6. *secular*: A Gallicism from *séculaire*; literally 'centuries old' but, more generally, 'of great age'.

7. *'Live rightly, die, die . . .'*: The manuscript gives the maxim in its complete form, 'Live rightly, die nobly'.

8. *'The horror! The horror!'*: A possible allusion to Psalm 55:4–5: 'My heart is sore pained within me: and the terrors of death are fallen upon me. Fearfulness and trembling are come upon me, and horror hath overwhelmed me' (Watts 2002, p. 215). Kurtz's formulation is probably influenced by French, where the definite article would be required.

9. *No, they did not bury me*: Marlow's disillusioned response to Brussels in this paragraph, reminiscent of the returning Gulliver's

distaste for humankind, also bears a close resemblance to the narrators' final reflections on London in H. G. Wells's *The Island of Doctor Moreau* (1896) and *The War of the Worlds* (1898).

10. *some other feeling*: Conrad wrote that his African story offered a 'mere shadow of love interest just in the last pages' (2 January 1899, *Letters*, vol. II, pp. 145–6).

11. *sarcophagus*: A stone coffin, usually adorned with sculpture or inscription.

12. *never, never, never!*: Possibly recalling King Lear's response to the death of Cordelia in Shakespeare's *King Lear*: 'Thou'lt come no more, / Never, never, never, never, never!' (V.iii.309–10).

13. *familiar Shade*: Book VI of Virgil's *Aeneid* describes the Shades of the Underworld as stretching out their arms in longing to the boatman Charon as they stand on the shores of the Styx, river of darkness; they yearn for the boatman's help in order to cross the Styx and enter Elysium, the abode of the blessed.

14. *I felt . . . chest*: An awkwardly constructed sentence, perhaps influenced by French or Polish usage; 'felt something like' would be better English.

15. *The heavens . . . such a trifle*: An echo of the Latin maxim '*Fiat justitia, ruat caelum*' ('Let justice be done, though the heavens fall').

THE CONGO DIARY

1. *Matadi*: An important centre for trade about 30 miles (48 kilometres) upstream from Boma at the mouth of the Congo, where Conrad had arrived from Europe in the *Ville de Maceio* the previous day, 12 June.

2. *Gosse*: Joseph-Louis-Herbert Gosse had recently been made manager of the Matadi Station of the Société Anonyme du Haut-Congo.

3. *Casement*: Roger Casement (1864–1916; knighted 1911) was at this time working for the Compagnie du Chemin de fer du Congo as a supervisor of the railway that was planned to connect Matadi with Kinchasa. Conrad later elaborated: 'For some three weeks he lived in the same room in the Matadi Station . . . He knew the coast languages well. I went with him several times on short expeditions to hold "palavers" with neighbouring village-chiefs. The object of them was procuring porters for the Company's caravans from Matadi to Leopoldville' (24 May 1916, *Letters*,

vol. V, pp. 596–7). In 1898, Casement became British Consul for the Congo Free State and in 1903 prepared a widely publicized report on atrocities committed by Belgian colonists. After a distinguished diplomatic career, his involvement with the Irish National Volunteers and collusion with Germany during the First World War led to his arrest and execution for treason in 1916.

4. *Hatton & Cookson*: A Liverpool-based trading company, operating in the Lower Congo area.

5. *Simpson*: James H. Simpson of the Australian shipping firm Henry Simpson & Sons. Conrad had captained one of its ships, the *Otago*, from January 1888 to March 1889.

6. *Gov. B.*: Tadeusz Bobrowski (1824–94), Conrad's maternal uncle and guardian.

7. *Purd.*: Richard Curle identified this person as 'Captain Purdy, an acquaintance of Conrad' (*Last Essays*, p. 161).

8. *Hope*: See *Heart of Darkness*, Part I, note 1.

9. *Cap Froud*: Albert George Froud (1831–1901), the secretary of the London Shipmaster's Society, whose Fenchurch Street office Conrad had often visited in the later 1880s. A Somerset man by birth, he retired to Bristol. Conrad recalls him in *A Personal Record*.

10. *Mar.*: Marguerite Blanche-Marie Poradowska (née Gachet de la Fournière, 1848–1937), widow of Aleksander Poradowski, a distant relative of Conrad, was the 'aunt' who had used her influence in Brussels in 1890 to help him obtain his post in the Congo. Conrad wrote to her from Matadi on 18 June (*Letters*, vol. I, pp. 56–7), but if he wrote again on 24 June, this letter, like the others mentioned here, has not survived.

11. *People speaking ill of each other*: Cf. the account of life at the 'Central Station' (*Heart of Darkness*, 29–30).

12. *Harou*: Prosper Harou, a Belgian agent of the Société Anonyme du Haut-Congo, had arrived from Europe in the same ship as Conrad.

13. *Danes*: As *Heart of Darkness* also indicates, Scandinavians commonly served as officers in the Society's steamboats.

14. *Mosquitos*: Spelled in this form throughout the diary.

15. *andulating*: The 'beginning "u" in "undulating" is pronounced like the Polish "a"' (Zdzisław Najder, ed., *Congo Diary and Other Uncollected Pieces*, Garden City, NY: Doubleday, 1978, p. 48).

16. *the missionary*: Rev. Charles E. Ingham, author of *Congo Read-*

ing Book, 2 vols. (London: East London Missions Institute, 1890–91).

17. *Backongo*: Properly 'Bakongo', the name of a large tribe inhabiting the coastal regions of the Congo and Angola.

18. *Zanzibari*: Natives of Zanzibar were often employed by the Congo Free State to act as soldiers or policemen.

19. *Palma Christi*: The Latin name, meaning 'the palm of Christ', for the castor oil plant.

20. *cal[a]bashes*: Various species of gourd and pumpkin-like fruit.

21. *malafu*: Palm wine.

22. *ressembling*: After the French *ressemblant*.

23. *accidented*: A Gallicism, from *accidenté* ('uneven, hilly').

24. *manioc plantations*: The 'stuff like half-cooked cold dough' that Marlow sees the Bangala crew eating (*Heart of Darkness*, 50) is made from the tuberous roots of the manioc.

25. *Messrs Heyn & Jaeger*: Agents of the Société Anonyme du Haut-Congo. Reginald Heyn, an Englishman, managed a transport base at Manyanga.

26. *Stayed here till the 25*: Conrad never fully explained the reason for this protracted stay. For a detailed discussion, see Zdzisław Najder, *Joseph Conrad: A Chronicle*, trans. Halina Carroll-Najder (Cambridge: Cambridge University Press, 1983), pp. 130–31.

27. *Nkenghe*: William Holman Bentley provides the key to the first two columns of this list, noting: 'Markets in these parts are held once in every four days; the names of the days being *Nsona*, *Nkandu*, *Konzo*, *Nkenge*' (*Pioneering in the Congo*, London: Religious Tract Society, 1900, vol. I, p. 358). He later elaborates: 'The Congo week consists of four days ... The markets are named after the day of the week and the town near which they are held' (vol. I, p. 399). Here planning his itinerary for the next two weeks, Conrad converts the seven days of the European week into the four days of the Congo week, presumably to calculate when his journey would coincide with market-day. The places listed in the third column probably represent the camp-sites used on the journey.

28. *Mrs Comber*: Annie Comber (née Smith), who had only recently arrived at the mission, would be dead before Conrad returned to Europe. She had come out from England in early 1890 and married Percy Comber, a Baptist missionary, at Matadi in June. After repeated fevers, she died at Banana on 19 December 1890 while waiting for a homeward-bound steamship.

29. *Davis*: Philip Davis, a Baptist missionary, arrived in the Congo with Percy Comber in 1885. From October 1886 he was stationed at Wathen, where he died in December 1895.

30. *Rev. Bentley*: The Baptist missionary William Holman Bentley (1855–1905), author of *Pioneering in the Congo* and several other works on the cultures and languages of the Congo. He and his wife Hendrina (née Kloekers) had gone to Tungwa, near Makuta (Bentley, vol. II, p. 341).

31. *much more trees*: An unidiomatic phrase, influenced by the Polish *wiele więcej drzew*.

32. *One wrecked*: The ship Conrad had expected to command, the *Floride*, was wrecked on 18 July, but was re-floated and brought back to Kinchasa within five days (Sherry, p. 41). Cf. *Heart of Darkness*: 'One of them . . . informed me with great volubility and many digressions . . . that my steamer was at the bottom of the river' (24–5).

33. *shimbek*: An African term for a few huts occupied by people of the same employment (for example, railway builders).

34. *Ipeca*: That is, Ipecacuanha, a herbal medicine used to combat dysentery.

35. *Row . . . carriers*: Cf. *Heart of Darkness*: 'Then he got fever, and had to be carried in a hammock slung under a pole. As he weighed sixteen stone I had no end of rows with the carriers' (24).

36. *speech . . . understand*: Cf. *Heart of Darkness*: 'one evening, I made a speech in English with gestures, not one of which was lost to the sixty pairs of eyes before me' (24).

Glossary of Nautical Terms

This glossary briefly explains all nautical terms used in *Heart of Darkness*. Admiral W. H. Smyth's *The Sailor's Word-Book: An Alphabetical Digest of Nautical Terms* (1867; rpt. London: Conway Maritime Press, 1991) can be recommended as providing useful detailed description relevant to the period in which Conrad was writing.

bow: the forward part of a ship, from the point at which she begins to curve to the stern
brought up: halted and anchored the vessel

decked scow: a large, flat-bottomed boat with broad, square ends, used for carrying freight
dug-out: a canoe made from a hollowed-out tree-trunk

fairway: navigable part of a river
float: one of the blades of a ship's paddle-wheel

hard a-starboard: as far as possible to the right
helm: the handle or tiller (in large ships the wheel) by which the rudder is managed; occasionally extended to include the whole steering gear

offing: the more distant part of the sea or river in view
opened the reach more: sailed further round the bend into the open stretch

purchases: leverage equipment for raising or lowering heavy objects

reach: (a) portion of a river that lies between two bends; (b) as much as can be seen in one view

sheered: swerved or changed course

snag: a hazard to navigation, particularly a submerged obstacle

sounding-pole: a pole used to measure the depth of water close to the land

sprits: small spars set diagonally upwards from the mast, on which sails are extended on fore-and-aft rigged vessels

stanchion: upright bar or post serving as a support

trip the anchor: raise clear the ship's anchor from its bed

trireme: an ancient Greek and Roman warship; a type of galley with three tiers of oars on each side

yawl: two-masted sailing vessel, rigged fore-and-aft, with a large mainmast and a small mizzenmast (rear mast)

CLICK ON A CLASSIC
www.penguinclassics.com

The world's greatest literature at your fingertips

Constantly updated information on more than a thousand titles,
from Icelandic sagas to ancient Indian epics, Russian drama to
Italian romance, American greats to African masterpieces

•

The latest news on recent additions to the list, updated
editions, and specially commissioned translations

•

Original essays by leading writers

•

A wealth of background material, including biographies
of every classic author from Aristotle to Zamyatin, plot
synopses, readers' and teachers' guides, useful Web links

•

Online desk and examination copy assistance for academics

•

Trivia quizzes, competitions, giveaways, news on
forthcoming screen adaptations

THE STORY OF PENGUIN CLASSICS

Before 1946 . . . "Classics" are mainly the domain of academics and students; readable editions for everyone else are almost unheard of. This all changes when a little-known classicist, E. V. Rieu, presents Penguin founder Allen Lane with the translation of Homer's *Odyssey* that he has been working on in his spare time.

1946 Penguin Classics debuts with *The Odyssey*, which promptly sells three million copies. Suddenly, classics are no longer for the privileged few.

1950s Rieu, now series editor, turns to professional writers for the best modern, readable translations, including Dorothy L. Sayers's *Inferno* and Robert Graves's unexpurgated *Twelve Caesars*.

1960s The Classics are given the distinctive black covers that have remained a constant throughout the life of the series. Rieu retires in 1964, hailing the Penguin Classics list as "the greatest educative force of the twentieth century."

1970s A new generation of translators swells the Penguin Classics ranks, introducing readers of English to classics of world literature from more than twenty languages. The list grows to encompass more history, philosophy, science, religion, and politics.

1980s The Penguin American Library launches with titles such as *Uncle Tom's Cabin* and joins forces with Penguin Classics to provide the most comprehensive library of world literature available from any paperback publisher.

1990s The launch of Penguin Audiobooks brings the classics to a listening audience for the first time, and in 1999 the worldwide launch of the Penguin Classics Web site extends their reach to the global online community.

The 21st Century Penguin Classics are completely redesigned for the first time in nearly twenty years. This world-famous series now consists of more than 1,300 titles, making the widest range of the best books ever written available to millions—and constantly redefining what makes a "classic."

The Odyssey continues . . .

The best books ever written

PENGUIN CLASSICS

SINCE 1946

Find out more at www.penguinclassics.com

Visit www.vpbookclub.com